Male instinct ruled.

While Maria was still recovering from the shock of seeing him, he pulled her close and claimed her lips with his own. He savored the spicy taste of her, the scent and texture of her hair as he cupped her head, the lush curves of her body as he pressed the length of her body to his own.

Nothing mattered but this.

He would have devoured her completely if he could, but the indignant shrieks of a nearby woman eventually penetrated his consciousness. At the same time, he felt Maria's hands against his chest, actually pushing him away.

"My Lord!" the older woman cried. "Unhand Lady Maria this instant!"

Nick kept his eyes locked on Maria's. All he could see reflected in those glorious irises was panic.

Her lips were swollen by his kiss, but they were trembling. She took a step back— And slapped him…!

Praise for Margo Maguire's previous titles

Dryden's Bride
"Exquisitely detailed...an entrancing tale that will enchant and envelop you as love conquers all."
—*Rendezvous*

"A warm-hearted tale...Ms. Maguire skillfully draws the reader into her deftly woven tale."
—*Romantic Times*

The Bride of Windermere
"Packed with action...fast, humorous, and familiar...*The Bride of Windermere* will fit into your weekend just right."
—*Romantic Times*

HIS LADY FAIR

MARGO MAGUIRE

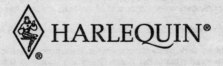 HARLEQUIN®

TORONTO • NEW YORK • LONDON
AMSTERDAM • PARIS • SYDNEY • HAMBURG
STOCKHOLM • ATHENS • TOKYO • MILAN • MADRID
PRAGUE • WARSAW • BUDAPEST • AUCKLAND

ISBN 0-373-29196-5

HIS LADY FAIR

Copyright © 2002 by Margo Wider

All rights reserved. Except for use in any review, the reproduction or utilization of this work in whole or in part in any form by any electronic, mechanical or other means, now known or hereafter invented, including xerography, photocopying and recording, or in any information storage or retrieval system, is forbidden without the written permission of the publisher, Harlequin Enterprises Limited, 225 Duncan Mill Road, Don Mills, Ontario, Canada M3B 3K9.

All characters in this book have no existence outside the imagination of the author and have no relation whatsoever to anyone bearing the same name or names. They are not even distantly inspired by any individual known or unknown to the author, and all incidents are pure invention.

This edition published by arrangement with Harlequin Books S.A.

® and TM are trademarks of the publisher. Trademarks indicated with ® are registered in the United States Patent and Trademark Office, the Canadian Trade Marks Office and in other countries.

Visit us at www.eHarlequin.com

Printed in U.S.A.

Please address questions and book requests to:
Harlequin Reader Service
U.S.: 3010 Walden Ave., P.O. Box 1325, Buffalo, NY 14269
Canadian: P.O. Box 609, Fort Erie, Ont. L2A 5X3

This book is for Mike.

Chapter One

Alderton Keep. Early Spring, 1429

Ria stole into the buttery and smoothed the wrinkles from the front of her new gown. Not that the gown was truly new, for it had belonged to Cecilia Morley, Ria's sophisticated, young, *legitimate* cousin. But even if it was not a perfect fit, the elegant castoff, once a lovely blue silk dress, was a decided improvement over the threadbare gown Ria had been wearing these last few years.

Ria allowed herself a moment to savor the sensation of the fine silk against her skin. She was glad Cecilia had had the fur lining removed. Ria had no use for it. Nor had she any use for the jeweled collar that had once adorned the neckline. With the hard work that was required of her, Ria knew those fineries would quickly be ruined.

Besides, she had her own jewelry, a precious locket—a bauble of gold with a secret latch that held a lock of her mother's golden hair within. Ria always carried it with her, though she kept it tied up in a square of linen so that no one would ever see it. And take it from her.

She spun around and gave herself leave to imagine that, just this once, she was dressed in the glorious gown before its lining and jeweled collar had been ripped from it. She could almost feel the weight of the gems, and dream she was tall and slender and lovely like Cecilia, making heads turn and eyes glitter with envy.

'Twas a foolish fancy, Ria knew, but her little dreams made life at Alderton Keep bearable. Her life had always been harsh, and it seemed to grow worse with every passing year.

Her aunt Olivia had made it quite clear that Ria would never be recognized as a member of the family. The Morleys would provide her a roof, food for her belly and the occasional bit of cast-off clothing. But Ria would be required to work for it.

The bastard daughter of Lady Sarah Morley deserved no better.

"Ria!" Cook's harsh voice interrupted her wandering thoughts. Ria quickly tied a scratchy woolen shawl 'round her shoulders—more to cover up the shortcomings of Cecilia's dress than for warmth—and flew out of the buttery, into the kitchen.

"Where've yer been, girl?" Cook demanded.

"I—I've just—"

"Get the pot out of the fire fer me now," the sour-tempered cook ordered, "then give it a good stir."

Ria lifted the heavy cauldron from its hook in the huge blackened fireplace and carried it to a sturdy wooden table in the center of the kitchen.

"Ye slopped some of m' stew over the side, ye beef-witted dewberry!" Cook screeched at her, cuffing the side of her head and nearly knocking Ria down as she struggled with the heavy pot. "Now wipe up the mess ye made!"

"It wouldn't have sloshed if you'd put it in two smaller pots like I told you before," Ria retorted just as Cook cuffed her again.

She knew better than to sass Cook, but it went against her nature to keep silent over unfair criticism. Ria rubbed the bruised spot on the side of her head and picked up a rag. She said nothing more, but began cleaning up the spill.

"When yer done there, yer to take this tray up to Lady Olivia's solar," Cook said. "She's got a guest wi' her, so try not to splash or spill while yer up there."

Ria glanced up to see a large wooden tray laden with ale and other refreshments. She was bone weary, but it did not matter. She would take the tray to her aunt Olivia, then await further orders. Just as she always did, and always would.

Within the warmth and comfort of her solar, with its thick walls and narrow windows, its warm fire and colorful tapestries, Olivia Morley poured warm wine for her visitor from London, a justice from the high court, and tried to conceal her agitation.

The widow of Jerrold Morley, Olivia was still a comely woman, with nary a gray hair in her thick sable mane—at least none that had a chance to flourish before being plucked out. Her eyes were of the same soft brown as her hair, though their softness was deceiving. Her vision and acuity were as sharp as ever.

"No, my lord," Olivia Morley said to the visitor. "There never was a child. And even if Sarah's issue had survived, she would not, *could not* have inherited Rockbury." She maintained an even, well-modulated tone as she spoke to Lord Roland, as distinguished a gentleman as she'd ever encountered. Not the slightest hint of Olivia's discomposure showed as she lied.

"But my lady, the property is en—"

"I care not how the property is entailed," Olivia continued in a haughty tone, "*or* who wrote Sarah Morley's will."

"Sarah *Burton*."

Olivia shrugged indifferently. "I will not allow my husband's property to go to the child of a harlot!"

"But Rockbury was never your husband's property—"

"Of course it was!" Olivia raged as she stood up from her chair. She paced in front of the fire, her hands twisting angrily in front of her. It was so unlike her to lose control of her temper, and she worked to subdue it. "Whoever heard of such a bequest? The very notion of a bastard inheriting such an estate is ridiculous. Absurd. Preposterous! As Sarah's next of kin, my husband—"

"I assure you, Lady Olivia," the visitor replied calmly, "the estate in Staffordshire was clearly, and quite legally, a gift to Lady Sarah from King Henry IV. The property was hers...to bequeath to whomever she chose. And as to the bastardy of—"

"Nonsense!" Olivia persisted. "The will can be broken. Surely the king did not intend to *reward* my husband's sister for her wanton behavior."

"My lady, you are speaking of the late Duchess of Sterlyng," Sir Roland said through clenched teeth. "And she had every right to bequeath Rockbury where she would. King Henry's papers indicate that he gave the title to Rockbury to your sister-in-law as a reward for her loyalty to his cause, in spite of her family's ostracism for it.

"And according to Lady Sarah's last will and testament, the property was properly, *legally,* bequeathed to her offspring, a girl-child named…Maria Elizabeth."

"It was our understanding that the child perished," Olivia said tightly.

"But there have been rumors—"

"None of them true, I assure you."

"Then Rockbury reverts to the crown," Sir Roland said as he arose from the comfortable settee near the fire.

"But that is impossible, sir!" Olivia declared with her hands clasped tightly in front of her gilt girdle. "Rockbury should be part of my son's estate! He *will* have it!"

"Nay, my lady," Roland replied quietly. "The crown will have it back."

A light tap at the door failed to penetrate Olivia's distracted state, so Lord Roland bade the newcomer to enter.

A young serving maid appeared, a lovely girl whose mass of wavy, honey-gold hair was more out of its chignon than in. Her eyes remained downcast.

He could not help but notice the young woman's delicately crafted face, with skin as clear and sweet as fresh cream. By her looks, she could have been a highborn lady, he thought, but for her subservient manner and the reddened, chafed skin of her hands.

The justice turned his attention from the serving maid and spoke to the well-dressed woman who stood before the fireplace, her expression one of controlled fury. "I had hoped to find Lady Maria and discharge my duty to her this afternoon, and be well on my way to Chester before nightfall," he said, easily dismissing Lady Olivia's unpleasant mood.

Olivia tightened her lips slightly before speaking. "I am sorry. As I said before, there was no chi—" she said, then spoke sharply to the maid. "Go on! Out with you!"

The servant girl turned and moved quickly from the room, closing the door gently behind her. Perhaps she was simple, Roland thought.

"I am loath to keep you from your appointment in Chester...." Olivia said. But perhaps, she thought, if she kept him at Morley, she would manage to convince him of Geoffrey's right to Rockbury. Then the justice would prevail upon the ruling council in London to grant Rockbury's title to her son.

"Please," she said, extending a gracious arm toward the food that Ria had just placed on the table. "Refresh yourself before you continue on your journey. Chester is a good two-hour ride from Morley. But the weather is fine and after your meal you will be fit again for travel."

Ria stood outside the door trembling. She had not been able to hear all of what had been said behind Lady Olivia's door, nor did she know what to do about what she *had* heard. 'Twas more than likely she'd misunderstood everything. Certainly that possibility made her hesitate to speak up, along with knowing she'd take a beating later for impertinence if she spoke to Lady Olivia's guest. Especially if Ria happened to be wrong.

If she *had* heard correctly, and she *was* to have an inheritance from her mother, then there was time enough to receive the news. One hour, or even two, did not matter, not when her whole life was about to change.

And what a change 'twould be! She would have a home, a place where she belonged, without question.

Empty-handed, floating on air, Ria made her way down the stairs and entered the kitchen, where an oversize basket full of dirty laundry was shoved into her hands.

Ria smiled and took it outside.

Chapter Two

Nicholas Hawken, Marquis of Kirkham, set several small stones upon a wall of rock. Then he picked up his whip and walked twenty paces away.

Snapping the lethal strip of leather several times in quick succession, he hit each rock separately, without touching its neighbor, and knocked every piece down.

At one time he'd have thought it quite an accomplishment. Now 'twas just another idle pastime.

Nicholas was restless. At the rate he and his companions were traveling, 'twould take another two days to reach Kirkham. That is, if the men didn't decide to stay here at the Tusk and Ale Inn, where the serving wenches were uncommonly pretty and more than accommodating.

Mayhap he would avail himself of their services later, but for now, this exacting exercise would work to dissipate his foul and melancholy mood. For it had been on this day, exactly twelve years before, that his brother, Edmund, was slain on a blood-soaked battlefield in France.

The two brothers had fought side by side under King Henry himself, proud and happy to be part of the conquest of France. They'd been determined to distinguish themselves on the field and achieve glory for the Hawken name.

Nick lined up the stones again and once more whipped each one off with the precision he'd learned from an Italian nobleman.

So many years, so many regrets.

'Twas his own fault Edmund had been killed before his twentieth year. Had Nicholas not persuaded his brother to accompany him to France, Edmund would be firmly ensconced as marquis at Kirkham, with Lady Alyce Palton as his wife.

Instead, poor Alyce had wept herself into an early grave over Edmund's loss, and Nicholas himself had become the heir, a man as unworthy as any could be.

He turned and, with a flick of his wrist, viciously whipped the long, narrow strip of leather around the trunk of a nearby tree. Would the icy grip of guilt ever let him free?

Nick didn't think so. He could not imagine living without it.

"There you are!"

Nicholas turned to see two of his traveling companions crossing the narrow field to approach him. The two intruders retained their cheerful demeanors in spite of Nick's scowling face.

"Lofton sent us in search of you, Kirkham," one man announced.

"He said to tell you he saved the frisky one for you," the other added.

"Frisky what?" Nick asked, winding his whip into a neat loop.

"Frisky blond wench!" the man said with a hearty slap on his back. "Knows you're partial to 'em!"

Blond or bald, it hardly mattered. Oblivion was all Nicholas sought. He raised an eyebrow and gave a good impression of a knavish grin, then started the walk back to the inn.

Oblivion.

Ria wondered why, after so many years, anyone bothered about Sarah Morley's—no, Sarah *Burton's*—child. No one had thought of her since her birth twenty-two years before. What did they want with her now?

Rarely did she think of herself as Sarah's daughter, or even as Olivia's niece. Ria was no one, had never been anyone. At least, not since the death of her nursemaid, Tilda, the old woman who'd brought her here to Alderton Keep when her mother had died.

Tilda was the one who'd started calling her Ria, a pet name, really. But when Tilda died, it had become something less. It was no longer a name, but merely a sound people barked when they wanted something.

Happily, that was about to change. No longer would she be the no-name girl of Alderton. She was *Ma*ria Elizabeth Burton, a *legitimately* born person of consequence.

And if she were legitimate, it meant she had a father.

Ria stopped in her tracks when that thought dawned on her. The man in Aunt Olivia's solar had referred to her mother as Sarah Burton, Duchess of Sterlyng. That would make Ria's father a duke—the Duke of Sterlyng.

Ria scrubbed the soiled linens in the washtub, wrung them out and hung every piece on the line that was strung across the bailey. She frowned and wondered what all this meant, reminding herself she could very well have been mistaken about what she'd heard. Why had she never heard of the Duke of Sterlyng before?

Why hadn't her aunt and uncle known of Sarah's marriage to this duke?

Or *had* they known, and chosen to keep Ria from her inheritance…and possibly, from her father?

She picked up the empty basket and walked around to the kitchen, where she set it in a corner. When she noticed that there was too little firewood stacked by the hearth, she picked up the heavy canvas cloth and went outside to retrieve more before Cook had yet another reason to cuff her.

Soon, Ria thought…soon she would be known as the daughter of a duke. She shook her head, dislodging more unkempt tendrils from her braid. 'Twas all beyond any of her wildest imaginings.

She stacked the wood outside the kitchen. Though it was still early afternoon, Ria began to worry. She had hoped to be summoned sooner rather than later, but the gentleman in Aunt Olivia's solar had not yet called for her. Was it possible she had entirely misunderstood what had been said?

Nay, she assured herself, 'twas not conceivable. Ria was Sarah's daughter—no one had ever denied that. Her mother had been despised by the Morleys when she'd gone with King Henry. They'd been firm supporters of King Richard, and Sarah's defection had caused a terrible rift in the family.

But now Ria knew her mother had wed a duke. She'd been a duchess with an estate of her own. A place called Rockbury. There was no mistake about the name. Ria had heard it clearly.

Feeling more optimistic again, she decided to go to her little nook beneath the back stairs and pack her belongings. Not that she owned very much, but all that she had was precious to her, though her most valuable possession—her locket—was never far from her person.

Tamping down her growing excitement at the prospect of leaving Morley, Ria thought of her journey ahead. How far was Rockbury? she wondered. In Staffordshire, she'd heard the man say, but she did not even know where that was. Would she have to travel for days, or merely hours to get there? And what would they think of her once she arrived?

Would her father be there, or was he long dead, just like her mother?

The idea of a father was compelling. Ria could hardly imagine how it would be to have someone who cared, someone who would champion her and protect her from all who would harm her.

Ria looked down at her clothes. Better to turn up at Rockbury wearing her own modest, rough kirtle, she decided, than Cecilia's cast-off gown with its low-riding neckline and too-long hem. It only emphasized her short stature and too-full figure.

She entered her tiny chamber and lit a tallow candle, since there was no window to provide light. The dark, cramped room contained only a narrow pallet on which she slept, and a stand that she'd fashioned out of stones from the fields. A threadbare kirtle and a dingy linen underkirtle lay neatly folded on the end of the bed.

After peeling off the shawl that covered her bodice, and slipping down the shoulders of the gown, Ria poured water from a cracked clay pitcher and began to wash off the grime from the morning's work. She was only partly finished when she heard the commotion.

Ria tried to ignore most of the disturbances around the keep unless she was directly involved, but it suddenly occurred to her that Olivia's visitor might be leaving.

Without her!

She hastily pulled the gown back on and tied the shawl around her shoulders as she quit her room, running through the dark passageway that led from her nook to a side entrance of the keep. If she could only make it to the stable before the man left...

She managed to shove the heavy door open, and quickly flew outside, tripping over a crate holding several chickens. Painful scrapes on the heel of her hand and on her knee did not deter her. She just scrambled up and continued on, hurrying to intercept the visitor before he left.

"Ria!"

The female voice came from above. Ria paused long enough to see that it was her aunt, leaning from the window of her solar.

"Stop this instant, you clumsy girl!"

Ria ignored Olivia and circled the keep, then ran down the path to the stable. Her cousin, Geoffrey Morley, and young Thomas Newson, son of a neighboring baron, stood at the entrance. Though they were a few years younger than Ria, they were much larger and a good deal stronger. The two youths eyed her indolently.

"Where is he?" Ria cried in frustration. How could the visitor have left so quickly?

"Who?" Geoffrey asked with feigned ignorance.

"You know—the gentleman who came to see your mother!" Ria replied, in a panic. "Has he left?"

"Now why would you care about that?" Thomas said. The two young men crowded around Ria, forcing her to back up into the stable. She glanced quickly around the yard. There was no one nearby—no one to

call for help, not that any of the Morley servants would
have come to her aid.

"'Tis none of your concern, Thomas Newson," she
said, holding her ground, poking one finger into the fellow's chest. Ria had never liked Thomas, not since he
was a young lad, sneaking around and pulling mean
pranks on her. In the intervening years, Ria had been
ever on her guard when he was near.

She suppressed a shudder. "Where is the gentleman?" she demanded in spite of their intimidation.
"You must know!" She would not cower before them,
even though they clearly had the upper hand, in terms
of brute strength. Between them, though, Ria didn't believe they had half her brains.

"Well, let's just see...." Thomas grabbed her arm
and pulling her deep into the stable. "Perhaps he is
here, eh?"

They shoved her into the first stall, but found one of
Morley's old horses standing there. A second stall was
open, empty.

"This where that fancy mount was, Geoff?" Thomas
asked, grinning.

Ria yanked her arm away and turned to leave, but
Geoffrey blocked her way. Thomas grabbed her shawl
and pulled her into the empty stall. Geoff knocked her
down.

"Get away from me, you oafs!" she cried, kicking
at their legs when they tried to approach. Pain stabbed
through her elbow where it hit the ground.

"Hold her down!" Thomas said.

A terrible, dark fear gripped her, but she refused to
be paralyzed by it. The outcome of this incident depended upon her ability to keep her wits about her. With

one arm immobilized, she tried to roll, but couldn't do it while she fought off two pairs of strong, male hands.

Thomas got hold of her feet while Geoffrey held her shoulders. He knocked her head on the ground, stunning her for a moment. When she came to her senses, she doubled her resistance.

She fell a pull and heard something tear. She swallowed the bitter bile that rose in her throat and braced herself. There had to be something she could do, she thought as instinct made her lash out with one foot.

One of her hands slipped loose, and Ria quickly reached up and wrenched a handful of Geoffrey's hair. She yanked viciously, tearing it out by the roots. He howled and fell back for an instant, just long enough for her to knock Thomas off balance and roll away from him. When she was on her feet again, Geoffrey was an absolute puddle, holding his head, lost in his own misery.

Thomas, however, was still a serious threat. There was an innate meanness about him that Ria and every other servant at Morley recognized. Everyone kept clear of him.

Ria knew it would take a miracle to save her. She wanted to cry when she thought of her near escape from Morley, of her impossible dream of leaving with the stranger.

She should have known better.

Thomas started to circle. "You aren't going anywhere, Ria," he jeered. "You've flaunted your arse in my face once too many times to go free now."

Ria turned as he moved, never letting him out of her sight. *Flaunted?* She'd stayed as far as possible from Thomas Newson. Why would she have tried to attract the attentions of this slimy toad?

He lunged suddenly, catching her shawl, pulling her close. Ria shoved her knee up as forcefully as possible between his legs, and he cried out, grabbing his belly and falling to the ground.

Ria knew he wouldn't stay down forever. Gathering her aching, bruised body, she made a run for the stall door, knowing perfectly well she could not stay at Morley any longer. 'Twas clearly time to leave, even though she had to go alone.

She moved quickly, daringly. 'Twas a hanging offense to steal a horse, but that was what she meant to do. It took only a second to run from the stall where Thomas and Geoffrey nursed their wounds, and open the next one. She hauled a mounting block over and climbed onto it, then threw one leg over the old mare's bare back. Without a backward glance, Ria rode out of the stable, then out of the yard. Heading southeast, she had only one thought, one destination in mind.

Rockbury.

Chapter Three

Lord Kirkham gave a lazy smile in response to a lame jest by one of his companions. His party of noble wastrels was finally nearing Castle Kirkham, prepared to enjoy a month of diversions far from the tedium of London.

And Kirkham was a most inventive host.

Legends had grown around his prowess in the hunt, his fondness for ale and his talents in the bedchamber. His brawling abilities were celebrated across the kingdom, and his finesse with a whip was unparalleled.

"Hand me your flask, Lofton," Nicholas drawled. "Mine's empty." He carelessly tossed his own tin container into the forest beside the horse path.

"What say we race to Kirkham's gate?" asked Viscount Sheffield. "Loser pays the tavern bill."

Nicholas swayed in his saddle.

"You up to it, mate?" Lord Lofton asked him.

"Aye. But I say the *winner* has his choice of the comeliest wench in the castle," Nicholas declared, throwing his dark head back with a laugh.

"Agreed!" Lofton hooted. Kirkham's changeable moods as well as his capacity for drink were a constant

source of amusement to his friends and acquaintances.
"Let's go."

They were off as abruptly as if a flag had been
dropped at a tournament. Nicholas dug in his heels and
hugged his horse's back as they urged their mounts to
a gallop, side by side on the path. Only three of them
joined in the race, the others following casually behind,
jesting and laughing, too inebriated to manage much
speed.

It was just as well. The horse path was narrow and
barely allowed space for the three horses to ride abreast.
Nicholas rode on the outside, with Lofton in the middle.
No matter how much ale he'd consumed, the others
knew Nick liked to win, and would do what was necessary to accomplish it.

The horses were nose to nose, but there was still a
good distance to go before they reached Castle Kirkham's gate. Just down this track a bit, then around the
bend where the eastern road bisected—

A rider turned onto the road ahead. The horse reared,
and there was a quick flash of blue and gold as the rider
was thrown into the path of the galloping horses. Nick
pulled back sharply and slowed his mount, while the
others scrambled in confusion. Dismounting before his
horse had come to a halt, he ran to the woman, who lay
unconscious in the road.

She was young. And clearly of noble birth, judging
by her clothes.

Her head was uncovered. Her hair, a glorious honey
color that looked as if it had been tipped by a monk's
gilded brush, spilled on the ground around her. At one
time Nicholas would have called her lovely. Now the
cynic in him knew there was little true beauty in this

world. Still, he was well able to appreciate her attributes.

Thick eyelashes formed crescents over her high cheekbones, and her eyes themselves were framed by delicately arched brows. Her nose was unremarkable, but her mouth, those lips, full and inviting...

Nick licked his own and spoke. "Madam..."

A soft moan was the response he got, and he had the most remarkable sense of another time, another place. That moan could easily be mistaken for one of pleasure, and he could almost imagine that lush, fantastic hair spread out on his bed.

Yet something about her pose struck him as entirely innocent and without guile. She would have need of his *protection,* not his—

Nick shook his head to clear it of the ridiculous notion, and turned to the men who were now dismounting to surround him and the maid. His cohorts were chuckling and talking about Kirkham's wenches, and having a piece of *this* comely one.

Their crude talk riled Nicholas unaccountably. "Go on to Kirkham," he said roughly. "I'll see to the maiden and join you shortly."

"*Maiden,* eh?" one of the ruffians behind him muttered.

"Not one of your castle wenches, then?"

"Go," Nicholas said harshly, turning toward the men gathered behind him. Quickly composing himself, he added in a more amicable tone, "Rooms have been made ready for all of you, and we'll meet in one hour for the evening's festivities. Please. Leave me now. I will deal with this."

Reluctantly, the men moved away, while the young woman lying on the path moaned again and turned slightly. Nicholas could see her pulse beating at the base of her delicate neck, and he envisioned himself pressing his lips to the spot.

"Madam," he repeated as he slid one hand under the maid's head.

She opened her eyes abruptly. Without a moment's hesitation, she raised a fist and delivered a solid punch to Nicholas's jaw. It was the surprise, as much as the force of the blow, that threw him back on his rear. While he was down, the girl scrambled to her feet. But before she could take one step in flight, she crumpled to the ground again, muttering.

Nicholas felt fortunate that his comrades were far up the path and not present to witness his inglorious dumping by this slip of a maiden. Clearly, she felt no remorse for her actions, for she grumbled angrily about mothers who should have drowned their clumsy, half-witted children at birth.

She turned onto her hands and knees and began to crawl away. Fully appreciative of the view she presented, he held back a grin and spoke. "D'you accost every man you meet," he said sarcastically, "or do I alone enjoy the honor?"

"Only bumble-headed fools who terrorize the countryside with their horseplay," she muttered.

Nicholas frowned, gritting his teeth. His reputation might not be the purest, but *no one* spoke to him in this manner! "Bumble-head—!"

"Go away," she said, turning to flash the most incredible eyes at him.

He vaguely remembered once before having seen clear amber eyes like hers, but he could not recall where or when. Nor did he care. Their unusual, seductive color intrigued him every bit as much as their scornful expression.

His ire was quickly replaced by something else. Suddenly, the only thought he could entertain was how those disdainful eyes would flare with passion when he took—and gave—the ultimate pleasure between her thighs. By the look of her, though, he would have to put some effort into her seduction. She was no easy tavern wench, ripe and willing.

Nay, this golden beauty was indecipherable. She seemed as delicate as a young maid, fresh and untried, yet she was as spirited and feisty as the most jaded courtesan he'd ever known. 'Twould be amusing to discover which she truly was.

And what sport *that* would be. He almost smiled in anticipation of the game.

"Are you hurt?" he asked, raising himself up to crouch near her. He was on his guard lest she turn around and deliver another punch…nay, he almost welcomed her to try it.

Ria turned back again and eyed him warily. Yes, she was hurt, and she doubted she'd be able to walk. But could she trust this man?

His powerful body was richly clad. He moved with the physical confidence of a warrior, but he smelled of ale and his demeanor was one of casual indifference. He was a drunkard. A lecher.

His gray eyes darkened perceptibly as he watched her, and Ria knew that, drunk or not, this was no raw lad whom she could best with a quick kick to his privates. Though he gave a superficial impression of indolence, she sensed there was more to him than what he presented.

His hair was dark, nearly black, and its extra length

gave its owner an appearance of sensual laziness. Thick black lashes framed stormy gray eyes. His nose was long and straight, but for a small bump near the bridge—where Ria assumed it might once have been broken. His cheekbones were sharply carved in a face that would have appeared harsh, but was made more human by his mouth. His lips betrayed a sensitivity that was otherwise well hidden by a dark and disagreeable expression.

Ria licked her lips nervously and wondered if she should apologize for striking him. She decided the less said about that blow, the better. She needed to get away from here as quickly as possible, and on her way to Rockbury. Luckily, she had learned in a little village a few miles back that the estate she sought was not far off.

"I've twisted my ankle," she said, once she was out of close reach. "If you would just—"

"Let me see."

"Nay, sir."

Ria had no intention of allowing herself to be handled by this man or any other. She'd fought for her freedom from her kin at Alderton, and now she was going to Rockbury. Nothing was going to deter her. Not her sniveling young cousin, Geoffrey Morley, and his vicious cohort; not this flagrantly masculine nobleman. She was going to find out the truth of her birth, even if the words she'd heard in her aunt's solar turned out to be a misunderstanding.

She dragged her skirt over her legs and scooted away. But the man lunged before she could move very far, and grabbed her leg near the knee, holding her fast.

"What's the hurry?" he said. The words were innocuous, but there was more than a hint of danger in his voice. He changed position, then turned her, pinning her beneath him in the damp grass next to the path.

His scent was not just that of ale. He smelled of horse and leather, and man. Dark whiskers shadowed the lower half of his face, emphasizing the devilishly attractive creases in his cheeks. He was a great deal larger than she, and his long, hard frame provoked a physical reaction she did not recognize.

When she shivered, his eyes went nearly black.

Ria could not move. Her breath was trapped in her throat, just as surely as her arms were trapped by his powerful hands at her sides. Her legs had lost all ability to move.

Their breaths intermingled. His chest touched her breasts. She felt weightless. Feathers replaced the organs in her belly, tickling her insides, from the tips of her breasts to her loins.

One of his hands pressed against her waist, and his legs shifted. Ria squirmed, eliciting a groan from him. He lifted his torso, framing her shoulders with his powerful arms, then moved one leg between hers. Keeping her eyes imprisoned by his own, he moved again, making contact with the most intimate part of her. He increased the pressure and a shot of molten heat burst through her.

Shocked by his scorching touch, Ria shoved him away with all her strength. She suspected he allowed her to do so, but nevertheless took advantage of the distance.

Sitting up quickly, she drew her legs under her. It was a moment before she was able to catch enough breath to speak. "M-my horse, my lord," she said stiffly, summoning the nerve to brazenly look him in the eyes. "If you would be k-kind enough to help me remount, I will be on my way...."

Nicholas did not move. He had never been one to force himself on a woman, but this one was different. He knew she'd been affected by his touch. Even now her voice was breathless, husky. There was confusion in her eyes.

Bits of dried grass laced her hair, and the deep blue silk of her gown was damp in places. She had the look of a woman who'd been well pleasured, though they'd not come close to what could have been.

Nick could not believe he'd lost his touch. He'd have this girl writhing beneath him again. Soon.

Her form pleased him; her soft curves had fit him perfectly before her sudden attack of conscience forced her to push him away. He'd have liked to remove the ugly shawl she had tied around her shoulders, to see what lay beneath, but hadn't had time to manage it.

Contrary to his usual inclinations, Nicholas was curious about her. He wondered what had brought her to his lands, mounted on a broken-down mare, without a saddle or any other baggage. As far as he could see, she had only the clothes on her back and a golden locket hanging on a delicate chain about her neck. Was she some nobleman's discarded mistress, or an innocent maid, somehow lost, perhaps separated from her guardian?

He smiled a little to himself. Clearly, she had nowhere to go. He would keep her with him.

"No," he finally replied.

The young woman's eyes widened as her brows lowered. "Sir," she said, pushing up onto her knees. "My lord..."

"You will accompany me to Kirkham," he said, "where someone will tend to your injured ankle."

"But I—"

"I insist," he said, with a tight smile that did not reach his frosty eyes. "After all, 'twas my fault you were thrown from your horse. 'Tis only fair that I offer you the hospitality of my home."

Nicholas stood and assisted her to her feet, even as he noted the surprise in her eyes. She had not realized that *he* was the lord of Kirkham. Supporting her weak side, he helped her step up to a jutting rock, then lifted her onto her horse.

"No saddle?" he asked as he mounted his own gray roan.

Ria shook her head as she considered making a run for it. Unfortunately, though, she was lost and needed guidance if she was ever to find Rockbury. She'd been riding for two days...two very long days without food or shelter. Two days of wondering when Geoffrey Morley would catch up with her.

She was not certain she wanted to tell Lord Kirkham who she was, or where she was headed....

"Come with me," he said, his voice warm and inviting. "The hour grows late and Castle Kirkham is just ahead. I'll see that you get that ankle bound and have a hot meal before you continue on your journey."

Ria had learned that it was better to say too little rather than too much, so she kept silent as they rode. She certainly had no objection to helping herself to a meal at Kirkham, and perhaps along the way she could discover Rockbury's location from one of Kirkham's servants.

She straightened her posture and assumed a haughty air so that Kirkham would not think her such an inno-

cent miss, easily flattered and seduced. Far better to
pose as a woman of sophistication so that this handsome
and worldly nobleman would not attempt to take further
advantage of her.

Nicholas made no pretense of watching the road. He
let his eyes wander over the maid who rode alongside
him, fascinated as much by the questions she presented
as her comely form. Her speech was *usually* as refined
as that of any noblewoman, yet she met his eyes with
a challenge and the kind of defiance not often seen in
young women of his class. Her clothing was torn and
ill-fitting, though it was made of as fine a material as
he'd ever seen. Her sun-kissed hair was magnificent,
and her features delicate and alluring. But her hands
were reddened and chafed.

She was not an expert equestrian, but she chose to
ride without a saddle. The horse she rode posed questions, too. Her mare was far from being prime horse-
flesh, but Nicholas knew of no villein who could afford
even the poorest horse.

Had she stolen this hapless mare?

"I am Nicholas Hawken," he said. "Marquis of
Kirkham."

The young woman kept her eyes on the road ahead.
Nicholas watched her profile, unable to take his gaze
from her throat as she swallowed before speaking.
"How do you do, my lord?" she said.

Nicholas smiled. She did not intend to give her name.

"'Tis my estate upon which you trespass."

"I do most heartily beg your pardon, my lord," she
said lightly. "'Twas not my intention to infringe upon
private property."

"Of course not," he said, watching, fascinated, as
she secured the ugly woolen shawl over the neck of her

gown. It was a crime to cover such smooth and enticing skin with that coarse brown wool. "You have yet to speak your name, my lady fair."

Again she rode on quietly, taking in the scenery around her. Nicholas knew she was procrastinating, and wondered why she hesitated to give her name. Was she running from her family? Wanted by a sheriff somewhere, perhaps?

"My name is...Maria. Of S-Staffordshire."

"Ahh..." Now he was getting somewhere, though the manner in which she spoke the name led him to suspect she'd made it up. "No surname?"

"N-nay, my lord," she replied, as if it were commonplace for a young maid of quality to be traveling about the countryside unescorted, riding bareback on an old nag, wearing ruined clothes and having no name other than "Maria of Staffordshire."

He would send inquiries to the nearby estates when he had her settled at Kirkham.

Chapter Four

Lord Kirkham had noticed the rough skin of her hands, so Ria tried to keep them hidden as Kirkham's secretary bound her ankle in the privacy of a well-appointed chamber near the chapel. 'Twas a comfortable room with long mullioned windows facing out over a quaint courtyard full of statuary and early greenery.

The secretary, Henric Tournay, was a young man scarcely older than Ria, she thought, with pale hair and even paler skin. His deep brown eyes were set starkly into the light backdrop of his complexion. All his features, in combination, gave him the appearance of being startled, at all times.

His hands were as white and clammy as the underbelly of a fish, and his touch repelled her. Still, he was trying to help, so she kept her unease to herself.

"'Tis bruised nearly to the toes, my lady,'' Tournay said as he wrapped Ria's foot and ankle. ''You must stay off it for a few days.''

''But that is impossible,'' Ria said. She glanced out the window and saw that it was nearly dusk. Daylight would be gone within the hour. ''I must be on my way. On the morrow at the latest.''

Tournay raised his nearly nonexistent brows and shrugged. "'Tis for you to decide, my lady. But Lord Kirkham—"

A burst of laughter in Kirkham's distant hall interrupted the man. Other male voices joined in, along with spurts of music. Instruments began to play, and voices joined in song, then all dissolved into discord and gave way to raucous laughter, only to be repeated again.

Ria bit her lower lip. How would she get out of Castle Kirkham without encountering the lord's guests? She was completely out of her element here.

She halted her dismal thoughts and decided she must take control of the situation. If she were to pass as a lady—nay, if she truly *were* the Burton daughter—she would have to act accordingly, and not be cowed by every chance encounter. She had spent years mimicking Cecilia, and knew she could make her speech and her bearing seem every bit as regal as her noble cousin's. Ria had plenty of experience in grooming, having played lady's maid to both her cousin and her aunt on many occasions.

It should pose no problem for her to appear as a noblewoman.

Yet why did the thought of carrying out her deception with Lord Kirkham make her tremble?

A light tap at the door had the secretary on his feet in an instant. He opened to a burly knight, who stepped in and glanced shyly at Ria.

"Lord Kirkham sent me to carry the lady to her chamber," he said.

"Very good, Sir Gyles," Tournay said. "I'll light your way."

Relief settled in Ria's heart. They must not be going through the hall, where Kirkham's party was gathered, or they would not need extra light. Silently, Sir Gyles gathered her into his arms and carried her through the door, then down a dark passageway until he reached a narrow, circular stone staircase. Here he climbed, following Tournay, until he reached the top, and again turned down a dark passage.

Tournay walked ahead, and finally reached a heavy oaken door, which he pushed open. In the chamber beyond, Gyles gently set Ria down on a chair next to the fireplace, while Tournay set the candelabra on a table.

Ria could not help but wonder where her host was, not that she was anxious to see him again. Merely curious.

"A tray will be sent to you presently, my lady," the secretary said as Sir Gyles turned to leave. "Lord Kirkham said to tell you that whatever clothing you find in these chests is at your disposal," he added, gesturing to two large wooden chests on the floor near the washstand. "No one uses them now, and Lord Kirkham noticed you had no...er, that your baggage was lost and he thought... Well, help yourself."

When the men were gone, Ria lowered her feet to the floor. She attempted to stand, only gradually adding weight to the injured ankle. Pain shot through the joint, all the way to her knee, making her dizzy and nauseated. Quickly, she sat back down.

This would never do, she thought. She had to leave Kirkham *soon*. There had to be a way to deal with this infernal ankle.

Standing again, she hopped on one foot to the other wooden chair, near the hearth, and took hold of it like a crutch. That was all she needed. A staff, or a crutch, to help her move about until the joint healed. There was no reason why she couldn't *ride* to Rockbury, and once there, everything would be settled while she limped on her bad ankle.

Hobbling around her chamber with the aid of the chair, Ria went to the basin of water that had been set out for her, and started to wash. She felt grimy after her flight from Morley, and the warmth and shelter of the room was a relief.

But she was only a guest here. Once she reached Rockbury and claimed her legacy from her mother, Ria would have her own home—a place where she really and truly belonged.

At least she *hoped* she belonged there.

Ria shook off the worry. Surely she had not completely misunderstood what had been said in Aunt Olivia's solar. She *had* to be Maria Burton. She had vague memories of Tilda calling her Maria, and shortening the name fondly.

Ria pulled off her woolen shawl and let the rich, silk gown slip from her shoulders. Glancing up, she saw a clear reflection of herself for the first time in her life.

What a mess she was!

'Twould take more skill than she had to give herself the refined appearance of a noblewoman.

A noise at the door disrupted Ria's thoughts, and two maids entered the room. One held a tray laden with food and drink. The other carried an armful of things, including a hairbrush and various other items used in a lady's toilette.

They both curtsied and set down their burdens. Piqued by the intrusion, Ria wondered if anyone at Castle Kirkham waited for leave to enter before barging in, but her annoyance was assuaged by the pleasant smiles and obliging manner of the two women. She knew her annoyance was misplaced.

"Lord Kirkham said you would have some trouble getting around," the short one said.

"So he sent us to help," the other added.

Nicholas Hawken paced the length of his chamber, dangling a folded missive from one hand. Tournay had handed him the letter, which had arrived a few hours before his own return to Kirkham, and the accusations stated therein were compelling.

If only the actual evidence of treachery, a letter to the Duke of Alençon, had not been lost.

For years Nick had played the lecherous drunkard, a superficial sot who cared for nothing beyond his next diversion. His recklessness and dissipation were renowned, and understood to be his reaction to losing his brother in France.

Not even his secretary suspected the truth.

'Twas the perfect ploy for gleaning information that could be used to further the English cause in France, and bring about a swift end to the interminable war. More than any other motive, Nicholas was committed to his purpose of reducing the number of Englishmen who perished in the French wars each year.

No more should have to die like Edmund.

While it was true that Nicholas still felt tremendous guilt for his brother's death, in reality his wild and wicked reputation had been carefully cultivated in order to allay any suspicions of him. While he went on his supposed drunken binges with his waterfront cronies, he was well able to cull information for the Duke of Bedford, Regent of France.

In short, he was Bedford's spy, and his missions had been both dangerous as well as amusing at times.

Over the past few months, however, sensitive information had repeatedly been diverted to the French dauphin in Chinon, information that had already had detrimental effects on a few small skirmishes. Whoever was channeling this information had to be stopped, or England's interests in France would be seriously compromised.

Nick looked down at the vellum in his hand. As impossible as it was to believe, the letter implicated John Burton, Duke of Sterlyng, as the traitor who had sent secret information to Jean, Duke of Alençon, regarding the numbers and status of English troops at Orléans.

How could that be? Nicholas wondered. Sterlyng's reputation was beyond reproach. The man's family lines went back to the Conqueror! He'd been a trusted advisor of King Henry V, as well as of Henry's father. Even now, the duke was part of the council that would rule England until Henry VI reached his majority.

And he was the Duke of Bedford's closest friend and advisor. With the disintegrating situation in France, Sterlyng's treason would be a terrible blow to Bedford and *all* the knights fighting for the English cause.

Nicholas threw the missive into the fire and clasped his hands behind his back. He'd invited a couple of dozen noblemen from London in order to ferret out their secrets. When the wine flowed and the wenches were willing, Nick often learned what he needed to know, with his pigeon never the wiser.

Now he wondered if there was any point in continuing this party.

Yes, he thought. He must do all that he could to verify the charges he'd just read. One intercepted letter bearing a fragment of Sterlyng's ducal seal was not adequate proof of treason. Before he could accuse John Burton of such a heinous crime, the case against him had to be ironclad.

Nicholas would continue with the party as planned. Most of his guests traveled in Sterlyng's circles, and one of them might know something. Nick took a swig of ale and swished it around in his mouth. Then he spat it out in the basin next to his bed. He only had to *appear* the drunkard. 'Twould never do to be caught truly incapacitated.

He left his chamber, intent upon the activity in the great hall, and gave a passing thought to the woman he'd brought home. He wondered how she fared, and considered summoning Tournay for a report. Then he decided to see for himself. Those glorious eyes alone were worth a short delay of his mission below.

Besides, her chamber was adjacent to his own. 'Twould not make much of a detour to see to her.

'Twas odd for Ria to watch her hair taking shape into a stylish coiffure. She who had never before seen her entire face in a mirror observed closely as one of the maids finished pinning the elaborate braids in place. Ria could hardly believe it was truly her own reflection she saw before her.

While one maid helped her remove Cecilia's gown, the other searched through the trunks and discovered a delicate chemise made of fine chainsil, as well as two beautiful gowns, which she laid out on the bed.

Ria did not believe she was dressing for any particular reason, for Lord Kirkham had not mentioned anything about joining the party in the hall. And she was grateful. She had no interest in testing her playacting abilities on so large an audience. Fooling a couple of young maids was one thing. Keeping up her charade before Lord Kirkham and his companions was far different.

"There, my lady," the maid with the gowns said, "you have your choice between the green and the orange. Both suit your coloring."

To Ria, the two gowns could not be described in such simple terms. The green one was finely made of velvet, and as deep a color as the forest at dusk, with lovely white fur trim around the neckline and hips. The orange looked more like a shaft of iron turned to rust. Its neckline was cut in a dramatic square, with tiny balls of gold sewn along the edge, and a golden girdle to match. Contrasting yellow silk was set into the flowing sleeves and train.

"I prefer the orange," said a deep, male voice.

Ria whirled to see that Kirkham had come in and was standing only a few paces from her. She did not know how he had entered without her hearing, though admittedly, her attention had been completely engaged by the beautiful gowns.

"Leave us," he said to the maids.

Ria opened her mouth to protest, but the two maids hurried to do his bidding while Lord Kirkham held her eyes. She felt naked, wearing only the thin chainsil. It left her neck and shoulders bare, as well as a goodly portion of her bosom—much more than was appropriate or comfortable in the presence of this man...this stranger.

As he came closer, she raised her hands instinctively to cover the exposed expanse of flesh. She would have taken a step backward, but knew her ankle would not support her.

"You were lovely lying on the ground with your hair in disarray, your clothes wet with dew," he said. "But now, my lady fair, you take my breath away."

Chapter Five

He should not have been so stunned by her transformation. She was the same maiden he'd accosted on the road, but now, with her hair artfully arranged and her shoulders bare, he was able to fully appreciate the fine bones of her face and neck, the creamy purity of her skin.

Lady Maria was exquisite.

"My lord," she said. She raised her chin and glared at him peremptorily, but he heard the slight tremor in her voice. He made her nervous.

He smiled and inclined his head as she tried to subtly cover her décolletage. To his great satisfaction, she was only partially successful.

"My own p-preference was…for the green," she said, her lovely eyes engaging his own. "But since you like the orange…" She picked up the gown and held it over her bare skin.

Nicholas paused a moment before replying. Lady Maria presented an odd mix of sophistication and naiveté. While she seemed to flirt and dally with him, he sensed a subtle unease in her demeanor. For the first time in many a year, Nick was unsure how to proceed.

Rather than moving forward to touch her, and perhaps steal a kiss to begin his seduction, he watched as she moved enticingly, holding the rich russet gown over her nakedness. Light and shadows played off her flawless skin, and Nick felt his muscles tense, his pulse rise. He was a master at seduction, yet felt *he* was the one being seduced.

'Twas not at all unpleasant.

Ria did not know what to do next.

The marquis stood looking at her, devouring her with his eyes, yet made no move to indicate what he expected from her. Perhaps that was to her advantage, she thought. She might be able to keep charge of the situation if she stayed one step ahead of him.

She moistened her lips and turned slightly away from Lord Kirkham, unwilling to display any more of herself than she had already. She was vastly uncomfortable, standing unclothed before him. It had been pure inspiration to take the gown and hold it in front of herself, interfering with his blatant perusal of her form.

But what now? She could not very well toss Lord Kirkham out of one of his own chambers. Could she?

"My lord," she said, tipping her head regally. "You very graciously provided maids to help me dress. If you would be so good as to call them back…?"

Lord Kirkham shrugged casually. "We won't need them."

Somehow Ria managed to refrain from gasping in shock. Surely he did not mean to dress her.

"On the contrary, my lord," she said, surprising herself with her audacity. She tipped up her chin and attempted to look down her nose at him. "*I* will need the maids."

He smiled.

"Please summon them on your way out," she added as she put one hand on Lord Kirkham's shoulder and turned him. Then she gave him a gentle shove toward the door.

When he was just outside, he turned to look back at her, his visage dark and frightening. Ria felt a slight palpitation of her heart and wondered if she had made a dangerous mistake.

Then he smiled tightly and turned away.

She closed the door and leaned against it, letting out the breath she hadn't realized she was holding.

Quickly, before Lord Kirkham changed his mind, Ria hobbled back to the bed and struggled to pull on the gown. She got caught up in the sleeves and neckline, but one of the maids arrived just in time to rescue her before her coif was ruined.

"Oh, my lady," the young woman said, hurrying into the chamber, "here, let me help you with that!"

Ria allowed the maid to pull the gown over her head and then help her with the buttons and laces. She was anxious to be fully dressed, lest the dark lord pay her another visit.

She did not know what to make of him. One moment he was surly and out of sorts, the next he was seductive and overly familiar. Was this the kind of behavior noblewomen were forced to endure from their men? Ria was unsure, her only experience with noblemen being her observations of the guests at Alderton.

She only knew that his effect on her was a powerful one, the likes of which she'd never experienced before.

She sensed that he was a dangerous man. Lord Kirkham was not dangerous in the same way that Geoffrey and Thomas threatened her...nay, the danger was much more subtle, and a far greater threat to her well-being.

Nicholas had no stomach for the game tonight. He sat quietly at the long table in the center of his hall and observed his peers as they indulged in their vices.

He surveyed his realm. *His realm! Ha!*

Kirkham. The title and estate he'd never thought would be his. The irony of his situation never escaped him. 'Twas only through Nick's own folly that Edmund had been killed, making Nicholas marquis.

Nick damned himself once again for the callowness of his youth and his unwavering belief that he and Edmund were invincible. 'Twas his own reckless desire for adventure and fame that had driven him to join King Henry's troops in France, and coerce Edmund into going along for the glory. Little had he known he'd leave his elder brother in an unmarked grave, buried deep under French soil.

Nicholas hadn't had the heart to return home right away...to his father, who had been devastated by news of Edmund's death, nor to Edmund's betrothed, the daughter of a neighboring earl. Nay, he'd wandered over Europe, punishing himself for Edmund's death until he'd been able to stay away no longer.

And when he'd returned to Kirkham, his father was dead. 'Twas one more regret to add to his list.

Naught had changed here since he was a lad. Kirkham's hall looked just the same, except for the company, of course.

Ale flowed freely. Men tossed dice and played at cards. Bawdy songs were played and drunken voices chimed in sporadically. There were willing wenches aplenty in the hall, and Nicholas was certain there were more in various nooks and crannies throughout the castle. But none were so interesting as the one in residence in the south tower.

Maria. Of Staffordshire.

Maria with the fascinating eyes.

He was now achingly familiar with some of her other attributes, and regretted his decision to leave her for the time being. It had been nigh on impossible to turn away from those seductive curves that she'd barely managed to hide behind the russet gown.

Enough had been left uncovered to whet his appetite.

Nicholas took a gulp of mulled wine. 'Twas no matter now. He'd made his decision and he would let it stand. He would not intrude upon Lady Maria tonight. Better to let her rest her ankle overnight and let it heal some before he seduced her. Besides wanting her willing, he'd also like her able.

Harry, Lord Lofton, sat down next to Nicholas and reached for one of the pitchers of ale on the table. He poured himself a cup.

"Not interested in dice tonight, Kirkham?" Nick's guest asked with a sly gleam in his eye.

"I rather prefer the minstrels' songs at the moment," he replied lazily. He leaned back in his chair and stretched his legs to their full length, crossing his ankles indolently atop the table.

"You wouldn't be thinking of visiting a mysterious lady abovestairs, would you now?"

Nick raised an eyebrow and shrugged. Most assuredly, the thought had crossed his mind repeatedly, though he was working to dissuade himself from that notion. He'd like nothing better than to see her in that russet gown…and then see her out of it again.

"What do you hear of Carrington these days?" Nicholas asked, changing the subject. The Earl of Carrington was a close friend of the Duke of Sterlyng, and news of him could very well shed light on Sterlyng's activities.

"Gone to the Continent," Harry replied. "Bexhill mentioned that Carrington's taken 'is wife and daughters to Italy for a month or two."

Nicholas preferred never to take the word of the Earl of Bexhill, a pompous London sot, and had difficulty believing it now. Despite rumors to the contrary, Nick knew that Carrington was not on close terms with his wife, who usually remained at their country estate while the earl lived in London. The man's departure with his family bore closer scrutiny, regardless of what that fool Bexhill might have said.

"What's in Italy?" Nicholas asked, taking another sip of wine. He made it appear quite the generous gulp.

"The weather," Harry replied. "Bexhill said that Carrington's countess suffers from…aah, but you've diverted me from a more interesting topic." Harry grinned wickedly. "The lady you've stashed in your tower."

"The woman is not your concern."

"Ah, but Kirkham," Harry cajoled, "if you're not interested, then what say you let me—"

Nicholas swung his feet down from the table. "The lady is under my protection," he said, choosing his words carefully. "And as long as she remains so, I—"

"Want her for yourself, s'that it?" Harry asked drunkenly.

"Do you not see another female here to interest you?" Nicholas asked, reining in his temper. Lofton had to be the most thick-skulled of all the wastrels known to Nick, but he often had access to information that Nicholas might otherwise miss. "The fairest and most willing young maids in all of Staffordshire are under Kirkham's roof tonight."

"Ah, but the one you shroud in mystery is not—"

"Mystery?" Nicholas scoffed.

"You never allowed any of us to see her, did you?"

"Certainly not," Nick said indignantly. "Throw an innocent maiden to the wolves? I think not."

Hal laughed. "Don't tell me you've sprouted a conscience, Kirkham. I say she's fair game."

"But then, you're an ass, Lofton."

Hal barked out another laugh and furrowed his brow as he looked at his host speculatively. "That I am, Kirkham," he said. "That I am."

Chapter Six

Ria awoke chilled.

She sat up in her bed, disoriented for a moment in the dark chamber. Then she remembered where she was.

The thin gown she wore was little use against the cold, and Ria now wished she'd found something more substantial to wear to bed. Instead, she'd been enamored of a lovely white silk chemise with tiny sleeves and delicate embroidery along the neckline. There was no drawstring at the neck to close it, and it gaped, slipping off one shoulder, adding to her chill. Ria pulled it up, only to have the other side slide down.

The castle was quiet now, without the sounds of revelry that had accompanied her drifting off to sleep. In fact, 'twas surprising she'd been able to sleep at all, with all the voices and music and laughter floating up to her from the hall.

The draught given her by one of the maids must have aided her in falling asleep, Ria thought as she swung her legs out of the bed. She stepped down gingerly and half hopped to the hearth, taking care not to put weight on her injured ankle.

Ria would have made it but for the low stool standing

in her path. Invisible in the dark, it tripped her up as
she neared the fire. She fell hard, letting out a yelp and
pulling a chair down with her.

She was not seriously injured, but couldn't help
groaning as she sat up. She must have roused everyone
in the castle with all the clatter.

Just as she feared, there was a sudden spate of voices
outside her door. Embarrassed to have made such a disturbance, Ria started to pull herself up just as the door
opened.

"Return to your beds," Lord Kirkham said to those
who had gathered outside Ria's chamber. His back was
to her, but she sighed, knowing she would soon have
to face him in all her clumsy splendor. When he turned,
she saw that he carried a lamp.

And he was only partially dressed.

She clambered awkwardly to her feet as he closed the
door behind him. On the tip of Ria's tongue was an
apology for the disturbance she'd caused, but she suddenly remembered who she was pretending to be. A
woman of noble birth. A lady who would not think
twice about rousing an entire household if there was
something she needed.

Nor would she quake at the sight of a half-dressed
man coming to her aid. She was the daughter of a duchess, after all. The sight of a brawny chest with an intriguing mat of dark hair sprinkled across it meant
naught to her. Nor was she particularly moved by the
sight of his powerful legs, clad in hose and braes that
were scandalously exposed by his lack of tunic.

Not at all.

She wiped her clammy hands on her gown and stood
up, determined to play the noblewoman.

"Have a care, Lady Maria," Kirkham said as he approached her. "Else you'll fall again. Are you hurt?"

"Nay, my lord," Ria replied lightly. "Only my pride."

"Mmm," he said, setting the lamp on a low table near the bed. "Your pride is likely to be sporting a few new bruises on the morrow."

Ria bristled at the unmistakable sound of humor in his voice. After all, it was at *her* expense, and she did not appreciate bearing the brunt of his ridicule.

"Let me help you."

Before she could react, he lifted her in his muscular arms and carried her away from the hearth.

Kirkham's scent pervaded her senses. He did not smell of strong drink. Nay, his scent was warm and masculine, and altogether too appealing. Alluring, somehow. Ria had never before experienced the kind of longing he aroused with a mere touch, and she remembered thinking him a dangerous man.

This was the danger.

The candle in the lamp flickered, and shadows played over Kirkham's face. Ria could not read the expressions crossing his visage, but his eyes held a dark intensity as he carried her to the bed.

Instead of placing her on the mattress, he let her feet slide to the floor, her body slipping down the length of his own, like a caress. The heat of his chest burned through the thin silk of her chemise, and she knew he felt it, too, when he glanced down.

Ria's eyes followed Lord Kirkham's, and she saw that they were skin to skin. Somehow, between falling and being rescued, the neck of the overlarge chemise had become askew. Steeling herself to keep from reacting like a naive bumpkin, Ria raised her chin and blinked.

Nicholas felt he might burst. Surely the woman knew what she was doing to him. She had only to feel the evidence of his arousal to know how this contact of her body against his affected him.

The naked tips of her breasts brushed against his chest, setting his skin on fire. Her breath caught, sending a tremor of fierce desire through him. She wanted him as wildly as he wanted her.

His lips touched the madly beating pulse in her neck as she tipped her head back to give him better access. Her skin tasted faintly of flowers, soft and feminine. He kept one hand on her back to keep her clamped to him, while his other hand cupped her shoulder, then touched the delicate bones of her throat. Softly, seductively, he moved it to the fullness of her breast, where he caressed her and made her whimper with need.

He found her mouth then, and absorbed the small noises she made, sounds that only inflamed him further. He soothed her trembling with his kisses, and slid one hand down to her buttocks. Pulling her ever closer, he moved against her in a rhythm that clearly demonstrated his intent.

His tongue boldly sought hers, and their mouths engaged in an intimate match that set his senses reeling.

Her responses to him gave an impression of shyness and innocence, yet he remembered the seductive expression in her eyes, the calculated shrug of her shoulders…the enticing gown that barely cloaked her lush attributes.

No one who looked like Lady Maria could still be chaste.

As soon as her ankle healed—

God's teeth, what was he doing? The woman was injured due to his lack of caution, and now he was making love to her before her injury healed. She likely had new bruises from her most recent fall, as well.

"Maria..." he whispered, breaking off the kiss.

She looked up at him, those amazing amber eyes glazed with arousal. He could have her now; he knew that without a doubt. But he wanted her full participation. And that was not likely to happen until her body was intact, without bumps or bruises.

There would be another night. A full night, hours and hours together, when her stamina would be reduced neither by pain nor by an inconvenient draught of valerian to ease it.

He wanted her fully awake when she succumbed to him.

Morning dawned, bright and sunny.

Maria lay quietly in her bed and listened to the birdsong outside her window. All else was quiet at Kirkham.

Except for the thundering of her heart. She did not know what had come over her during the night when she had nearly allowed Lord Kirkham to bed her. Nor did she understand why he had stopped his seduction.

She was grateful that Nicholas's advances had not progressed too far while she was under the influence of the drug she'd drunk earlier in the evening. Yet his departure from her chamber had caused a terrible longing that persisted through her dreams and even upon awakening this morning.

She'd never experienced anything like what he'd shown her last night. Never an inkling of what a man's touch could do.

But not just any man, Ria suspected. Only the hands and lips of Nicholas Hawken would ever have the power to excite her that way.

She shivered with the chill of morning and glanced about her room. *This* was how it would be to arise in her own chamber at Rockbury, she thought, in a deliberate attempt to remove Lord Nicholas Hawken from her mind.

With sunlight bursting through the windows, a soft bed with adequate quilts—mayhap even a curtain—to ensure ample warmth, and fresh rushes on the floor, she would have more than she'd ever known in her life. Peace. Comfort. Contentment. A place—a *home*—where she belonged.

She drew her knees to her chest, pulled the soft quilts up around her shoulders and thought about leaving Castle Kirkham. She was torn between her need to get to Rockbury and her desire to stay and explore the possibilities with Lord Kirkham.

What were his intentions toward her? Surely they were honorable, for he believed her to be a noblewoman. No man in Nicholas Hawken's position would seduce a woman of gentle birth. And Lord Kirkham believed she was "Lady Maria."

Ria told herself she truly *was* Lady Maria. She did not know if she would ever become accustomed to hearing herself addressed as Maria, or *Lady* Maria. 'Twas doubtful.

She considered telling Lord Kirkham of her quest for Rockbury, then decided against it. She was not sure of anything regarding her inheritance, and did not want to be embarrassed if it turned out she was wrong. She could not tell Nicholas she was the daughter of a duchess and heir to Rockbury until she verified the truth of the matter. Better to remain quiet until then.

Still, there was the matter of this attraction that blazed between them. How would a noblewoman act in these circumstances?

Ria thought about the many times young men had visited Alderton, and how her cousin Cecilia had behaved in their presence. Cecilia had spent several seasons at court in London, and was quite adept at managing all her young suitors.

Ria wondered if *she* could be as brazen and flirtatious, yet modest and demure as Cecilia was. Surely Cecilia would have known how to deal with Lord Kirkham when he'd arrived in her room last night.

"Oh! My lady!" a pert young voice said quietly. "'Tis early...I didn't expect you to be awake yet!"

'Twas one of the young maids from the previous night. She turned and picked up a basin of steaming water she'd set behind her, then entered the room, closing the door behind her.

The prospect of hot water was appealing, and Ria slipped her legs out from the warmth of the quilts. She had decided nothing about her actions today, but much depended on the condition of her ankle. If it was well enough to travel, she would go.

If not, then another day or so at Kirkham would not harm her.

All was quiet in Kirkham's stables. None of the grooms were about as yet, and Nicholas enjoyed the serenity of the morning. All too soon his guests would be up and about, searching for new and ever more wicked diversions, even as they suffered the effects of the previous night's festivities.

Nick paced the length of the low building until he reached the last stall, where Lady Maria's mount had been stabled for the night. Unlatching the gate, he stepped in with the aging mare and looked her over, though his attention was not fully on the horse.

Instead, he could only think of the hour he'd spent after his encounter with Maria during the night, tossing about in his bed, deliberately restraining himself from returning to join the lady in hers. He hadn't been so stirred by a woman in…well, in quite some time. Perhaps never.

And he did not know why.

'Twas not any one feature that made Lady Maria so enticing, though she intrigued him as no woman had managed to do before. Nay, he could not quite determine what made her so attractive to him.

Perhaps it was her injury that made him feel so protective, so possessive. After all, he'd been the one responsible for her fall from this sorry nag.

Nicholas ran one hand down the horse's forehead to its muzzle, then glanced at the teeth. He wondered how far Maria intended to travel on this ancient beast.

More than that, he wondered how he had allowed his attention to become so sidetracked by Lady Maria that he'd spent no time at all considering the Duke of Sterlyng and his treachery against England.

Nicholas barely knew John Burton. The man was of his father's generation, and his friends were older noblemen. As far as Nicholas knew, Sterlyng had never expressed any wild tendencies in his youth, as so many well-born young men often did. The duke had been in the service of Henry of Lancaster when Henry had taken the throne from King Richard, and had been a loyal Lancastrian ever since.

To Nick's knowledge, the man had no family, but was entirely dedicated to the service of England.

Was it possible he'd gone traitor?

If he had, Nicholas would prove it. Then he would personally see to the man's execution.

Chapter Seven

Typically, Henric Tournay had seen to all the details for the day's hunt. There was nothing left for Nicholas to do but ruminate over the letter he'd received on his arrival at Kirkham, regarding Sterlyng's alleged treason.

Thinking of the methods he would employ in his investigation of Sterlyng, Nick took a leisurely stroll back to the keep and circled 'round toward the garden in back, where he and Edmund used to play as children.

The gardeners had done their work well, for the flower beds were raked out, and there were new, young shoots just beginning to poke through the winter-ravaged ground. 'Twas difficult for Nicholas to understand how anything could grow after the past winter, which had been uncharacteristically harsh, but he supposed that was life. It always seemed to renew itself.

He followed the footpath through the squat fruit trees with their gnarled branches covered with early buds, and headed for the secret part of the garden where he and Edmund used to hide from their tutor. Though not quite a maze, it was a winding path, and the deeper one followed it into the garden, the farther away from the world it seemed.

He had nearly reached the low wall where the vines grew thick when he heard a low, feminine voice speaking.

"Come down, you fierce little beast!"

Vaguely, Nicholas recalled similar words being spoken to *him* years before.

He grinned and walked on, following the cooing voice, and stopped when he rounded a set of tall evergreens. Lady Maria stood on her toes, trying to coax a kitten out of the crotch of a tree.

Regrettably, she was quite properly dressed this morning, in a deep blue velvet gown with long, flowing sleeves and a high neckline that would have pleased a nun. Her head was covered, as well, though her golden tresses were partially visible through the headpiece and veil.

He wondered how she'd managed to walk all this way unaided.

Unless her ankle was better...?

"Come now, poor kitty," she said, unaware of Nicholas's quiet approach behind her. She raised one hand invitingly toward the tree, and Nick hoped the kitten wouldn't give her a nasty scratch. "I do not want you to fall. Where is your mama?"

The kitten finally relented and moved tentatively, stretching its paws and taking one step toward Maria. She reached up and allowed the kitten to come to her. When it was close enough, Maria took it gently in her hands and cuddled it to her breast.

Nicholas stopped to observe the sensuous stroking of Maria's small hands over the tawny fur of the cat. A stab of desire, as fierce as any he'd ever known, shot through him as he watched.

He regained some semblance of self-possession and approached her, taking care not to startle her.

"I daresay I wouldn't mind your hands doing that to me, my lady fair," he said. To his delight, she blushed sweetly and allowed the kitten to drop to the ground and scamper away. Then she reached awkwardly for the crutch that was propped against the tree.

"My lord," she said. "You should not say such things."

"No?" he asked, moving closer. He lifted her chin with one finger and looked into her eyes. "Your little friend shed his fur all over you." Keeping his eyes locked on hers, he gently began to brush away the cat hair from the velvet bodice.

He knew he was out of order, touching her this way, but when she trembled at his touch, he could not seem to help himself. He did not *want* to help himself.

Again he was unsure of her reaction to him, though he remembered how she'd felt against him during the night. Soft. Lush. Inviting. His palms itched to have her naked beneath them again, with her breasts tightening in response to his caress.

His body screamed with the urgency to touch her, and he wanted her more in that moment than he could remember ever wanting anyone.

She suddenly moved her crutch and stepped away, breaking all physical contact with him. She turned and surveyed the area between herself and the garden wall.

"This part of the garden is unusual," Ria said once she was able to trust her voice. It had never occurred to her that Lord Kirkham would be out wandering the garden while he had so many guests to attend to. And somehow he'd done it again—managed to disconcert her with his eyes, and a mere brush of his hand. "I've never seen vines that grow so thick...."

Nicholas cleared his throat. "My brother and I used to hide here," he said as he approached her again. He looked dark and cross, and more dangerous than ever. Maria could not keep herself from envisioning his naked chest, broad and muscular, with its spattering of dark hair and flat brown nipples. She hoped he did not notice her unease.

"We had a particularly nasty tutor," he continued, his voice low and intimate, "who liked nothing better than to thrash us whenever we slipped away from our lessons."

"And your parents allowed this thrashing?"

He shrugged. "I suppose your parents coddled you?"

Maria averted her eyes so he would not be able to read the truth in them. "Of course."

She jumped a bit when he lifted her locket from its resting place against her breast.

"This is an interesting piece," he remarked, gazing intently into her eyes again. The back of his hand rested against her heart, and Maria was certain he could feel it racing. "What secrets does it hold?"

"None of any interest to you, my lord," Ria said, whisking it out of his hand and moving away. "'Twas my mother's." She knew she should not be alone with him here in the garden, since he'd proved himself anything but trustworthy. She could not trust *herself* when she was alone with him, either.

"Where did you get the crutch?" he asked as he followed.

"Aggie...your maid gave it to me," Maria replied. "Her younger brother is lame and he outgrew this crutch."

"It looks awkward," Nicholas said. "Take my arm instead."

"This will do, my lord," Maria said. She did not want to touch him, nor could she allow him to touch her again. The experience was all too disturbing.

She only wanted her ankle to heal enough for her to leave Kirkham and head for Rockbury. The sooner she knew whether or not she was Maria Burton, the better.

"Have you broken your fast?" he asked, taking the crutch from her anyway, and then tucking her arm in his.

Maria did not know how to protest this familiarity and still maintain her semblance of a noble demeanor. She let it go, and hobbled alongside him. "Nay, my lord."

"Then you will do so with me," he said.

"But I—"

"No one will be up and about for hours," he said. "'Twill give us an opportunity to become better acquainted."

"I thought we became rather more acquainted than we should last night, my lord," Maria said, then wished she had bitten her tongue. Oh, why had she said such a thing?

"Nowhere near as well acquainted as we will be, my lady," he said, clearly amused by her discomfiture.

His remark caused a slight hitch in her step, but Maria could think of no retort. She kept silent as she limped beside him. She could feel the warmth of his upper arm against the side of her breast, even though she'd worn a heavy velvet gown.

She pulled away slightly and walked on, ignoring the vaguely devilish smile that quirked Lord Kirkham's lips.

They entered the keep through a wooden door that opened into the gardens, and went into the richly appointed room where Henric Tournay had bound her ankle the night before. Sir Gyles was there ahead of them, looking big and burly in his gray hauberk with his sword sheathed at his side.

"Good morn, my lord," he said, then turned to give a slight bow to Maria. "My lady."

All this deference was so strange. Ria—nay, *Ma*ria, as she had to think of herself—did not know how she would ever become used to it.

Nicholas ushered her to a soft chair near a large oaken desk. A fire flickered cozily in the fireplace, making the room warm and comfortable. "You will rest more easily here than in the great hall," he said. "'Tis cavernous and cold when there are only a few occupants."

"Thank you, my lord," she said warily. Lord Kirkham's eyes raked over her appreciatively, and Maria felt less than covered by the modest gown she'd chosen to wear. She was glad of Sir Gyles's presence, but caught a disapproving look in his eye before he had a chance to mask it. She wondered if he disapproved of her or of something Lord Kirkham had done.

Uneasy with both men, Maria sank back in the chair and closed her fingers around the locket, which hung from its long chain about her neck.

"Gyles," Nicholas said as he sat down at the massive desk. Maria watched him take a sheet of clean vellum, then dip a tapered quill into ink. He filled the page with a thick, bold script. "I should like you to take a few men and ride to London with this message." He remained silent until he finished writing his missive, sanded it, then folded and sealed it. He handed it to Sir Gyles.

Maria's eyes followed Lord Kirkham's hands, strong and powerful, their backs dusted with dark hair. Hands that had touched her more intimately than they should.

"Shall I await a reply?" Gyles asked.

"Nay, 'twill not be necessary," Nicholas replied as Gyles turned to leave. "And you need not hurry back to Kirkham. Return at your leisure."

"Aye, my lord."

"By the way, Gyles…my lady has not yet broken her fast. Nor have I." Nicholas glanced at Maria, and she felt his smoldering look all the way to her toes. "Before you leave, send a footman to the kitchen for a meal…to be served here."

"Aye, my lord," Gyles said as he bowed again to Maria and left the chamber.

Lord Kirkham stood and came around to Maria's side of the desk. "So, the ankle is still quite sore today?"

She nodded ruefully. "I had hoped to be on my way this morn."

Nicholas leaned back against his desk and crossed his ankles. "And what exactly is your destination, my lady fair?" he asked.

Maria hesitated only an instant. "H-home," she said, knowing perfectly well that he would next ask specifically where home was. She glanced toward the fire to avoid his gaze.

Lord Kirkham let out a bark of laughter. She glanced up at him and saw bemusement in his eyes. 'Twas a little better than the sarcasm in his tone when he called her his "lady fair."

"It has been a long while since a woman has intrigued me so," he said as he knit his brows and shook his head slightly. "If I ask where 'home' is, will you answer me honestly?"

"In truth, my lord?" she said haughtily. "No."

That earned her another bolt of laughter, and Maria bit her lip in consternation. This was not at all how Cecilia would have conducted a conversation with a gentleman at Alderton. Maria's dauntless cousin would have stood up to the man and said that her destination was not his concern. Then she would have batted her eyes and postured outrageously, dislodging all questions from the poor, unsuspecting suitor's mind.

The trouble was Maria did not for a moment believe that Lord Nicholas Hawken was poor or unsuspecting. Nor did she believe *she* possessed the kind of allure that was second nature to Cecilia. Her cousin was tall and willowy, with beautiful sable hair and lovely brown eyes.

"I'll leave you to your secrets then," Nicholas said as he pulled a low stool next to her. "You are welcome to stay at Kirkham as long as you wish."

Maria thought his choice of words strange, but did not dwell on it. She did wonder, however, why he would think she would stay any longer than was necessary for her ankle to heal.

She contained her astonishment when Lord Kirkham crouched down and picked up her injured foot, placing it gently on the stool. He did not take his hands from her leg, but caressed her through the thin wool of her hose.

His attention...his bold touch...unnerved her.

She should not be able to feel his heat so well through her hose, and that heat should not have had the power to make her recall the sensations caused by his hands, his lips, his body, during the previous night.

"My lord…" Maria said, quite breathlessly.

"There does not seem to be any swelling," Nicholas said, ignoring her alarmed tone, "but…'tis quite bruised?"

She nodded in response.

One of his hands moved up to cradle her calf, and his eyes met hers. He was seducing her with a mere touch of her leg! "Was nothing else injured?"

"N-nay, my lord."

She'd begun to pull away when Nicholas removed his hand and stood. "Ah, here is the footman with our meal," he said.

Maria let out the breath she was holding and marveled that Lord Kirkham had been aware of the footman's arrival long before she herself had noticed anyone else's presence.

She did not doubt that that was the only reason she'd gotten a reprieve from his attentions.

The footman carried in a tray laden with bread, fruit and mugs of warm cider, which he placed on a low table near Maria.

Lord Kirkham pulled up a chair and sat next to her.

"I hope you are hungry," he said to her as the footman took his leave.

"Aye," she replied. "I am. Quite famished."

And by the expression on his face, Maria felt as though she'd said something entirely improper.

The day's hunt was successful, although Nicholas did not succeed in learning anything useful about the Duke of Sterlyng. Rumor had it that the duke had a secret heir stashed somewhere, but Nick was uninterested in Sterlyng's personal affairs. It was the affairs of England that concerned him.

If Sterlyng had any nefarious dealings with the French, he was somehow managing to keep all suspicion away from himself. None of the guests had anything to say about him other than to remark on the folly of searching for his missing offspring after so many years.

Considering Sterlyng's wealth and status, it was assumed by all the noblemen present that impostors would begin to seep through the woodwork and try to lay claim to the Sterlyng fortune.

And so the discussion went, until all the men returned to the keep for refreshments, then to their chambers to rest before the evening's entertainments. Nicholas paced the floor of his private study on the main floor of the keep.

'Twas his favorite room, the office, as his father had called it. Here was the collection of books his grandfather had begun decades before, and to which his father and he had added precious tomes throughout the years. There were various Hawken keepsakes stored here, as well, under lock and key. Business was discussed here with Nick's steward, and 'twas in this chamber that he reviewed important lawsuits brought by the people of the village.

Here, in the office, was where he'd barely reined in his desire for the lovely Lady Maria.

Nicholas did not want to think about the Duke of Sterlyng anymore. He had no interest in trying to wheedle information from his guests while playing the debauched nobleman.

Lady Maria had his full attention.

He gave a moment's thought to the clothes he'd put at her disposal—clothes that would have belonged to Edmund's wife, had his brother married Alyce.

Lady Alyce had been a charming girl, the daughter of a neighboring earl. Yet Nicholas could not recall that she had ever looked as well in deep blue as Lady Maria did. Or that Alyce had ever filled out a gown as enticingly. He could not think of Alyce as anything other than the child who'd grown into the young lady Edmund had loved.

Nick certainly could not have imagined Alyce in the wispy gown that had slipped from Maria's shoulders the night before as he carried her to her bed.

He shuddered with the memory of that moment.

And tried to think of a way to keep his preoccupation with Lady Maria at bay.

Chapter Eight

Aggie placed the last bone hairpin in Maria's coif and stepped back to admire her handiwork. "I doubt Lord Kirkham has ever seen one as lovely as yourself, my lady," she said. "'Tis no wonder he wishes to sup with you alone."

Maria blushed in dismay. "I have no intention of joining Lord Kirkham in the solar, Aggie," she said. He stirred her too deeply for comfort. 'Twas best she keep away from him for the duration of her stay at Kirkham, which she hoped would not be more than another day.

"But Lady Maria," Aggie protested, "his lordship specifically requested that—"

"He has important guests here," Maria interrupted. "There is no need for Lord Kirkham to cater to me...."

Aggie remained silent for once, and Maria appreciated it. She needed to think more about getting to Rockbury, and less about Nicholas Hawken.

The marquis had deftly turned her over to Sir Roger and Tessa Malloy, Kirkham's steward and his wife. Maria thought he'd done it to keep her out of the way of his other guests. In truth, she did not mind. Tessa Malloy was a friendly, talkative soul, so much so that Maria did not have to explain herself or her reasons for being at Kirkham. She'd passed the afternoon pleasantly with the older couple, learning about Kirkham and the villages in the district.

She'd also discovered the location of Rockbury.

Her mother's estate had been mentioned only in passing, but Maria's casual questioning gained her the information she needed. Rockbury was merely a day's ride from Kirkham. She should be able to hobble out to the stable and get her horse. And she knew she could ride.

The only question was whether she could mount and dismount. Maria hoped that by morning her ankle would support her.

"I'll just have Cook prepare a tray for you here in your room, my lady," Aggie finally said, "if that's what you prefer."

"Thank you," Maria replied. "I do."

She stood and, supported by her crutch, made her way to the window that overlooked the garden where she and Nicholas had walked that morning. He'd left her soon after their morning meal, and Maria had been grateful for the reprieve. The man never let up with his seductive overtures.

She had nearly succumbed.

"Tell me about Staffordshire, Aggie," Maria said now. She knew she needed to take the east road from Kirkham to get to Rockbury, but more information about the district would be welcome. She did not ask specifically about Rockbury, preferring to keep her interest in the estate to herself. Since she did not know how her situation would work out there, she was hesitant to mention any of her plans...or hopes.

Eventually, Aggie left Maria alone.

Dusk began to fall, and Maria lit the lamps in her room to ward off the gloom. She was unaccustomed to so much inactivity and found herself growing restless. With her ankle still so tender, she was a virtual prisoner, since she could not walk very far, even with the help of the crutch.

Music began to play in the great hall, and Maria assumed Lord Kirkham would be occupied again, drinking and feasting with his guests. She did not know what pastime they'd enjoyed all afternoon, but most of the guests had been away from the castle while she had visited with the steward and his wife.

Voices drew Maria to her chamber window, and she hobbled over to look. A couple of men and a woman wandered out into the garden. The lady's laughter filled the air, though the men's voices remained low and indiscernible. Then one of the men laughed and the three strolled away, out of Maria's sight.

Leaning on her crutch, she went back to her chair by the fire and sat down. It was going to be a long, dull night.

The games were afoot. Lord Lofton and Viscount Sheffield played drunkenly at swords on the upper landing of the hall. Music played while several men danced with the loose women who'd been hired for the purpose. Men gambled with dice at one end of the large room, and raucous laughter broke out in the other.

In one quiet alcove, the wench on Nicholas's lap wiggled suggestively and batted her lashes at him. She reached across him, brushing her breasts against his arm, and picked up her mug from the table next to them. She took a long draught of ale, then touched her tongue to her lips, implying all the wicked things she would be willing to do for him...for a price.

He wasn't interested.

Awareness of his disinterest appalled him. The wench was as willing as any woman could be, and he was a fool not to take advantage of her enthusiasm.

Nick tried to tell himself his distraction was due to the lack of news about Sterlyng. He had pursued all avenues of information available to him at Kirkham. He'd subtly questioned all his guests about the Duke of Sterlyng and his friend Carrington, who'd supposedly gone off to Italy just as England's most pleasant season was upon them. Nicholas had subtly questioned his guests about every nobleman who was known to have financial or other dealings with the Orléanist faction.

But he had learned nothing, beyond the rumors that had been rife about the duke's missing heir.

Perhaps that was the connection. Nicholas would have to determine who the mother of this supposed heir was...a Frenchwoman, perhaps? If that were the case, and heaven knew Sterlyng had spent sufficient time in France with Bedford, was it not possible that he'd taken a French mistress and sired a bastard on her? The dauphin himself was rumored to be illegitimate....

Since Sterlyng left no other heir, he might be strongly tied to this offspring.

'Twas worth investigating, though by no means would the duke be exonerated if this theory turned out not to be true. The letter to the Duke of Alençon, affixed with Sterlyng's official seal, was incriminating in and of itself.

One thing was certain—there was no more Nicholas could do tonight. He could pass the time as he would, with no thought to England or the men serving the king's cause in France.

Which brought his attention back to the lusty harlot in his arms. Her eyes were a deep, liquid brown and oh, so seductive. Her gown was cut low, all the better to display her ample charms. 'Twould take very little to coax the lass up to his chamber in the south tower.

Right next to the one occupied by Lady Maria.

Nicholas stood, easing the woman off his lap. "My lord?" she asked.

Nick frowned as he found himself without an explanation for what he would do now, or why.

After he'd returned from the hunt, Maria had told him—through her maid—that she was resting and did not care to be disturbed. Then she'd declined his invitation to dine with him in the solar, making her aversion to him clear.

He had no good reason to allow the woman to preoccupy his every waking thought.

He grinned wickedly at the woman before him. She possessed a coarse beauty that would serve him well enough. One long night with this one in his bed would give him respite from his political speculations, and mayhap even dispel his fixation on Lady Maria. He took the wench's shoulders in his hands and dragged her to him, planting his lips on hers.

She speared his mouth with her tongue and grabbed his buttocks, grinding her pelvis against him. She pivoted, dragging him with her, and pushed him onto the chair he'd just vacated. Then she sat on him again, only this time she straddled his hips with her legs.

"Lord Nicky..." she whined. She wriggled against him, pressing her hips to his loins. She took one of his hands and placed it on her breast, startling him when he realized he hadn't put it there himself.

He doubled his effort to seduce her, though she clearly required no wooing. Unaccountably irritated with himself, *and* with her, Nicholas rolled her nipple between his thumb and forefinger. He pulled her gown down in order to have better access to her bountiful flesh.

But he was pitifully unaffected by the wanton, willing female sprawled across what were usually his most sensitive parts.

Nicholas felt smothered by her. She smelled of onions and…of something else he couldn't quite determine. 'Twas not the pleasantest of aromas, though.

She moaned into his mouth and detached herself enough to whisper a suggestion that they find a private place where she could show him a few tricks she knew with her tongue.

Again Nicholas was remarkably unmoved by her proposition. In truth, he thought that if she wriggled against him once more, or tried to shove her tongue any farther down his throat, he would be compelled to dump her off his lap without ceremony.

A loud crash brought him abruptly to his feet, and he carelessly set the woman away from him as he headed toward the disturbance.

Sheffield had managed to lose his footing while engaged in his game of swordplay with Lofton, and had pitched down the steps. He lay at the bottom, unmoving, but at least he was not dead, judging by the moans emanating from him.

Nicholas shoved through the drunken crowd around Sheffield and knelt next to the injured man. He did not want to appear too competently sober, yet he needed to see that Sheffield got the care and attention he needed.

Fortunately, Henric Tournay arrived and began issuing orders. Hardly any time elapsed before footmen came and carried Sheffield to the chamber where he was lodged. Henric ran his hands all over the man, checking for fractures, for internal bleeding. Finding nothing more than a cracked rib and a few nasty bumps and bruises, Tournay bade the man swallow a sleeping draught, and assigned a footman to sit with the nobleman whilst he slept.

Nicholas felt the need for sleep, as well, so he avoided the crowd in the hall and made his way up a back staircase and through a cold, dim passage that led to the south tower. Mayhap he was not so much in need of sleep as of escape, he thought, approaching his chamber.

These evenings of drunken debauchery were wearing on him. For the first time he began to wonder if he would ever finish his mission, if the wars in France would ever be concluded.

He thanked God for Tournay, for all the times his secretary had acted swiftly, with good sense and competence. The man, young as he was, had become indispensable these last few months.

As Nicholas entered the gallery near his bedchamber, he stopped short. Ahead of him an awkward figure was hobbling away, toward the main staircase. 'Twas a woman's form, clad in a voluminous white gown, using a crutch to support herself as she walked.

Intrigued, Nicholas followed quietly behind, inhaling the fresh, elusive scent left in her wake.

She followed the curve of the tower until she reached

the top of the stairs. There she remained in the shadows, gazing down on the scene below.

Nicholas looked his fill at the delicate figure before him. She wore a much more modest gown than last eve. But for all its bulk, it did not hide the sumptuous figure beneath. Its sleeves were full and reached the lady's wrists. The skirt touched the floor and then some, swirling around ankles that were sure to entice him. The neck was high and virginal.

The fabric of the gown was some diaphanous concoction that allowed the light of the chandelier at the top of the stairs to pass through it, giving Nicholas a tempting view of the soft curves hidden beneath.

His reaction to the view was sharp and sweet. And quite reassuring after his recent debacle with the harlot belowstairs.

"Lady Maria," he said quietly.

Though he tried to avoid sneaking up on her, she was startled by his voice. She whirled around and nearly lost her balance. He caught her and righted her just in time.

"My lord!"

He did not respond verbally, but raked his eyes over her appreciatively, from her gloriously golden curls to her suspicious eyes. He dwelled on her shoulders and the perfect hollow of her throat. His eyes wandered to the enticing abundance of her breasts and shuddered as he noted the way the gown floated softly down from their taut peaks.

His fingers fairly burned with the need to touch her.

"There was a noise…"

"True enough," Nicholas said when he finally found his voice. "One of my guests fell."

She composed herself visibly before speaking. Again she was transformed from the naive maiden to a woman of experience. Nick could not say which of the two fascinated him more.

"Poor man, I hope he was not too severely injured."

"Nay," Nicholas said, taking the crutch from her and leaning it against the wall. "He was not. At least not according to my secretary."

"Please, my lord," Maria said, "let us not vie for my crutch again."

"You *do* recall who won our battle this morn?"

"Of course I do, but you mustn't—"

"Ah, but I must," he said, picking her up in his arms. He snagged up her crutch, then carried her with ease, stopping only after they'd stepped into her chamber.

Maria knew she could not allow him to repeat his actions of the night before. That was why she'd avoided him all afternoon, knowing full well he was bent on seducing her. And Maria was determined to avoid it.

What would Cecilia do?

It occurred to Maria that her cousin would likely coerce Lord Kirkham into leaving her by promising more…later.

Forcing a flirtatious smile to her lips, Maria touched Kirkham's chin with one finger, than turned her hand and ran the back of it down his chest. She kept her eyes on his, but felt a shudder rock through him.

Her smile wavered for an instant, and she was afraid she'd taken the wrong tack. But she quickly squirmed out of his arms, took her crutch from his hand and gently pushed him out of her room. "Until tomorrow, my lord," she said in a quiet, seductive voice.

Then she closed the door.

Chapter Nine

The following morning, Nicholas was still shaking his head over the way Lady Maria had managed to maneuver him out of her chamber, but he wasn't about to let her escape him today.

His guests had all gone on the hunt—all except Sheffield, who remained abed. The man was merely bruised and sore, not badly injured, so Nicholas had no qualms about leaving him in the care of Kirkham's servants.

After considering the possibilities with Maria, Nick sent a footman and maids out to his hunting lodge, a rustic cottage located deep in the forest at the farthest reaches of the estate. 'Twas also the scene of many a successful seduction in the past.

The servants had orders to air out the lodge and make it habitable, then return to the castle. In the meantime, Nick planned to invite Maria on a tour of the estate. During the course of their tour, they would happen upon the building in the forest.

Nick grinned wickedly to himself. The romantic little lodge had never failed him yet.

He instructed a groom to have two horses saddled, then headed for the south tower.

* * *

Maria tested the strength of her ankle as she walked back and forth across the length of her chamber. 'Twas still sore, but she could walk on it.

She had to leave. Soon.

Nicholas Hawken was too much a threat to all she had striven to attain. She would not jeopardize her inheritance by dallying too long at Kirkham, no matter how compelling the interlude might be.

Lord Kirkham was a difficult man to judge. At times he seemed wholly intemperate and irresponsible, an outrageous flirt. Yet at other times he was kind and gentle, considerate to a fault. She had yet to see him act harshly with the castle servants, even when mistakes were made, and he was solicitous of Tessa Malloy, the steward's elderly wife.

Maria did not know what to make of him.

In any case, it did not matter. It *could not* matter. She was going home.

She'd gotten information about Rockbury from Tessa Malloy, as well as from Aggie and one of the footmen. Putting it all together, she knew the estate's approximate location. She knew how many hours' travel it was from Kirkham, and what road she would have to take to get there. Now all she needed was for her ankle to be sound enough for her to complete her journey.

Once Maria arrived at Rockbury and discovered whether she truly was the heiress, all the pieces of her life would fall into place. She desperately hoped Rockbury would be the place where she belonged.

Mayhap in time she would find a husband, and have a family of her own. What more could she ask? She might be old for marriage at two and twenty, but she knew it was not an impossible dream.

'Twas what was expected of the noble class. To wed and beget heirs. Hadn't Tessa Malloy just told her that the people of Kirkham anxiously awaited the day their master would bring a bride to the estate?

An odd question crossed Maria's mind. Was it possible that the marquis considered her a likely choice? What would she say if he asked her?

Maria gave a little shake of her head and let out a derisive sigh, dismissing such foolish notions. Kirkham's designs on her had been clear from the beginning. His intentions were no different than those of that abominable friend of her cousin, the fellow she'd narrowly escaped at Alderton only a few days before.

Testing the ankle once more, she took another awkward stroll across the room and was startled by a knock at the door. "Come in," she called.

The Marquis of Kirkham entered. "You're off your crutch," he said as he pushed the chamber door open. To Maria, he seemed the consummate scoundrel with his sinful gaze and irreverent smiles. A wayward lock of hair dipped low over his forehead, and in spite of herself, Maria's fingers itched to smooth it back for him.

She nodded. "'Tis much better today," she said, catching a fleeting expression in his eyes. He was pleased with her improvement.

"I've planned a trip around the estate this afternoon, and I'd be honored to have your company."

Surprised by his invitation, Maria took a few careful steps to the window, giving herself a moment to consider Nicholas's request. She could not see anything untoward about Kirkham's invitation, no indication of anything improper, however unexpected it was. Maria had thought Nicholas Hawken simply bent on seduction. Clearly, she would have to give more thought to Tessa Malloy's words.

Even as Maria lamented her inexperience in these matters, she was determined not to display her ignorance openly. Thinking of her earlier conversation with Lady Malloy, Maria had to believe it might just be possible that Lord Kirkham's invitation was an honorable one.

Could it be that he was interested in more than merely enticing her into his bed?

Warming to the idea of keeping company with the handsome and worldly marquis, Maria found her heart swelling at the prospect of becoming wife to a man she knew and admired. Would Kirkham be the one?

"When do you wish to leave?" she asked.

The village of Kirkham was a prosperous one. The men were out planting their spring seed in the ridges and furrows of the fields, and a good many of the women remained in the village itself, working at their various tasks at home.

Maria looked around her. Chickens pecked at the ground outside the small cottages, and pigs rooted around at will. Children ran free, playing at games with which Maria was wholly unfamiliar.

As she and Nicholas rode down the lane, a multitude of children surrounded them, squealing with glee and begging Nicholas for treats. They stopped next to the alehouse, and Maria's eyes grew wide when he dropped down from his horse, patted several of them on their heads and lifted the smallest into his arms. He then reached into a saddle pack to pull out a satchel of honey-eyed biscuits—sweets enough for all of them.

Maria's heart beat a little faster at the sight of his

smile. She would never allow herself to wed an ungenerous man, and now she knew she would not have to. Nicholas was genuinely enjoying himself.

He set the small child on her feet again, and the children scampered away, as fast as they had descended upon them. Then Nicholas stepped over to Maria and helped her from her horse, easing her down to her feet.

She descended slowly, her body caressed by the length of his, and he did not release her even when she was standing on her own two feet. His hands remained around her waist, with his thumbs brushing over the dangerous territory just beneath her breasts. He dipped his head and had barely touched her lips with his own when a voice in the distance interrupted them.

"Lord Kirkham!" called a man who approached from the alehouse. "You honor my poor establishment with this visit. Will you stop in for a mug?"

"Master Lucomb," Nicholas said as he put a little space between himself and Maria. He ran the fingers of one hand through his hair, even as he supported Maria with the other. "'Twould be my pleasure." He ushered Maria to the entrance of the tavern and went inside.

It took a few moments for their eyes to adjust to the dim light within, but Maria walked ahead of Nicholas, with his hand at her waist, until they reached a table where the landlord bade them to sit. "Dulcie! Mags!" the man shouted. "Drinks for Lord Kirkham and his lady!"

Two buxom young women scuttled out from a back room and hurried to do the proprietor's bidding. One of them poured drinks while the other sliced bread and cheese and put it on a platter. Both women tried to catch Nicholas's eye, but he studiously kept his gaze off them, unwilling to acknowledge them while he was in the company of a lady.

Besides, the game was on. Nicholas would not win Lady Maria by exchanging lecherous glances with serving wenches. Nay, he would do all in his power to lure his lady fair into his arms.

Maria spoke charmingly with Lucomb, easily winning the man over with her polite, but demure, manner. Her hair, though partially covered, shone brightly in the weak light that filtered in through the high windows of the tavern, and 'twas all Nicholas could do to keep his hands from touching it. Her eyes sparkled like gems as she threaded her arm through his, in a manner that could only be considered proprietary.

She wanted him—as badly as he wanted her.

They drank their ale and sampled the bread and cheese while Nicholas spoke of having casks of Lucomb's ale sent up to the castle. When Nicholas finally stood and offered his hand to Maria, the proprietor stopped him with a question. "Did you know Mattie Tailor was ailing, my lord?"

Nicholas frowned. "Nay," he said. Mattie had nursed him as a babe, when his own mother had perished in childbirth. She'd cared for him, loved him, when he'd had no mother of his own to do it. "What ails her?"

"'Tis the dropsy. She is short on breath," Lucomb replied. "But Anna tends her and sees to her needs."

Nicholas nodded, and considered whether to put off a visit until the morrow. He decided against it. The game could wait a bit. "Lady Maria, will your ankle tolerate a short walk?" he asked.

"Yes, my lord," she replied. "It hardly bothers me at all."

He helped her down the lane to a small cottage,

where a young woman came to the door and let them in.

"Nicky?" queried a voice from deep in the darkness.

"Yes, Mother Mattie," he replied, going to the bed against the far wall. Maria took a few more steps inside and watched as Nicholas sat on the bed and took the hand of the sick woman who lay there, rasping with every breath.

"Ah, 'tis good to see you, lad," she said. "You've come back to Kirkham to stay this time?"

"We'll see, Mattie," he replied. "You know I've my life in London…I can't just give it up."

"You're a rascal, you are," she said. She lifted one hand and cupped his jaw affectionately. "But a worthy one. Who've you brought with you?" she asked, squinting in Maria's direction.

"Ah," he said, arising. 'Twas almost as if he'd forgotten she was with him. "This is Lady Maria. My lady, meet Mattie Tailor, who may not have given birth to me, but nurtured and raised me in my mother's stead until I was old enough for fostering."

"'Tis happy I am to know you, my lady," Mattie said. "Forgive me if I do not get out of m' bed. I've been ill of late…."

"Do not fret, ma'am," Maria said, coming closer and taking the sick woman's hand in her own. "Rest easy. I am pleased to know you."

"You and my Nicky—"

"Is there aught that you need?" Nicholas interrupted. "Food or ale? Blankets?" he asked. "I'll hire a lad to cut peat for you…."

"Nay, Lord Kirkham," said the young woman who had let them in. "We are well provisioned—as always—and we thank you."

In the dim light of the cottage, Maria could not be sure, but she thought Lord Kirkham blushed, and it endeared him to her. He cared deeply for this old woman and saw to her needs. They chatted for a while, in the manner of friends long acquainted, and included Maria as etiquette required.

"You will send word if...there is any change in her?" Nicholas said to the young woman when their visit had come to an end and they'd stepped to the door.

"Aye, my lord," she said. "Of course."

Then Nicholas made a quick farewell and ushered Maria outside.

"What say we ride a bit?" he asked, after pausing to breathe deeply of the fresh air outside Mattie's cottage. His careworn expression vanished and the wicked gleam returned to his eye. Maria was hesitant, but decided there would be no harm in an innocent ride through his demesne.

They mounted their horses, and soon he led the way down a well-used path, past rich fields bordered by low hedges. The day was fine, and Maria thoroughly enjoyed the ride, even though she was unaccustomed to riding on horseback. 'Twas a fine vantage point from which to view the world, and to consider all that she'd seen that morning.

For all his appearance of being a wastrel, Nicholas Hawken was no true rogue. With her own eyes she'd seen that the people of the village revered him, and he knew so many of them by name. Even the children were known to him.

She rode behind him into a dense forest, and Nicholas called to her to follow him closely. She did so, and soon they came upon a cottage near a swiftly flowing brook. The setting was quiet, and seemed magical to Maria.

"What is this place?" she asked as he helped her down.

The cottage was nothing like the ones she'd seen in the village. True enough, the roof was thatched, but there were several mullioned windows like the ones in Lord Kirkham's office chamber at the castle, well-tended shrubs that framed the house prettily, blue and gray cobbles leading up to the ornately carved front door.

"My hunting lodge," he replied. "Come. We'll lunch here…rest awhile."

"'Tis supplied with food?"

"Ah…on occasion," Nicholas said, taking her hand and placing it in the crook of his elbow.

Maria went inside with him, not wanting to appear as if she'd never been on an outing of this nature before. She remembered two occasions at Alderton when a whole company of guests had gone on an excursion to a nearby lake. It had been a nightmare of work for the servants, who had had to manage all the details to make the affair possible.

As far as Maria knew, the party had enjoyed a lovely time.

On one wall of the cottage was a massive stone fireplace, with a comfortable, stuffed settle and a low wooden table nearby. The fireplace was laid for a fire and Nicholas knelt to light it. Also in the room were several more comfortable-looking chairs, as well as a locked cabinet, full of books. At the other end of the room was a sturdy oaken table with a clean linen cloth spread over it, and two plates, set for a meal.

Maria had no doubt that the basket in the center of the table was full of food. She clasped her hands together to keep from wringing them, and reminded herself that Nicholas's intentions were honorable. After all, he'd taken her to visit his village, and had introduced her to Mattie Tailor, a woman to whom he had strong emotional ties. Surely that was not the kind of thing a man did lightly.

"My grandfather had this lodge built years ago," Nicholas said from his place at the hearth. Then he gave a wry smile. "To escape my grandmother."

Maria replied with a shy smile of her own as she stood at the far end of the room—as far away from him as possible, Nicholas thought. She looked delightful, as usual, even though she was dressed in the overprim, blue velvet gown tightly laced up to her throat and below her wrists. Nary an inch of her enticing flesh was exposed to his admiring gaze.

For now.

Once he had the fire going, Nicholas stepped over to the table to view the contents of the basket. He found it laden with food, and began to take out the neatly wrapped packages.

Glancing up at Maria, he noted her tentative expression again. Her golden eyes flickered hotly in the firelight and she pulled one side of her lower lip through her teeth. Every muscle in his body clenched.

He wanted to be the one to do that.

"We shall have a veritable feast, my lady fair," he said, uncorking a bottle of wine. He poured the rich red liquid into two goblets, handing one to Maria, locking her eyes with his own as they sipped.

Heat simmered between them. Nicholas was tempted to throw her over his shoulder and head for the bedchamber, but he was certain she expected more finesse of him than that. She was skittish, perhaps from the long

ride through the forest, or because of their isolated location. For they truly were far from anywhere.

It did not matter. He would calm her, woo her until
she surrendered to their mutual attraction and found herself in the master's large, comfortable bed with him. He
would see that she had no regrets.

"There are cold meat pies and fowl," he finally said,
"cheese, spiced bread, dried fruit...."

Nick filled both plates, then picked them up and took
them to the low table near the fire. Then he seated himself on the cushioned settle and glanced back at Maria.

"Come and sit," he said.

He smiled with confidence as she picked up the wine
goblets and joined him. She started to sit at the far end
of the settle, but seemed to change her mind, moving
closer to the middle.

Her invitation could not have been clearer.

He slid closer to her, then reached over and broke off
a piece of meat pie. He offered it to Maria, intent on
the game to win her. Though she seemed charmingly
unsure for a moment, she opened her lips and accepted
the tidbit, savoring the taste without chewing, closing
her eyes in appreciation.

Nicholas almost groaned aloud, but he was too much
the master to show her his reaction so soon.

She started chewing, then opened her eyes and took
a morsel from her own plate, dropping it into Nicholas's
mouth.

He caught one slender finger with his lips.

She did not pull away. Her amber eyes grew huge,
the pupils turning them nearly black, and Nicholas
could not help but notice the way her breasts rose and
fell with the tension of the moment. The pulse at the
base of her throat quickened and her eyelids lowered.

He cupped her hand with his own, then pulled it away slightly, placing a kiss on her palm.

One of Maria's hands flattened over her chest, as if to try to contain the beating of her heart. Nicholas was heartened by her reaction. She did not speak, so he continued.

Another kiss touched the inside of her wrist. This time, he used his tongue.

"My lord..."

"Nicholas," he corrected, even as he pulled her body closer.

"N-Nicholas," Maria repeated.

He did not let go of her hand, but leaned toward her and touched his lips to a sensitive point just below her ear. He loosened the veil that covered her hair, letting it fall behind her. Then, as he moved his lips closer to hers, he pulled out hairpins, causing her flaxen curls to shimmer around her shoulders.

"You are so beautiful...." he breathed. Her eyes were on his mouth, and she sighed as he moved to kiss her lips.

Sensation sparked through him when their mouths met. 'Twas as if they'd moved from the settle into the fireplace. Nothing existed but Maria and him. Her scent, something floral and a little bit spicy, surrounded him. Her lips were soft and moist, and the little sound she made beckoned for more.

He dipped one hand into the silken curls at the back of her head, intensifying the kiss. Her lips parted and he slipped in his tongue, eliciting an incredibly sweet response from her.

She pulled him closer.

She speared her fingers through his hair, cradling his head, even as he laid her back on the settle. Her form fit him perfectly. One of his hands worked on the laces of her bodice, the other teased with experience and purpose what lay underneath.

He groaned into her mouth when the cloth fell away and he was able to touch her bare skin.

Maria felt as if she were floating in a haze of sensual heat. Fire shot through the tips of her breasts to a place low in her center—a sensitive spot she'd only recently discovered, during the one other occasion when Nicholas had kissed her.

She moved against him to relieve the building tension, and he eased one powerful thigh between her legs. The slight pressure he exerted was enough to send her spiraling to heaven and back.

Even as she shuddered, she ached for more. She did not know what he'd done to her, but she knew it was not finished yet. She was driven to discover what all he could teach her, what more there was to know.

His tongue plundered her mouth wildly and his movements became even more demanding. Maria wanted to feel his naked chest against her breasts, wanted to kiss and suckle his nipples as he was doing to hers.

"Yes, love," he said as she pulled on his tunic, "that's it."

He sat up only for as long as it took to yank the tunic over his head, then he stood and leaned over to pick her up. He carried her to an adjoining room, which was chilly and dim.

A large bed dominated the space, and Nicholas set her down next to it, speaking endearments in hushed tones.

He made her feel beautiful, wanted, cherished.

Earlier, she'd seen that he was a kind and generous

man, a man worthy of her devotion. She would have no qualms about binding herself to him for life.

She was kissing her way across his chest when a sound in the distance penetrated her consciousness. She ignored it, finding his nipple beaded and wanting, just like her own.

She laved it with her tongue, circling it, suckling it, growing more aroused with every moment.

She felt Nicholas's hands on her shoulders. They squeezed and drew her closer, then suddenly pushed her sharply away.

"Damn!"

She looked up at his distraught expression and wondered if she'd somehow erred. Then she heard the voices. People were approaching the cottage.

"Stay here," Nicholas said, taking her lips again in a searing kiss. "I'll deal with this."

Maria leaned back against the wall and took a deep breath. After a moment, she heard the door open and then voices—a woman and a man, conversing with Nicholas.

Her breasts were still excruciatingly sensitive from Nicholas's caresses. She covered them with her hands and tried to compose herself while she waited.

But the visitors were not leaving.

In fact, Maria clearly heard the sound of footsteps and voices in the main room of the lodge. They had come inside to stay.

Chapter Ten

Nicholas could not believe his bad luck. Or the even worse timing of Sir Roger and his wife. He threw on his tunic and fumbled with the laces before opening the heavy door to the cottage.

"Why, I had no idea you were here, my lord," Tessa said as her eyes perused the room. She and Roger *had* to have known he was here, and must have expected to find Maria, as well. Their horses were tethered right outside.

"What brings you to my remote hunting lodge, Tessa?" he asked as he attempted to feel the kindness he forced into his tone.

"'Tis our habit to come here for days at a time, my lord," Roger said, "especially when you, er, when the company at the castle is so…spirited."

Nicholas felt a twinge of guilt. Of course they would feel uneasy with the kind of activities going on at Castle Kirkham. And he had always recognized the Malloys' need to get away. Sir Roger had regularly turned a blind eye toward Nicholas's excesses, though in private, Nick knew Roger disapproved of his intemperate behavior.

He avoided meeting Roger's eyes. Though he knew

the old steward would never consider judging him harshly, Nicholas sharply felt the cost of his masquerade. He disliked deceiving the old fellow and his wife, who had known him since he and Edmund were children.

They had to be disappointed in him.

Someday, he would be free to tell them—

The door to the bedroom opened and Maria stepped out. She had dressed and somehow managed to put her hair to rights. Her cheeks were flushed and her lips rosy, but she appeared otherwise composed.

"Lady Malloy," she said graciously. Nicholas suppressed a grin as Maria entered the room with the courtly air of a queen. "How nice to see you. Will you join us in our meal? We have plenty..."

Ignoring the plates abandoned by the fireplace, Maria went directly to the table and took new plates from the basket. Tessa Malloy protested as Maria began to serve the food herself, insisting that she and her husband had not meant to intrude.

"Think nothing of it," Maria said amiably. "Your company is most welcome."

Nicholas could not help the rude sound that spilled out at this exaggeration, but he covered it with an artfully executed cough.

Lady Malloy sat down with Maria at the table, and Roger joined them. Nicholas reluctantly sat with them, feeling cross and irritable. He did not know how Maria managed to socialize with these intruders with such poise. He was so frustrated he was ready to burst.

Looking at the woman only inflamed him more. Her eyes sparkled and a delightful blush crept up her neck and into her cheeks. Her eyes flashed—apparently with interest at the conversation, though Nicholas took great pleasure in the knowledge that she was as aroused as he.

No longer did he merely have to imagine the sight of her flesh, naked and quivering under his hands. He'd seen the pale perfection of her breasts and knew that their tips were as velvety as the petals of the most delicate rose. They had pebbled with arousal at his touch, and presaged a wildly climactic response when he finally made love to his lady Maria.

Tonight.

He would wait no longer. She wanted him as badly as he wanted her, and her ankle was no longer an impediment.

Tiny gold-tipped tendrils of hair escaped Maria's repaired coif and teased the flesh below her ear. Nicholas could almost taste the spot, nearly feel her speeding pulse upon his tongue. She popped a morsel of cheese into her mouth, and he watched as she sucked gently on the piece before chewing and swallowing.

Nicholas felt the blood drain from his head and flow directly to the part of his anatomy that already stood in rapt attention. Without having to think rationally, he knew that mouth was made to give pleasure.

If only he could wait long enough.

Tessa chatted interminably about inconsequential nonsense, and Nicholas thought she would never stop. When Maria placed her hand on his thigh under the table, every muscle in his body clenched. His reaction was primitive—he felt like some kind of barbarian warrior who should throw his woman over his shoulder and carry her off to have his way with her.

"You plan to stay here tonight?" Maria asked Tessa. The older woman nodded. "Lord Kirkham has no need of my husband at the moment, and we like the quiet out here…that is, if you do not mind, my lord.''

Maria thought Nicholas looked about to strangle on his own words, but he replied, ''Not at all, Tess. You know you are always welcome here.''

'''Tis getting late, my lord,'' Maria said, anxious to be away. She had managed to contain her embarrassment at being found in such delicate circumstances with Nicholas, but dearly wished she could be anywhere but here. Nicholas's behavior had not helped, either. The heat in his eyes when he looked at her was enough to burn her on the spot, and she'd made a colossal mistake in thinking that her hidden touch under the table would calm him.

On the contrary, his fire had come close to consuming her.

''Aye,'' he said. '''Tis time we took our leave.''

''My lord,'' Sir Roger said, ''we do not wish to chase you from your own—''

''Not to worry, Roger,'' Nicholas said as he took Maria's arm and headed toward the door. ''We'll see you back at Kirkham in a day or two. Enjoy your respite.''

Maria and Nicholas hardly spoke on the ride back, but the air fairly sizzled between them. 'Twas late afternoon. No one was about when they rode up to Kirkham's keep, and Maria wondered where all of the guests were, especially the ladies. She knew there were some about—she had seen at least one of them.

She was about to ask Nicholas, when one of the grooms came to them, helped her dismount and took the horses' reins.

"Ah, milord…" the groom said. "Master Henric has been anxious for your return."

"Is aught amiss?" Nicholas asked.

"'Tis Lord Sheffield…."

"Where is Tournay?"

"I believe you'll find him in Lord Sheffield's chamber."

Maria had not met any of Nicholas's guests, but she assumed Sheffield was one of them.

"What is it?" Nicholas called over his shoulder to the groom as they moved off down the passageway. "What's wrong?"

"Lord Sheffield's injuries are worse than Master Henric first believed."

"Damnation," he said as he led Maria through a side entrance to the keep. His jaws clenched tightly for a moment before he turned to Maria. He took her hand and raised it to his lips. "We will sup together tonight, my lady fair."

"Nay, my lord," she said, backing away till she bumped into the wall behind her. The day's events had shown clearly that she was out of her element with Lord Kirkham. She needed to establish some distance between them in order to keep her virtue. "I think 'twould be better—"

"Aye, you think too much," he said, placing one hand on the wall on each side of her head.

Maria took a shaky breath. She could have moved if she'd wanted to. She *should* move, she thought. And escape to her chamber as fast as her legs could carry her.

But he brushed his lips over hers, then crooked one knee artfully, exerting just enough pressure to elicit the same kind of raging sensations that had burst through her at the lodge, when he'd had her nearly naked before the fire.

His breath was warm on her mouth, his lips and teeth lightly teasing.

"Please..."

"Please what, my lady fair?" Nicholas breathed. "Please take you here? Now?"

"Nay, Nicholas," Maria said weakly. His physical presence was overwhelming. She wanted him to continue, yet she knew she had to stop him...stop herself.

She pulled away from the wall and ducked under his arm.

Nicholas stood looking at her with hooded, dangerous eyes. Maria remained still only for a moment, then she turned and fled.

Nick stood in the dark hall, waiting for his breathing to slow, his pulse to settle. It took more than a couple of minutes before he felt composed enough to seek Tournay.

'Twould not do to arrive in Sheffield's chamber in an obvious state of arousal. He was no randy youth chasing after his first skirt. On the contrary, he had to safeguard his reputation as one of England's foremost rogues.

What was it about Maria that made him react so spectacularly? She was merely a woman. A comely one, true enough, but he'd known many a beauty both in England and abroad. How did this one make him lose possession of his wits? How did she manage to tantalize him to the very brink with hardly a touch?

He shuddered once more and walked toward Sheffield's room.

"My lord," Henric Tournay said when Nicholas entered. The injured man was awake and moaning, wheezing with every breath. "Lord Sheffield has taken ill since his fall."

Nicholas could see that. The man was flushed with fever and grimacing. His face was moist with sweat. "What is it?"

"A fever of the lung," he replied. "The fractured rib must have punctured it."

"Send for a physician," Nicholas said, coming 'round the bed to speak to Sheffield.

"Done," Henric replied. "The closest physician of any reputation is at Malvern Castle."

"That's nearly a day's ride."

"Aye," Henric said, "but I sent a rider out early. They'll start back in the morning and be here by midday."

"No sooner?"

Henric shook his head. "'Tis doubtful, but possible, I suppose. In the meantime, we've had the healer from the village up here...."

Nicholas touched Sheffield's hand. "William...can you hear me?"

The injured man groaned and tried to lift his hand.

"A physician is coming," Nick said.

"Hurts...with every breath."

Nicholas turned to Henric. "Is there anything we can give him to help him sleep?"

Henric nodded. "Aye. And a poultice on his chest will relieve him so that he can rest," he said. "It should take effect soon."

Sheffield's eyes closed, and Nick knew there was naught he could do for the man, besides wait for the physician. He was in good hands with Henric watching over him, and the healer from the village was a decent one—a midwife, but the woman had knowledge of the healing arts, as well.

Nick hoped Sheffield's youth and usual robust health would see him through.

"Notify me if his condition worsens."

"Aye, my lord," Henric said. "I've…called for the priest."

Nick was taken aback by this dire statement, though he knew Henric was only doing what was right. There was no telling what would happen now, and the man deserved to be shriven. Nicholas gave a resigned nod and left the chamber.

He was met by his other guests, who were irritatingly oblivious of Sheffield's situation. Young Lord Lofton paced restlessly before the fireplace in the great hall, clearly anxious for the night's entertainment to begin.

Nicholas had no interest in dealing with any of the men, and begged off, advising the company to engage themselves in whatever diversions pleased them.

Then he climbed the staircase and went to his own chamber.

Maria would take her leave in the morning. Before dawn.

Thanks to her outing today, she knew the location of the stable, and exactly where her horse was kept. She'd become familiar with the east road, so she would have no difficulty finding it again, and riding all the way to Rockbury.

She had to leave. All her good sense fled when Nicholas was near, and she knew she had to get away from him before everything spiraled out of her control.

She had behaved exactly the way Cecilia would have done, yet Maria doubted Cecilia had ever been so thoroughly charmed by such a skilled suitor. Without a doubt, men like Nicholas were the reason for ladies' guardians. No one was safe from such an expert womanizer. He was much too comely for her sanity, and his engaging manner weakened her wits. She *had* to get away from him.

When Maria arrived at Rockbury and ascertained her position there, she would send word to Kirkham, informing Nicholas where to find her. Thereafter, he would be able to come to terms with her father or guardian, as the case might be, for her hand.

Maria knew she could not encounter him alone again and keep her virtue intact. He had a way of overwhelming her sensibilities. One moment he was merely breathing on her ear and speaking sweet nonsense to her, the next, she was standing half-unclothed, with his talented fingers teasing her most sensitive parts! No man had ever managed to seduce her to the point of forgetting herself.

'Twas fortunate that Lady Malloy and her husband had arrived at the hunting lodge when they did.

The thought of what had transpired at the lodge caused heat to pool in uncomfortable places. Maria stood abruptly. She went to the window, then unlatched it and pushed it aside to let in some cool evening air. She leaned out and breathed deeply.

Music began to play in the hall, and then Maria heard disembodied voices drifting up from the courtyard below. Male laughter and feminine giggles...

It sounded like great fun. Mayhap she would join the gathering in the hall later in the eve. Her ruse as a true lady had worked well enough with Lord Kirkham, so why not the others?

"My lady?" a voice called, accompanied by a light

tap. The door was already swinging open by the time Maria went to answer it, and Aggie was there with a tray of food.

"I'll just set this on the table 'ere, by the fire," she said.

Maria blushed in remembrance of the meal she and Nicholas had begun to share by the fireplace at the lodge. How sensual it had been, merely eating…touching fingers to mouths…. She had not been able to resist him then, and she was terribly afraid that in truth, she did not *want* to resist him.

"Thank you, Aggie," she said, her voice sounding small and choked.

"Is aught amiss, my lady?" the maid asked.

"Nay, 'tis fine," she replied. "And I thank you for your trouble," she added, before remembering her facade as the imperious noblewoman.

Ah, well…she would be gone on the morrow, and it no longer mattered what the servants thought of her.

Maria lit a lamp and sat down after Aggie left. How very easy it had been to fall in love with Nicholas, especially after their visit to the village. He'd been kind and generous, showering various boons and gifts on the people. He'd known every person by name, even the tiniest babe among them. The people had respect for Nicholas, and affection.

That did not occur without effort. Maria had seen how the people near Alderton behaved toward her aunt and cousins—keeping a respectful distance. They clearly had no desire to interact with her Morley relatives any more than necessary.

But Nicholas was different.

Her heart swelled at the thought that even now he was taking his turn, sitting with his injured guest while

the poor man lay helpless. Maria doubted that Geoffrey
Morley would ever have the wherewithal to—

The door to her chamber opened and Maria turned.
Nicholas stepped in, closing the door behind him. He
crossed his arms over his broad chest and stood silently,
waiting for her to speak.

She could not.

He was so unbearably handsome. His hair was damp
from bathing, and his jaw freshly shaved. His eyes
raked over her with an intensity that made her quiver,
and she knew she no longer possessed a will of her own.

He dropped his arms to his sides and came toward
her.

Without speaking, he took one of her hands and drew
her up, until her body was flush with his. "Your lips
were made for this," he breathed. Then he kissed her,
taking full control of her mouth. The tip of his tongue
teased hers, then his teeth nipped and taunted. Maria
felt as if her bones had melted.

Nicholas's hands roved down her back until they
reached her hips. When he pressed her closer, she felt
the same all-consuming craving she'd experienced at
the hunting lodge, though it was more intense this time,
more demanding. When the hard ridge of his arousal
pressed into her, she curled her fingers into the fabric
at his shoulders and let out an unconscious plea from
the back of her throat, a sound that Nicholas swallowed
as his tongue plundered her mouth.

Maria did not know when his hands slipped between
them, but suddenly her laces were unfastened for the
second time today, and Nicholas was peeling her
sleeves down her arms.

Between playful kisses, he removed his own tunic.
Leaning down, he captured one rose-tipped breast in his

mouth, while his fingers hungrily plied the other. In the mindless grip of need, Maria plowed her fingers through his hair as her head fell back. She felt him shudder and knew that he wanted her with a wild ferocity that thrilled her as much as his touch.

He suckled her as he loosened the ties of her gown, which fell in a rich blue pool around her feet, unnoticed. He led her to the bed and eased her down, laying her amid the soft down of mattress and pillows. Seeing adoration in his eyes, Maria felt no embarrassment at her nudity. She opened herself to his loving attention.

He trailed kisses from her breasts to her belly.

"Nicholas..."

"You are beyond sweet..." he murmured, kissing her. "I've thought of nothing but this since you crossed my path."

When his mouth met hers again, his points and hose were gone, and he was as naked as she.

Maria's body vibrated when his hair-roughened skin touched her. He took infinite care with her, wooing and tantalizing as he learned every wildly aroused inch of her. Tension pooled somewhere deep in her core. "Nicholas...I...please..."

He touched her intimately, knowingly.

All conscious thought dissolved into liquid heat. Maria's body was consumed by sensation. Skin and bones melted. Blood boiled. She opened herself to the man she loved.

"That's it, love. Now."

Maria's climax nearly drove Nicholas to his own, but he intended to draw out their lovemaking. She was so responsive to his touch he had no doubt that she would reach it again. And he wanted to take her along with him when he reached his own peak.

Her breasts filled his hands. Her mouth tasted of sweet wine, and her skin smelled of exotic spices. Her hair was a mass of untamed curls, her golden eyes heavy with desire. Nicholas had never known a woman so uninhibited in her response, and it made him wild to possess her.

And he meant to enjoy her all night long.

He moved into position between her legs, then lowered himself to kiss her gently rounded belly. She was so soft, so perfect. She clutched at his head, his hair, his shoulders, and the small sounds she made incited him to a near frenzy. Never had he been so far gone, so out of control before sheathing himself intimately.

He had to be inside her. *Now.*

Positioning himself at the entrance of her body, he entered her with one powerful thrust.

And stopped.

God's breath! Blood pounded in his ears and his breath sounded wholly unfamiliar. This seduction was not at all what he'd planned.

He'd bedded a *virgin!*

Chapter Eleven

Had it been required of him an hour ago, Nicholas would have sworn she was no innocent. Her flirting and teasing had been as expert as any courtesan's. She had played him well. Unbelievably well.

His lust for her had been simmering since her arrival at Kirkham, and today's frustration at the lodge had been the last straw. After leaving Sheffield's sickbed, Nick had spent as short an interval as possible at his bath—though he'd taken extra care with shaving—in order to get back to her sooner.

"Nicholas?" Maria asked. Her voice was small and unsure.

His face was damp with perspiration; his muscles ached with the strain of holding back. He was feverish with need. "You might have told me, love...."

The muscles in her throat worked, but she said nothing. Instead, she closed her eyes and moved slightly, her delectable body torturing Nicholas into pulling back and driving into her again.

His movements quickened and became frenzied. She enveloped him in a cocoon of pure sensation and truth, urged on by need and want, lust and desire, all in one.

She played his body like an instrument, though unwittingly, for he knew she had no experience in this, the most intimate of acts.

Her nails scored his back, and as she met each possessive thrust, *she* possessed *him* entirely. Her whimpers caressed him. Her teeth scraped his jaw and neck. Her tears touched his soul.

He shattered within her.

And in that moment, everything he thought he knew about women and lovemaking was obliterated. The earth shifted, and as he fell alongside her, he could hardly believe they still remained upon the bed.

He pulled her close and kissed away the tear that slid into her hair. "Do you weep, my lady fair?" he asked gently. "Have I so wounded you?"

"N-nay, my lor—Nicholas," she said. "'Tis only that I never knew... I've never..."

He wanted to make light of her newfound feelings, to tell her that it was always so between a man and a woman.

Yet he could not lie. Instead, he rose up again and began to woo her as he should have at the start...gently, patiently, pleasuring her even as he tutored her.

Something woke her. 'Twas not just the strangeness of having Nicholas in her bed, but a sound that came through the open window of her chamber. Voices from below, and something else. What?

The desire to stay warm and safe within Nicholas's arms was strong. Yet something was going on outside.

Maria slipped out of bed. Ignoring twinges of discomfort in her tender flesh, she went to the open window and looked out.

Torchlight illuminated a small group below. They

chortled and laughed, then drunkenly hushed themselves, dissolving into laughter once again. Maria could not understand why Nicholas would surround himself with such buffoons.

They threw small stones at the window of the chamber next to hers, and Maria realized 'twas Nicholas they were trying to summon. A woman's voice called out in a loud whisper, "C'mon, Lord Nicky! Come and show us what yer got!"

"Eh, Nick!" the male voice was slurred. "F'get about the piece you've got stashed in the tower. This one'll give you what you need without such botheration!"

More laughter and giggles sounded, while Maria's heart dropped to her feet. Humiliated, she tried to block out the words, but could not help but hear them over and over again. *She* was the piece Nicholas had stashed in the tower. While she had been falling in love with him, he'd been lying in wait for her, to seduce her and take her virtue without any more thought than where he would find his next cup of ale.

Stones hit the window again. The woman's loud whisper drifted up again. "Aw, Lord Nicky! Come down!" she said. "Ye liked me wares well enough last eve!"

Shaken, Maria realized that tears were of no use to her, and she dashed them away. 'Twas pointless to feel hurt or misused. She had been used before, but never quite so coldly, or with such calculation. She had been such a fool, allowing herself to believe that Nicholas's motives were honorable.

Well, Nicholas Hawken could go to the devil.

She shoved away from the window and looked around the chamber in the dim light of the fire. Her vision was blurred from tears, but it did not matter. There was nothing here that belonged to her, no packing to do. She would leave now, and refuse to give him the opportunity to gloat over his damnable prize.

If naught else, she still had Rockbury—at least she *hoped* she had Rockbury—and Nicholas had no idea of her connection with the estate. Once she left Kirkham, she would never have to see him again.

In the shadows of the chamber, she found her gown on the floor and quickly laced herself into it. She slipped on her shoes, fastened them and let herself out.

At daybreak, the physician arrived and Nicholas was summoned to Sheffield's chamber. Maria's bed was empty as he left it, and he assumed she was visiting the garderobe, or had perhaps gone elsewhere to bathe. Despite the number of times he'd loved her during the night, he doubted she'd feel comfortable bathing before him in the light of day.

That would change, he thought. Tonight.

He felt a surge of sheer masculine pride in knowing that he'd been the one to show his lovely Maria the pleasures to be shared between a man and a woman. And not just *any* man.

Nicholas had been the one. The only one.

And tonight, when he took her to his bed, he would introduce her to even more sensual delights. He'd never known a woman as responsive as Maria. She was fresh and untutored, and entirely genuine in her lovemaking. She had taken exquisite enjoyment from *his* pleasure, treating him playfully, and with affection.

That was something new. 'Twas more than a bit unsettling, as well.

His lovers usually liked him well enough, or liked

what he could provide them, but he sensed more than a casual fondness here. She *cared* for him.

That was a disquieting thought. He certainly did not care for her in the same way, nor would he ever. He had no tenderness in him, at least not the kind needed by a woman. Besides, his task was all too important to be abandoned. He did dangerous work for Bedford, and his lack of family ties or other entanglements freed him from worry. No woman held his heart, making him vulnerable to an enemy who would use that weakness against him.

Bah! He would enjoy her for now, but he knew he would soon tire of her. Then they would part, and he would see that she was well compensated for her womanly devotion to him and...

His brows came together in a frown. *Who was Lady Maria, anyway?* he wondered as he made his way to Sheffield's chamber. The question had only fleetingly crossed his mind before, and now he wondered in earnest. He knew with certainty that she was not a discarded mistress, but the other possibilities were troubling. She'd been well dressed, and her speech was cultured. Yet young women of her class did not just ride the countryside unattended.

Puzzled, he dressed and left her chamber. He would probe for an explanation later, after he'd seen to Sheffield.

Maria could not believe her eyes.

If this was Rockbury, then she was truly a princess.

Of course, she had yet to discover whether or not she was the heir, but the dream was, for a moment, an intriguing one.

'Twas a grand manor house, with three stories, turrets

and towers, and a gravel drive that circled in front of an imposing entrance. Maria could not imagine a more majestic place than the king's palace itself.

Yet a palace was not what she needed. She merely wanted a home, a quiet haven where she could retreat and sort out all the recent events in her life. A place where she could begin her life anew and forget Nicholas Hawken.

With more than a little trepidation, she rode right up to the main entrance and dismounted. With her jaw agape, Maria stared at the place, well aware that 'twas likely she had it all wrong. A place as magnificent as this could never be hers.

The door opened noiselessly, and a small, elderly man stepped out. Maria closed her mouth, held her head high and looked the man in the eye, not insolently, but assertively. After all, she'd come to claim this fine house as her own. She would not appear the supplicant here.

Even if she were about to be sent away.

The old man's expression faltered as she approached him, and he suddenly turned and called into the house. Maria did not hear exactly what he said, but before she'd taken two more steps, an old woman—the other half of a matched set, Maria thought—appeared on the doorstep.

"Lord in heaven!" the woman cried.

"Aye, Mother," the man replied without taking his eyes off Maria. "'Tis Lady Sarah come back to us!"

To Maria's surprise, she had difficulty taking a deep breath. It was as if she'd been laced too tightly into her kirtle, so that not enough air could get into her lungs.

They thought she was Sarah.

They were not going to send her away!

"'Tis all right, lass," the man said. The woman came out and put one comforting arm around Maria's shoulders as if she'd known and cared for her all her life. "No need to weep. Yer home now."

She hadn't even realized there were tears in her eyes, running down her cheeks. Brushing the moisture away, she allowed the woman to lead her into the house.

"Yer father will be beside himself with joy," the woman said. "He's not given up hope of finding ye, ever since his hateful stepmo—er... Ever since the dowager duchess told him you went and survived when our poor Sarah was lost in childbed."

"My f-father?" Maria said, controlling the trembling of her voice.

"Aye," said the man. "The Duke of Sterlyng. John Burton. We'll be sending for him right away."

"Then...then you believe I'm Maria Burton?"

The older couple laughed at Maria's uncertainty. "Yer the very image of yer mother," the woman said, "and ye've got yer father's eyes. All golden they are, and warm as the sun on a spring morn."

"Now, Mother..."

"Ye know 'tis true, Elhart Twickham," she said. "And I don't mind sayin' it—his grace is a comely man still. And just look at this locket. Ye cannot deny it once belonged to our lady Sarah."

"We'll be sendin' for the duke right away," Master Twickham repeated as his wife led Maria deeper into the house. "Won't take him but a day to get here from London, once he hears ye're here."

Maria's knees felt weak.

She had a father! Someone who would be—as the servant had said—beside himself with joy to find her here. Maria had never needed him more than she did at this moment.

This was something she had never really counted on: Rockbury. Belonging here. She realized now that she'd never believed that it could be true.

Yet here she was, daughter of the Duke of Sterlyng. And he would be happy about it.

Where had Maria gone? And just as importantly, why had she left him? Hadn't their days—and their one glorious night—together been—

Hell's bells. He was beginning to think like a besotted idiot. *Glorious nights. Lovely days.*

She was no more or less than any other woman of his acquaintance. His *intimate* acquaintance. True, she'd been more enthusiastic than most, mayhap a bit more intriguing than any he'd known before.

What did it matter? If she was going to be so secretive, he was well rid of her. He had his own secrets to keep without having to deal with hers, too!

Nicholas paced back and forth before the fireplace in the great hall, restlessly pondering those questions and the hundred others that plagued him. He did not really know who she was, or where she was from, so he had no idea where to begin searching for her.

Aye, he would search for her.

She'd been gone several hours before he even realized she'd left Kirkham, so must have gotten a notable head start on one of any number of roads. When he finally managed to leave Sheffield's sickroom, Nick tried to pick up her trail, but a heavy rain in the late afternoon obliterated any tracks she might have made.

But he would find her. He would have her back in his bed before she could think twice.

"What's the word on Sheffield?" Lofton asked casually, breaking in on Nicholas's thoughts as he sat in a chair by the hearth.

Nick was dumbfounded by the man's flippant attitude. After all, Lofton had been the one responsible for Sheffield's fall. He could at least give an appearance of remorse.

"His lung is punctured," Nicholas replied. "His chances for survival are poor."

Lofton shook his head. "Shame," he said. "Well, at least *you* got a good night's rest."

Nicholas gave him a contemptuous glance. "Why so?"

"Trendall and I tried to rouse you in the wee hours," Lofton said. "Brought one of the whores to your window and tried to wake you, but—"

"*What?*" he demanded. "*When?*"

"I don't know…an hour or so before dawn…. Seems to me their caterwauling would have roused the dead," he said, then laughed. "But not Kirkham. Oh, no. Sleep deeper than the dead, you do."

Nicholas resisted the urge to jab his fingers through his hair. He could just imagine what had gone on in the courtyard below Maria's window. It must have awakened her.

He stood abruptly and stalked out of the hall. What in heaven's name had she heard? Something offensive, of course, but had it given her reason enough to go haring off into the night?

He slammed one fist into the wall. Evidently, it had.

Two days later, in the early evening, Maria sat at the edge of a small pool at the far end of the Rockbury garden. 'Twas a peaceful place, where birds nested, insects fed and small creatures chased each other and their own tails in the fresh spring weather. She dangled her feet in the water, kicking at the curious golden fish that seemed to have no fear of her.

Here, she could almost forget the face of Nicholas Hawken, and the seductive touch of his lips on her body. While she sat here in her own garden, she came close to denying that he'd had any affect on her at all.

She pulled her feet out of the water and wrapped her arms around herself. She could not think about Nicholas now, not when her father was expected at—

"My lady?"

The voice of the caretaker's wife interrupted her dismal thoughts. She rose to meet the woman, but was surprised by the appearance of a white-haired stranger. The man's step faltered slightly when he saw her, but he proceeded, anxious, yet strangely hesitant in his gait.

He was still handsome for his age, and Maria saw her own eyes when she looked into his. Her eyes burned and her throat felt so raw that she was unable to speak.

"Maria...?" he said when he reached her. His voice was deep and rich, but oddly breathless. He extended one hand and she saw that it trembled. His amber eyes glistened brightly as he reached out to her.

Maria swallowed and forced her voice to work. "Father?" she whispered tremulously.

He did not speak for a moment, but held both her hands tightly. Then he pulled her into his arms.

"My God, child," he said with a trembling voice. *"Maria!"*

Chapter Twelve

In her wildest imaginings, Maria could not have dreamed up a place as strange or as marvelous as London. People were everywhere. Colors dominated the markets, along with more noise than Maria had ever heard before. Mingled aromas of smoke, cooking food, waste, and the Thames itself were nearly overwhelming.

Her father's house was in Bridewell Lane, not far from the river, just northeast of Westminster Hall. Seamstresses, shoemakers and tutors had been in and out of the house during the last week, so often that Maria's head spun. She had new gowns and veils, jewelry, shoes and boots. A gentle mare for riding was now in her father's stable, and he'd purchased a lovely, ornate lady's saddle for her.

Maria had spent so many hours in her life mimicking her cousin Cecilia that her speech was nearly perfect and her manners impeccable. However, a tutor had been hired to teach her all that was still lacking: how to ride as befit a lady of her station; the rudiments of reading; the necessary skills to run a household.

After all, the duke would see his daughter married. She would marry well, and marry soon.

Maria sighed. She had awakened early and dressed with care as she thought of the previous evening's diversions. Her father had invited several well-born friends and acquaintances to meet his daughter, and several of them had asked his consent to pay court to her.

She should be content. Nay, she should be ecstatic with her change of circumstance. Her father was a kind and loving man, so delighted to have his daughter back that he spared no trouble or expense for her. He was protective, yet not stifling, allowing Maria a great deal more freedom than she suspected other noble daughters received.

The young men who'd attended her last night were handsome, wealthy and accomplished. Some sat in the House of Lords. A few were knights who had served the Duke of Bedford in France.

But none were Nicholas Hawken.

She had hoped to abolish Nicholas from her memory, but quickly discovered that 'twas not so easy a task. With every male smile that was bestowed upon her, Maria remembered Nicholas's teasing mouth and how his kisses had driven her mad. With every young man's attempt to touch her hand, she felt a painful twinge in the region of her heart.

But all this pining over Nicholas Hawken was absurd. She knew what kind of man he was—certainly not one who deserved any kind of devotion or fidelity from her! He was a lecherous scoundrel, a man with no compunction about seducing one woman after another.

In her mind, she could still hear the voice of the one in the courtyard, inviting Nicholas to return to her.

Maria left her chamber and walked down to the main floor of the house, to find Lady Alisia Preston, the woman in charge of her father's household, carrying two bundles of dried flowers into the house.

Alisia was a cousin of Sterlyng, and had married a common merchant against her father's wishes. Still a young woman when she'd been widowed, she had desperately needed employment to support herself and her young son. Sterlyng had provided that employment, as well as hearth and home for Lady Alisia and the boy, who was old enough now to be squire to an uncle in Surrey.

Alisia had immediately taken her young cousin, Maria, under her wing, much like a younger sister. Maria accepted her kinship *and* friendship with pleasure.

"Ah, my dear lady..." Alisia said when she saw Maria. "Here is yet another bouquet for you."

"Another...?" Maria looked around then, and saw that the tables held several vases and pots of dried flowers. She was astonished. This was beyond anything she had ever experienced, either at Alderton or Kirkham. "What is this all about?"

Alisia laughed. "They are gifts, my sweet girl," she said cheerily. "Tokens of esteem from all your young admirers."

"Who?"

"The young men who attended you last eve," she replied, "*and* the day before."

"But I—"

"And there are other gifts, as well," Alisia said. "Confections, lengths of cloth—fine wool, I believe— and even a joint of lamb for your table."

"A joint of..." Maria mused with puzzlement. She could hardly take it all in. "I don't understand."

"Your father intends to find you a suitable husband," Alisia told her. "And he has made it clear that you will have your choice of spouses. That is why we've had so many gentleman callers over the past few days. They know that only one will win you.'' Ignoring Maria's astonished expression, Alisia picked up another batch of greens from a table near the stairs.

A knock at the door had Alisia turning again to answer it, but her hands were full.

''I have it,'' Maria said.

Still trying to absorb all that Alisia had told her, Maria lifted the door latch and pulled it open. She could not have been more surprised if someone had slapped her.

'Twas Nicholas!

In the interminably long days since he'd last seen her, Maria had only become more beautiful.

And Nick didn't know whether to throttle her for leaving him or kiss her to the point of senselessness.

Male instinct ruled in this instance.

While she was still recovering from the shock of seeing him, he pulled her close and claimed her lips with his own. He savored the spicy taste of her, the scent and texture of her hair as he cupped her head, the lush curves of her body as he pressed the length of it to his own.

Nothing mattered but this.

He would have devoured her completely if he could, but the indignant shrieks of a nearby woman eventually penetrated his consciousness. At the same time, he felt Maria's hands against his chest, and she was pressing hard, actually pushing him away.

''My lord!'' the woman cried. ''Unhand Lady Maria this instant!''

Nick kept his eyes locked on Maria's. Hers were neither heavy-lidded with passion nor bright with excitement. All he could see reflected in those glorious golden irises was panic.

Her lips were swollen by his kiss, but they were trembling. She took a step back.

And slapped him.

Nicholas covered his injured jaw with his hand and rubbed. Perhaps 'twas not panic, exactly…but anger.

"Shall I call a footman, Lady Maria?"

Nicholas held his ground while he nursed his injury. "I thought you might be happier to see me, Maria," he said.

She looked like a deer caught in a bowman's sights— ready to bolt. He reached out and took her hand. Her eyes were shimmering with moisture and her lower lip trembled.

"I am no callet, Nicholas! If you've come to—"

Maria's companion gasped at her bold statement, and Nicholas winced. By no means had he ever treated her as a common whore. True enough, he'd seduced her and taken her innocence, and for that, he admitted to feeling some remorse. He had completely misjudged her, just as he had failed to discern her true circumstances when he'd waylaid her at Kirkham.

Nicholas had no intention of bedding her now—especially as long as she resided in her father's house. Nay, he intended to woo her as any of her many other suitors were wont to do. 'Twas as perfect a ploy as any he could have dreamed up for exposing Sterlyng's treachery against England.

"Of course not, my lady fair," he said, catching her hand and kissing it. He smiled guilelessly. "I've merely come to pay you my respects…and request an audience with you and your father later, at your convenience."

* * *

Maria felt faint.

Luckily, Alisia had been close by when Nicholas left, to lend support and usher her to a chair in the main sitting room of the house.

"'Tis not my business, Maria," Alisia finally said, "but he must have hurt you very badl—"

"Nay," Maria interjected shakily. "Nay, he did not hurt me, Alisia. 'Tis merely annoyance I feel. Nicholas Hawken hasn't the power to hurt me."

She did not notice the slight elevation of Alisia's brow. "If you wish, I can have your father—"

Maria shook her head. "I would prefer that my father not hear of this incident. Please," she said, taking Alisia's hands into her own, "do not tell him. I would not cause him worry." Nor did she wish to disclose her foolishness at Kirkham and jeopardize her father's good opinion of her. She knew that in his eyes, she could do no wrong. She would have it remain so.

"I don't suppose he would dare approach you again, not after your...reaction to him," Alisia said doubtfully.

Maria wrung her hands in her lap. Nearly two weeks away from the man, yet it seemed like only yesterday that he was wreaking tender havoc on her body, invading her senses, her heart. Would she never be free of the memory of those steely gray eyes raking her person with appreciation, or those marvelous, powerful hands working magic upon her body, her soul?

"Nay," she agreed. "He will not return."

It had taken nearly a week at Kirkham for Nicholas to hear of Maria's questions about Rockbury and for him to infer her intended destination. To say that he'd been shocked to learn she was Sterlyng's daughter would have understated the case.

He had suddenly recalled where he'd seen golden eyes like hers before. The Duke of Sterlyng had the same leonine eyes, as well as a thick mane of shockingly white hair.

And he was a traitor to England.

Nicholas had spent the last few days gathering information regarding Sterlyng's reunion with his long-lost daughter. He'd heard what everyone was saying about Maria and her desolate years at Alderton, and had known the stories were true. He'd seen the signs of her harsh life, yet he'd never put the evidence together.

Since his arrival in London, he'd learned that Maria rode every morning in the company of a groom, and Nick was determined to intercept her today. From her response to him that morning, he knew she was not immune to his touch, his kiss.

Nor was he unaffected by *her*. He could not keep himself from recalling everything about her, from the moment she'd struck him with her fist on the road near Kirkham, to the intimacies they'd shared on their last night together. He had not intended to ambush her that morning in her father's house.

To his dismay, he'd discovered that he could not keep his hands off her, keep his mouth from seeking hers.

He grinned. She was worth every bit of the trouble he'd gone to in order to find her. He should have expected her blistering response to him. She had more passion in her than a dozen other women of his acquaintance. He could barely wait until the next time he made love to her.

He would bed her again. Soon. But for now, he would have to bide his time.

Maria Burton provided Nicholas with his best opportunity to get close to Sterlyng, to prove that he was the one sending information to the Duke of Alenon. Though Nicholas would have to curb his wayward appetites whenever Maria was near, it was not beyond his abilities. It would be difficult, but he could do it.

He *would* do it.

He turned his mind to the matter at hand. Maria was in the habit of riding down to Westminster each morning with a groom. She usually rode along the paths near Westminster, then met her father at some point for a cool drink or a light meal.

Nicholas intended to waylay her before she met Sterlyng. He must make amends for his earlier behavior and get her to accept him as a suitor.

To that end, he had ridden to a remote meadow on the Westminster grounds to wait for her. If his sources were correct, and Maria followed her usual habit, she would be here soon.

Nick remained mounted, but found a spot that was not visible from the horsepath. He wanted to take her by surprise, just as he had this morning. Her reaction to him had been purely instinctual and genuine.

Clearly, she was not indifferent to him. His jaw still smarted with the evidence of that.

He smiled at the knowledge, and his body tensed with the notion of taking her to his bed again. Their one night together had been extraordinary. Even in her innocence, her responses to their lovemaking had been more spirited and intense than any he'd experienced before. Just the thought of having her naked in his bed, with her hair spread out across his sheets, her eyes locked with his and their bodies joined together, made him uncomfortable with anticipation of their next tryst.

The approach of a rider brought Nick's thoughts to the present. Judging by the speed of the horse's hoofs, 'twas a leisurely rider, and Nicholas had every reason to believe Maria would soon come down the path.

He wiped damp palms on his thighs when he saw her, and forced the air back into his lungs. She was as regal as any woman could be, dressed in fine silk and velvet, with a matching cap and veil covering her hair most properly. She sat her horse well, he noticed, even better than she had when she'd ridden with him across Kirkham lands.

He edged his horse out to meet with hers.

"Oh!" she cried, as one hand flew to her breast.

"My lady fair," he said wickedly. He reached out and took hold of the bridle to settle her mount. "What a coincidence."

"M'lady?" the groom asked as he came upon them.

Maria did not speak for a moment, seeming to weigh her options. "'Tis all right, Master Cole," she finally said, turning in her saddle to address the young man. "'Tis Lord Kirkham. We are a-acquainted."

"M'lady...his grace said—"

"Wait for us at the copse near the main drive, Cole," Nicholas said. "I will not keep Lady Maria long."

Maria did not appear to appreciate the way Nicholas assumed control. He believed she would have called out to Cole to keep him close by, but did not want to appear unnerved by Nicholas. Now that he knew her better, he saw that her method of dealing with uncertain situations was to brazen them out.

She tipped up her chin and rode on.

"Maria..."

"I have naught to say to you, my lord."

"Nicholas," he corrected as he tried to catch her eye.

She kept her gaze averted and shrugged.

"You are angry with me."

Maria kept her eyes on the path before her.

"I cannot believe you left Kirkham just because of a few buffoons singing ridiculous nonsense outside your window."

She gave him a cutting glance, then turned back to the path as if it contained the most fascinating scenery in all of London.

Clearly, he would have to take another tack.

As they rode silently, he studied her profile, the shimmering veil that did not quite cover her golden hair, the fashionable collar that teased the delicate bones of her neck, the way her gloved hands held the reins....

He shook his head to clear it of wayward thoughts that were of no consequence to his mission. For months someone had been channeling information to France. Nick had been grasping at straws for some evidence that would lead him to discover who the traitor was.

A beautiful face and an enticing body were not going to sway him from his purpose.

He reached for her bridle again and pulled her horse up short, aligning himself with her. "Maria," he said softly. "Do not torture me with your indifference. I apologize for my...my less-than-noble behavior with you at Kirkham. I did not realize... I never thought..."

If she did not quit staring at his mouth as he spoke, he was going to forget his resolve to act in a gentlemanly manner.

"Please go away, Nicholas," she said. If he was not mistaken, she was breathless as she spoke. "I am no longer an orphan without resources, without protection. My father intends to see me honorably wed. He knows nothing of what transpired at Kirkham—" she cast her eyes down in shame ''—and I would have it remain that way.''

Nicholas watched as she pulled the reins from him and turned her horse. As she rode away without another word, he rubbed the center of his chest with one hand. Try as he might, he could not ignore the fact that he had wronged her, and grievously.

'Twas frightening. If his guilty feelings were any indication, then he was not as great a scoundrel as he thought.

Chapter Thirteen

It took no time at all for Maria and her father to develop a deep closeness. They never experienced any awkwardness that might have occurred between strangers, but felt immediately connected to one another.

During the first few days, they spent every waking hour together, catching up on the lost years. Though Maria gave only sketchy information regarding her life at Alderton, Sterlyng surmised exactly how she had been treated, and was tempted to travel north to pay a visit to his Morley sister-in-law.

"Please, Father," Maria had protested. "That part of my life is over and done. I wish to move forward now. There is n-nothing about the past that is important. I have you now, and all my life ahead of me...."

"It goes against the grain, Maria," Sterlyng said. "I should enjoy seeing Olivia Morley pay for her ill treatment of you for all those years. And for not contacting me when she had to know—"

"But I do not believe she knew, Father," Maria said. "The Morleys would hear naught of my mother once she joined King Henry's court and they disowned her."

"Still..."

"I survived," she said, hugging him closely. "And I found you."

"No thanks to Olivia," Sterlyng countered. "Do you know that I sent a justice to Alderton? The man directly questioned Olivia about your existence and she denied you, child. She lied."

"I know," Maria whispered. "That is how I learned about Rockbury. But I would move on, Father...."

Beyond Alderton. Beyond Kirkham...

Maria never spoke of her interlude at Kirkham. She had no doubt that her father would have ridden off immediately to thrash Nicholas if he ever discovered what had transpired between them. She did not want that to happen.

After exchanging words with Nicholas on the path at Westminster, all Maria could hope was that he would stay away. His presence did nothing but bruise her already damaged heart. 'Twas difficult to see him, to be with him, when she knew that her feelings for him were not returned.

Nay, he had come to London not because he cared for her, but because she had offended his pride by leaving Kirkham as she did. She doubted many of his lovers left his bed in the dead of night.

There was a sudden chill in the room and Maria wrapped her old woolen shawl around her shoulders. She felt the cold clear through to her bones, yet the afternoon was bright with the warmth of the spring sun.

She chided herself for her maudlin thoughts and brushed away the foolish moisture from her eyes. Everything in her life had changed. She had not only a father who loved her, but the security of his name and his home.

Her father had made it plain that he wanted Maria

honorably—and quickly—wed. She was advanced in years for a first marriage, and Sterlyng thought it best to pursue the matter before her age became a detriment. He did not intend to rush her, nor would he make a betrothal contract without her consent. In fact, he'd told her that since she'd been given so few choices in her first twenty-two years, he would allow her to choose her own husband, as long as he was suitable.

Maria had no illusions about the marriage she would contract. Her father had introduced her to several proper noblemen, most of whom were quite pleasant.

But not one of them could make her blood boil.

It did not take much for Nicholas to improve his reputation in the House of Lords. He attended sessions over the next week, behaving responsibly and shunning his unruly cronies. He even put up a tolerant front when the arrogant Earl of Bexhill spoke his opinion, obtuse as it was. Nick knew that none of his actions would make him an intimate friend of Sterlyng, but would go far in getting the duke to allow him into his house.

To court his daughter.

Nick did not intend to wed the lady, but merely to court her as any other young man might do—thereby giving him access to the duke's house as well as to the duke himself.

Sterlyng's chambers at Westminster had been thoroughly searched, but his house had not yet been successfully breached, thanks to stout locks on the windows and doors, as well as the loyalty of the men and women Sterlyng employed. 'Twas up to Nicholas to gain access to Sterlyng's private quarters in his own home.

He had heard of several recent gatherings at the

duke's house in Bridewell Lane, and knew that the purpose of these soirees was to introduce Maria to various suitors.

Nick scowled at the thought of Sterlyng marrying her off. He did not examine his reaction too closely, but merely resolved to see that he insinuated himself into the duke's good graces as soon as was humanly possible.

The opportunity presented itself late one stormy evening when the king's uncle, the Duke of Gloucester, came to his office at Westminster.

"Kirkham," he said. Clearly ill and feverish, Gloucester coughed into a square of linen. He handed a letter to Nicholas. "This just arrived from France. Bedford asked me to have this taken to Sterlyng immediately. He also wanted you to see it."

Nick took the vellum from him and read the French words.

King of England, render account to the King of Heaven of your royal blood. Return the keys of all the good cities which you have seized, to the Maid. She is sent by God to reclaim the royal blood, and is fully prepared to make peace, if you will give her satisfaction; that is, you must render justice, and pay back all that you have taken.

After reading this much, Nicholas looked up, frowning. "What is this? Who wrote it?"

Gloucester sneezed, blew his nose and replied, "'The maid,'" he replied with a shrug. "A young woman in the service of the dauphin. Apparently, she feels that the power of God is on her side, and she is demanding that we give up all we have gained in France."

Nicholas read on to the end of the missive, where the "maid" suggested that she would destroy Bedford's forces if he did not withdraw from France. "Do we know anything more?"

"Bedford knows nothing…just that she has recently been at Chiens with the dauphin."

"This is confirmed?"

Gloucester nodded.

"She is no mere camp follower…?" Nicholas suggested, hoping that there was no more value to the letter than the ink and vellum used to compose it. Morale was poor among the English troops. A soldier-maiden with a mission from God could have the power to decimate them.

"Nay. 'Tis much more serious than that."

Nicholas could see that Gloucester was worried. Though the man was never the most astute politician, he had a fine intellect and was not easily duped. Nor was his brother, the Duke of Bedford, Regent of France. If they were both taking this missive seriously, then so would Nicholas.

"Shall I take this to Sterlyng?" Nicholas asked. It would give him the opportunity to see the duke's reaction to the letter, and perhaps gain some insight into the duke's treachery.

"I was hoping you would," Gloucester replied just as a clap of thunder rattled the windows. "The weather is rather too formidable for me tonight."

A footman at the gracious home in Bridewell Lane answered the door and let him inside, out of the rain. Nicholas could hear voices coming from deep within the house as he awaited word from Sterlyng.

When the footman returned, he took Nick's cloak and

led him to the gathering in the main room of the house, a great hall of sorts, with a huge hearth and fireplace, and high ceilings. Several people sat companionably in the warmth of the room.

Nicholas was chagrined to note that Bexhill was among them. Maria sat on a settle to his left—far too close, to Nick's way of thinking.

He had not seen her in a week, though he'd refused to dwell on how long it had been since he'd touched her. She was beautiful tonight, wearing a gown similar to one he'd have chosen for her at Kirkham. The russet color set off her honey-dipped hair to perfection. It fit her enticing form closely, and the low cut of the bodice showed her assets perhaps a little too well, Nick thought.

His fingers ached to touch her.

"Kirkham," Sterlyng said cordially as he came to his feet, "to what do we owe the honor?"

Nick dragged his eyes away from Maria and looked at her father. "Business, I'm afraid, your grace."

Sterlyng nodded. "You all know Kirkham?" he asked. "Maria? You mentioned a short visit to the marquis's estate?"

"Yes, Father," Maria replied quietly. A faint blush touched her cheeks. "We're acquainted."

"Well then," Sterlyng said as he began to usher Nicholas from the room. "If you'll excuse us…"

She should never have worn this gown.

Relieved to be called to the table for supper, Maria used the moment to pull a black silk shawl over her shoulders. She made sure she covered everything from her neck down. Her cousin Cecilia may have worn gowns like this, but Maria had felt too exposed from the moment Alisia had laced her into the bodice of the fashionable houppelande.

While the gentlemen had not quite leered at her, their assessing glances made her terribly uncomfortable. Worse was Nicholas's reaction. When he arrived, she'd felt positively naked.

She sagged with relief when her father led him out of the hall and into his study. It was too difficult to be in the same room with him and not be subject to his overpowering presence. She had enough trouble keeping him out of her thoughts when he wasn't even there.

She led the guests into the dining hall, where a large table was set to accommodate their party. Minstrels were already playing their instruments, and servants were carrying in trays of food and pouring wine. Maria busied herself with her duties as hostess, seeing that everyone had what they needed. Then she took her seat.

Talk revolved around the royal tournament of peace that would be held at week's end, as well as the London Fair, which had started that morning. Rain had put a damper on the fair, but had not shut down the stalls. Jests were made about the London merchants who would turn a profit, rain or shine.

When Maria's father returned with Nicholas alongside him and called for another place to be set, she locked her eyes on the Earl of Bexhill and tried to appear as if he had her rapt attention with his talk of lances and spears, jousts and other contests.

Nicholas smiled. Though Sterlyng's reaction to the letter had told him nothing, the evening would not be wasted. He'd made an impression on the duke—a favorable one—and now he was to dine with Sterlyng and his daughter, along with all their guests.

Unfortunately, Maria was still sitting next to Bexhill.

Nick had seen the color drain from her face when it became clear that he would stay to supper, and he'd heard her sharp intake of breath when he took the vacant seat next to her. No doubt she had expected her father to sit beside her.

"Lady Maria," he said, "you are most gracious to permit me to join your party." Then he leaned slightly toward her and spoke so that no one else could hear. "You are beautiful tonight, love...."

She picked up her goblet and drank deeply, then turned to Bexhill, who spoke loudly and earnestly about his prowess on the fields of battle in Aquitaine.

Maria kept her eyes on the pompous oaf, eating up his words rather than the food in her trencher.

"My lady fair," Nicholas whispered, pulling furtively at her shawl. "If you would let this scrap of silk slip but an inch, I would be that much closer to heaven with the sight of your pearly skin."

He watched the muscles of her delicate throat work as she swallowed. Then she sidled as far away from him as she could, short of landing on Bexhill's lap.

To Nick's delight, Maria lost control of her shawl and it fell. He reached down to pick it up, just as she did. "Your décolletage inflames me, love," he said when their heads met. "Would that I could touch you—"

She snapped back to her upright position and turned her wholehearted attention to the meal in front of her, ignoring Nicholas as he draped the silk shawl around her shoulders.

Her skin was flushed in the candlelight, though Nicholas believed he was the only one who noticed. Her body trembled, though he could not tell if it was from arousal or anger.

He knew that for himself, however, it was definitely from arousal.

Chapter Fourteen

Two days passed before Nicholas saw her again. He had gone to the house in Bridewell Lane the day before, but had been told that the lady was out.

Which was pure blather.

The house was being watched, and Nicholas knew all the comings and goings of the occupants. He knew full well that it had been Maria's choice not to see him.

"My lord," Henric Tournay said, entering Nicholas's chamber at Westminster with a stack of letters. The secretary's lean form was impeccably groomed, as always, though there was naught he could ever do to improve his sallow features. "Sir Roger sent word from Kirkham that Lord Sheffield has sufficiently recovered to return to his own estate in York."

"I'm relieved to hear it." Nicholas had been reluctant to leave him at Castle Kirkham, injured and ailing. But he'd had no choice—not if he intended to pursue Maria. And deal with Sterlyng.

"These letters arrived for you, my lord," Tournay continued, "and I need your signature on this."

Absently, Nick placed the vellum sheaves on his desk and went to the window. The morning had dawned fine

and sunny, and he had yet to figure a way to see Maria.
His motivation for seeking her out had become muddled
in his mind. He told himself repeatedly he had only one
purpose, and that was to gain access to her father.

"My lord?"

He turned absently to find that Tournay was still
there.

"Hmm?"

"Your signature."

"Ah, yes…" he said, returning to the desk. He
dipped a quill in ink and sifted through the documents
he had dropped on his desk just moments before. He
quickly read the document, then signed and handed it
to the secretary.

"Locate Sir Gyles and send him to me, Tournay,"
he said.

"I believe he is here at Westminster, my lord," the
secretary replied.

"Excellent," Nick said. "I'd like to see him as soon
as possible."

When Tournay left, Nicholas turned to his correspondence. Most of it contained the usual: reports from his
estates, an invitation to a feast at Fleet Castle and…

Nick took a deep breath, then slid into his chair to
study the last sheaf of vellum. It was a letter, folded
inside a cover sheet that was addressed to him.

The inner letter had Sterlyng's name on it. The message was terse. "Many thanks," it said. "Your numbers
were correct. It is clear now where the maid will be of
most use." It was signed with a flourish, "J."

Bits of blue wax had collected within the outer wrap-
ping—part of the seal, no doubt, but Nick could not
discern its origin.

He rose from his chair and went quickly to the door. "Tournay!" he called.

The secretary was already a fair distance from Nicholas's chambers, but he turned and walked back, his wan features unperturbed. "Yes, my lord?"

Nick stepped back into the chamber and closed the door behind Tournay. "Who delivered this?" he asked.

Tournay shook his head as he looked at the parchment in Nicholas's hand. "I do not know, my lord," he said. "'Twas under the door when I arrived this morning."

"Did you not think it strange to find it there?"

Tournay shrugged. "Not particularly, my lord," he replied. "Early missives are often slid under the doors of their intended recipients."

Nicholas supposed that was true, though he wished for an easier answer to the puzzle of "J." Who was "J," and who had intercepted this message, only to see that it reached Nicholas's hands?

Nicholas did not doubt the veracity of the letter, because of its reference to "the maid." Clearly, someone knew Nick was aware of Sterlyng's unlawful transfer of information to France, and was willing to assist in exposing him as a traitor.

Did it matter who this person was? As long as the evidence held up, why should Nicholas care who'd sent it?

Because it was too easy.

Sterlyng had seemed genuinely puzzled by the letter from "the maid" to the king. If he'd known of her, and if the dauphin was using this maiden to boost the morale of his armies, wouldn't Sterlyng have known?

"My lord?" Sir Gyles said as he tapped on the door,

then poked his head into Nicholas's chamber. "You wish to see me?"

"I do," he said. "Tournay, see if you can discover who was responsible for delivering that message."

The secretary nodded, then quit the room, leaving Nicholas alone with Gyles.

"Any odd activity at Bridewell Lane?" Nicholas asked, still disturbed by what he'd read in the intercepted letter. Someone was very anxious for Nick to condemn Sterlyng. Nick wondered why the informant did not make himself known.

"Nay, my lord," Gyles replied. "Just the usual comings and goings of the servants. Lady Maria stayed in all yesterday—'twas raining most of the day, if you recall—but this morn, she went out with Bexhill to Dunstan Fair."

Nick's jaw dropped, but he quickly recovered. "Bexhill!"

"Aye, my lord," Gyles said. "The earl arrived early, and escorted the lady and her companion—Lady Alisia Preston—to the fair."

Nick could hardly credit Maria having the poor judgment to leave the house with that dolt, Bexhill. He was naught but a blowhard, a boasting flap-dragon who could not keep from regaling everyone near and far with his exploits in France. Bexhill considered himself a knight without equal, and no doubt wanted to convince Maria he was beyond compare.

After all, Maria was as fine a catch as any noblewoman in the kingdom. To wed the daughter of a duke, a very wealthy, infinitely well respected duke of the realm, would be quite an accomplishment for Bexhill.

And 'twould happen only over Nick's dead body.

* * *

The fair in London was very different from any of the country fairs Maria had attended. Here in the city there were so many more goods to buy, foods to sample, entertainments to enjoy. Not only did she have her own coin to spend, but a suitor who was more than willing to spend his own on her!

Bexhill was a bit full of himself, but Maria did not mind his chatter. He was a decent enough companion. She felt quite like a princess, dressed in her new finery, with the handsome earl as her escort.

Of course, Alisia Preston had come along, and soon a number of Maria's new acquaintances had joined their party as well. Bexhill did not seem to mind that he had competition for Maria's attentions, but maintained a supreme confidence that he was superior to all her other suitors.

Alisia took Maria's arm and pulled her into a stall in which various bolts of cloth were artfully displayed. "'Twould be wise to 'manage' Bexhill a bit, Maria," she said when they were beyond the earl's range of hearing.

"What do you mean?" Maria asked.

"The earl has the two of you all but betrothed in his own mind," Alisia explained as she ran her hands over a bolt of dyed linen.

Maria's eyes went wide and her mouth gaped open. "He could not possibly... I've given him no reason...."

"Oh, Maria...you are so young...."

"But I'm not," she protested. "I am fully twen—"

"In terms of experience, my dear."

Maria blushed then. "Oh." She was certainly more experienced than Alisia ever knew. But the woman was correct in some ways. Maria was ridiculously naive—

having allowed herself to be duped and seduced by that reprobate, Nicholas Hawken. "What would you have me do?"

"Merely divide your attention among the others," Alisia said. "Do not give the earl any more confidence in your regard for him than is absolutely necessary."

A small frown furrowed Maria's brow as she considered Alisia's advice. "I think I understand," she said.

"Make him suffer a bit," Alisia added. "'Tis good for a man to feel he has fought for his lady-love."

Maria pondered Alisia's words. To be sure, this was a mistake she had made with Nicholas. She had never given him a moment's pause, but had been readily available to him. She had succumbed to his seductive charm and had never questioned his intentions. What a fool she had been.

And still she missed him. She had every intention of accepting other suitors, but none attracted her with the same audacity as Nicholas Hawken. Lecher and scoundrel he might be, but Maria still cared for him.

"Wrap this bolt of silk for me," a familiar masculine voice said. "And have it delivered to Lady Maria's residence."

Maria turned and saw Nicholas watching her with a hunger that he did not bother to disguise. Behind him, Sir Gyles paid for a roll of the finest, sheerest silk Maria had ever seen.

"My lord," Alisia protested, flushing deeply. "'Tis most improper for you to make such a purchase for Lady Maria. Why, one might mistake your—"

"What's this?" Bexhill's voice boomed. "Kirkham!"

"In the flesh," Nicholas said, bowing with a flourish, though 'twas by no means a friendly gesture.

"Looking for a fresh conquest to debauch?" Bexhill growled, ignoring Maria's gasp.

"Of course not, Bexhill, though 'tis clear you must have grown tired of your own vanity and come in search of an appreciative audience."

Maria was dismayed by the two men, who were behaving more like a couple of bull boars about to charge than two noblemen out to pass a pleasant morning at the fair. She turned and stormed out of the stall, leaving the two glaring at each other.

Maria took the arm of another suitor and strolled down a few stalls, though she could still hear Nicholas and Bexhill taunting each other.

"A sweet for a sweet lady?" Maria's escort asked as they stepped up to a baker's display.

"Thank you, no," Maria said, turning away from the sweet-smelling goods. Her stomach churned. The queasiness worsened as she listened to Lord Bexhill argue with Nicholas about his prowess in battle. Maria doubted whether she'd ever heard anything so ridiculous in her life.

Then Bexhill challenged Nicholas to joust against him in the coming tournament.

"'Twill be my pleasure to best you in battle, Bexhill," Nicholas said. He did not appear the indolent nobleman now. His gray eyes were furious, and Maria had never seen his color so high or his expression so angry.

"Idle threats from a tottering wastrel," Bexhill replied, standing toe to toe with Nicholas.

A crowd began to gather to watch the two noblemen spar with one another. Alisia tried to lead Maria away as Sir Gyles finally intervened and managed to turn Nicholas away from Bexhill.

Maria felt the blood drain from her head, becoming

slightly faint as the two men argued. Nicholas was by far the more powerful, but 'twas possible she was biased. She knew his body intimately—each muscle and tendon, every sensitive inch of him.

Even so, she worried that he would be injured if he jousted against Lord Bexhill. She had heard the earl's stories of his prowess on the battlefield, yet she knew nothing of Nicholas's military skills. All she'd heard of Nicholas were stories of a debauched nobleman, a dissipated rogue who wasted his life and his resources in the pursuit of pleasure.

What if Nicholas could not handle a sword or spear? What would happen then?

"'Tis time we returned home, Lady Maria," Alisia said, her voice betraying concern for Maria's well-being. Maria realized she must appear ill, or at least ill at ease.

She went with Alisia without resistance.

When they arrived at home in Bridewell Lane, Sterlyng had not yet returned from Westminster. Maria was aware that some dire event had occurred of late, but her father did not speak of his concerns to her. He did not want to worry her with England's affairs.

"You should lie down and rest so you are in good form tonight," Alisia said. "Every young nobleman for a hundred miles will be at Fleet Castle this eve. 'Twill be a prime opportunity for you to size up prospective husbands."

Maria groaned inwardly, but said nothing. She merely climbed the stairs to her chamber and lay down on her bed, falling instantly into a deep, restful sleep.

Nicholas could not believe he'd made such an ass of himself. Brawling in public with Bexhill, of all things!

The man was a useless popinjay, with a vastly inflated notion of his own worth.

But to argue with him outside a Flemish cloth stall at the Dunstan Fair…that was utter foolishness. Now Nick was committed to jousting with the man, in full view of the child king and all his councillors and advisors, as well as half the London population, both noble and common, who would come out to view the royal tourney.

And in the meantime, he had a traitor to catch and expose.

Henric Tournay could not find any indication of who had left the incriminating letter under Nicholas's door, and Nick was as puzzled as ever regarding the source of that information.

He had been invited to attend a fete at Fleet Castle that evening, and had planned to avoid it. Now, however, it seemed a more prudent decision to go. Perhaps he would be able to discover further information about Carrington's supposed trip to Italy, as well as the activities of a few other noblemen with access to his office at Westminster.

He knew that Maria would likely attend the festivities at Fleet Castle tonight, and anticipated seeing her again. 'Twas reason enough to travel all the way out to Fleet in spite of the threatening rain. He hadn't been able to get near her at the fair that morning, her companion having bustled her away from the site of his altercation with Bexhill.

But he had sent the bolt of silk to her in Bridewell Lane.

He smiled when he imagined her expression upon receiving it. True, 'twas a completely inappropriate gift for a man to give a woman who wasn't his wife. The fabric could only be used for the most intimate of garments.

He grinned wickedly. His reputation as a scoundrel was secure, and Maria...Maria would not be able to avoid remembering how intimately he knew her.

Chapter Fifteen

The heavy, low-hanging clouds passed without a drop of rain, and the evening at Fleet Castle progressed grandly. The food was sumptuous, the music splendid and the dancing lively. Many young gentlemen joined in the dance, and every one of them had an opportunity to touch hands with Maria—if only for a moment as they passed on to the next step, the next lady.

'Twas more exciting than anything Maria had ever experienced. She laughed and enjoyed herself under her father's watchful eye, engaging in lighthearted teasing and flirting all evening.

Until she saw Nicholas Hawken among the throng.

She could never keep her wits about her when he was nearby, and Maria had come to Fleet Castle with every intention of practicing her newly learned strategies on Lord Bexhill.

Bexhill was a man worthy of being a woman's suitor. Blond and handsome, he was charming and thoughtful. He never took undue liberties with her person, but always treated her with respect and deference.

He never created a fire within her.

But that was moot, Maria thought with a slight shrug

of her shoulders. She doubted anyone would ever have the same effect on her as Nicholas had, and she did not expect it. Her father wanted her to choose a husband soon, and she would do so. 'Twas only necessary to attend a few of these fetes, where she could meet *acceptable* young men of her father's acquaintance, and choose one from among them.

Bexhill was as likely a husband as any. Gossip was rife that he had decided to take a wife, and he was now surrounded by a horde of young ladies, many of whom had been nudged into the lord's circle by their mothers. Maria vowed never to appear quite so desperate for a man. Alisia's advice was sound, she thought. She was not going to fall too easily into matrimony with Bexhill, even though he was the most likely candidate.

Nay, as the music played on and the processional continued before her, Maria knew there were other likely young men to choose from. Or none at all.

Mayhap she would wait a time before committing to marriage. She was not that old and there was still time before 'twould be too late for her. After all, she'd only just found her father, and they were still getting to know one another. Why should she hasten into marriage?

She stood next to a pleasant young man, Lord Westby, heir to an earldom in Kent. He was handsome and kind, though a little too eager to please. There was no challenge in him, no boldness of spirit. She thought it might come with age, but he could not compare to...

Maria gave herself a mental kick. She could not allow herself to compare every young man to Nicholas Hawken. He was not the husband for her, as she well knew. Everyone spoke of him in negative terms. He was a scoundrel, a charming rascal, a—

Maria's heart sped up and her skin heated when a

deep masculine voice whispered in her ear, "One day, someone will compose a dance that allows a man to stay with his lady fair until the music ends." 'Twas not necessary for Maria to turn to know that Nicholas was standing behind her, teasing her sensitive flesh with his warm breath.

In sheer dismay, she realized that his scent, the sound of his voice, his touch, were etched forever on her soul.

But she would not allow the past to dictate her future.

Studiously ignoring him, she took hold of Westby's arm. "'Tis quite close, is it not, my lord?" she asked sweetly, looking up into the young man's eyes. "Shall we stroll in the garden for a bit?"

Nicholas watched them leave, cynically wishing he had a napkin with which to wipe the drool from Westby's chin. How could Maria lead the lad on so? She was no more interested in him than she was in the tapestry hanging above the fireplace.

Nick shoved his fingers through his hair, unaware and uncaring of what an unkempt ruffian it made him appear. If Westby so much as touched her...

Nicholas turned to a nearby table and picked up a mug of ale, downing half in one gulp. Whoever Maria involved herself with was not his concern, and he would do well to remember it. 'Twas her father who was his target, and Maria merely the means to reach him.

But rather than locating Sterlyng, Nick finished the rest of his ale and sauntered out to the garden. Night had fallen, but the hosts had lit torches to illuminate the path. Several couples and a few groups had taken advantage of the reprieve from rain, and were enjoying the fresh air out-of-doors.

It took but a moment for Nick to locate Maria.

She and Westby had not wandered far, but stood on

the path, looking north, where a storm was lighting up the sky. Lightning flashed in the distance, and the smell of rain was still on the air. When Westby put his hand at Maria's waist, Nicholas wasted no time, descending the steps by twos, quickly bypassing all who stood between him and Maria.

"Westby," he said when he reached them. "How fortunate to find you here. The Duke of Gloucester has been asking for you."

"G-Gloucester?" young Westby stuttered. "Asking for *me?*"

"He did not say why, but asked for you personally."

Westby was clearly torn between his duty to Lady Maria and his desire to see what the king's uncle could possibly want of him.

"You'd best go on, Westby," Nicholas said. "I'll see that the lady is returned to the hall unharmed."

"Thank you, Kirkham," the young lord said, even as he started up the path toward the castle. "I will repay you for your service when I can."

And then he was gone.

"'Twas unkind of you, Nicholas," Maria said.

"Nay, the lad will never know what happened."

"How so?"

"Gloucester and Lady Eleanor left Fleet only a few minutes ago. Westby will assume the duke was in a hurry to go, and could not wait." Nick was glad the weather was warm enough that Maria had left her damnable shawl inside. Her shoulders and neck were bare, as well as a goodly expanse of skin above the squared neckline. She was exquisite, and he could barely restrain himself from touching her.

"Will the storm come south, do you think, my lord?" she asked, looking up at the sky.

Right now, Nicholas could not have cared less whether or not they would have rain. "Mayhap," he said anyway. "You came to Fleet in a closed carriage, did you not?"

"Of course. My father is always well prepared."

"Except for misplacing a daughter at birth," he said, and immediately regretted it. He'd heard the incredible story of Sterlyng's lost daughter: how the duke had been in London at the time of Maria's birth, and that he'd been informed of his wife and newborn daughter's deaths by a letter from his stepmother. Word was that Sterlyng had been so overcome with grief that he hadn't returned to Sterlyng Castle until weeks later, during which time the infant's demented nurse had carried her to Alderton.

Nicholas could not fathom the enormity of Sterlyng's loss. For twenty-two years, he'd believed his daughter dead, only to learn recently from his devious stepmother, on her deathbed, that she had lied about the child.

Maria stepped away from him.

He took her arm. "I am sorry, Maria," he said. "'Twas ignorant of me to say such a thing."

She raised her chin and looked back at the sky, while he studied her lovely profile.

"'Tis beautiful, is it not?"

"Aye," he breathed, not taking his eyes from the vision she presented.

"You cannot understand how it is for him...for my father," she said quietly. "All those years he grieved for my mother and me...all those years alone."

Nicholas's brows quirked once. She thought of her father's pain, but what of her own? Had she not been kept by her aunt in the meanest of circumstances, treated worse than the lowest scullery maid?

'Twas remarkable that Maria never even considered her own losses. "Walk with me, my lady fair."

She turned then and looked at him warily. Finally, she put her hand upon his and agreed to go with him. "But not far, Nicholas."

Nick did not know what he was doing out there just then, when he should have been inside, questioning friends of the Countess of Carrington, whose health had suddenly driven her and her husband to Italy. He needed to discover the truth of the ailment that had her spending the season on the Continent with her husband. Nick knew he could charm the ladies into talking, but he did not have the heart for it now.

He wanted nothing more than to spend a few uninterrupted moments with Maria. Alone.

God's bones, she was exquisite. He could not keep himself from recalling every feminine inch of her, the way she'd responded to his every touch, or the depth of her passion when he'd spent himself inside her.

His body clenched.

And then he realized she was trembling. Surely she was not cold. Were her tremors from fear, or an acute awareness of him?

"Maria," he said, moving to position himself in front of her.

Looking at him warily, she took a step back.

Nicholas did not let her retreat. He approached until her back was against a hedge that was not yet full of spring greenery. Finally, she could go no farther without being skewered by a branch. Nicholas took her shoulders in his hands and looked down at her.

"This is a m-mistake, Nicholas," she said. "You do not want—"

He lowered his head and swiftly covered her reluctant lips with his own eager mouth.

She could not hide her reaction to him. With exquisite satisfaction, he moved his mouth over hers, tasting her desire. Heat throbbed through him. He pulled her close, pressing her soft curves against his hard length. He heard a groan from somewhere, but when her arms slid around his neck he lost all ability to think.

Her fingers sent shivers of delight through his body as they teased the hair at his nape. He had no awareness of their surroundings, no sense of time. He was entirely in her thrall, and he would have it no other way.

Abruptly, he broke the kiss, took her hand and led her farther down the path. Thunder rumbled in the distance, but they ignored it as Maria nearly ran to keep up with his long strides.

He pulled her behind a gardener's shed and pressed his kisses upon her again, even more hungrily this time. "I think of you wearing naught but the silk I bought for you," he said, tasting her ear, her jaw. "So sheer...your body enticingly visible, yet hidden from me."

One hand tantalized the plump flesh above the neckline of her gown, the other drew her hips to his own. He pressed their bodies together, even as he tried to relieve the intensity of sensations. "Would that I could suckle you..."

She suddenly went stiff and shuddered. Her breath came out in a high-pitched huff, and he realized she had reached her peak. She was incredible. He held her trembling body, trailing kisses from her throat to her breasts.

He looked 'round. There must be a place where he

could make love to her in private. He would not risk exposing her to anyone who happened by.

Maria was drowning.

She could not think or breathe, but merely feel. Her memory of Nicholas's power over her had not been inaccurate. His touch was all too potent for her to deal with. Clearly, he wanted nothing more than a few moments pleasure with her behind a shed in a castle garden.

She could not let that be.

Pushing away from him, she quickly gathered up her skirts and hurried down the path, breathlessly and on wobbly legs. She would find her father and get him to leave Fleet Castle immediately. She could not spend another moment here in Nicholas's presence.

"You are quiet, my dear," Sterlyng said as they rode through the dark on the road toward London. Random flashes of lightning and the rumble of distant thunder occasionally disturbed the night. "Did you not enjoy yourself at Fleet?"

"Oh yes, Father, 'twas a lovely time," she replied. "I was just weary and—and ready to return home."

The duke nodded, accepting his daughter's explanation. There had been many suppers at home and late evening entertainments that Sterlyng had wanted his daughter to attend. It was as if he wanted to make up for twenty-two years of deprivation in a few weeks, when Maria would have been content to spend quiet time with him alone.

She could not fault her father, though. She'd been convinced that 'twould be best to marry soon, and he was doing everything in his power to introduce her to as many eligible young men as was feasible. He couldn't possibly know how little these men interested her. She'd never given him reason to understand the turmoil Nicholas caused in her, or the depth of her feelings for that scoundrel.

If only he hadn't shown such generosity and kindness to others when they were at Kirkham. If only she could believe he was truly a knave to his very core.

But he was not. And Maria knew it, even if she refused to acknowledge it.

The carriage suddenly jolted and Maria was thrown off the seat, onto the floor. As her father helped her up, the carriage began to move faster, bumping erratically down the path. Men's voices pierced the night. Strange, crude voices, of men who were not part of their guard.

Maria was frightened. Who but outlaws would accost them on the road in this manner? What would keep them from killing her father once they had what they wanted?

"Hold on to the strap," Sterlyng said as he leaned toward the window. He pulled up the flap and looked out. Maria held on as they jostled down the road, but could not see much in the faint glow of the carriage lamps outside.

"Damnation!"

The voices outside rose angrily as the carriage came to a halt.

"What is it, Father?"

"Robbers," he said as he checked his weapons. His sword was sheathed at his side, and he carried a small knife inside his tunic. "The guards will deal with them."

Maria was unconscious of wringing her hands as the sounds of battle raged outside, but fully felt the fear that rumbled through her. How many guards traveled with them? What if they were unable to keep the villains out? What if the thieves managed to get past the guards and attacked her father? What would—

The door to the carriage was suddenly thrown open and a man lunged partway inside, grabbing Maria and pulling her out. She could hear her father protesting, but the thief used Maria to shield himself. Sterlyng could not get to him without injuring his daughter. Men were lying on the ground about her, and several masked robbers continued to fight on horseback.

Sterlyng drew his sword and joined the battle as the thief dragged Maria away. Even more terrified now than before, she sent silent prayers to heaven for their delivery from harm. She worried that her father might be injured, or even killed, over a few valuables that meant nothing to her!

The thief yanked her gold necklace and locket from her, tearing the skin at her neck. He wrenched the rings from her fingers, then started pulling at the gems in her hair. At the same time, Maria struggled, trying to remove her jewelry in order to give it to him, but the man seemed to have a dozen hands. She could not make him understand that she was not trying to escape him, but would willingly give him all that she had in her possession, even her mother's locket, if he would spare her father's life.

Amidst the chaos, racing hoofbeats approached, and as the confusion increased, Maria despaired. The thieves had reinforcements, and their horrible clash on this isolated patch of road was about to worsen.

A strange cracking sound suddenly pierced the night.

''Yeow!'' the man holding Maria cried. He let go of her and grabbed at his neck.

In a panic, Maria scrambled away. With only one

small carriage lantern still alight, she could see little of what was going on, but the sound of clashing swords was all around her. She was trapped where she stood, and could only hope that her father's guards would somehow win the day.

Nicholas Hawken's voice shouted curt orders in the darkness.

Nicholas Hawken? Maria thought her mind must be playing tricks on her. She had been praying for a miraculous rescue, but knew 'twas impossible for Nicholas to be right behind them on the road. She'd fled from him in the garden and then she and her father had left Fleet Castle. Nicholas would still be...

Maria shook her head. She did not know where Nicholas had gone after she'd run from him. It now seemed likely that he'd said his farewells right after she and her father had done so.

She let out a scream as one of the thieves grabbed her wrist and started to pull her from her spot of relative safety. She dug in her heels and fought him, but before she had to put up much resistance, she heard that odd crack again, and the man screamed and fell.

Nicholas was beside her then, lifting her off her feet, carrying her back into the carriage.

Her father was not inside.

"Stay here," Nicholas said, and then he was gone.

Maria waited an interminable length of time, listening to the swordplay, the cracking and the other sounds of battle that went along with it. She was filled with fear for her father, for Nicholas, even for the Sterlyng guards, who were risking their lives for her safety.

Suddenly, all was quiet.

In trepidation, Maria lifted the window shade slightly and strained her eyes to see what was going on. Her father stood at the edge of the darkness, next to Nicholas, while the guards subdued the last of blackguards who had attacked them.

She could not tell what her father and Nicholas were saying, only heard them murmuring in low voices. Then Nicholas disappeared into the darkness and Sterlyng returned to the carriage.

"Are you all right, Maria?" he asked, lighting the lamp in order to see her better.

"Yes, Father," she replied. She was badly shaken, her flesh was raw and scraped in places and her clothing was a mess. "I am unharmed."

"Thanks to Kirkham," Sterlyng said. He frowned. "I may have misjudged the man."

"How so?"

Sterlyng shook his head and gazed absently toward the window. "I'd thought him nothing more than an undisciplined wastrel since his brother's death," he said. "Never believed him capable of behaving responsibly...certainly not heroically."

"He *did* rescue us, didn't he, Father?"

"Without a doubt," Sterlyng replied. "I've never seen a man use a whip quite the way Kirkham did."

"A whip?"

Sterlyng shifted and refocused his gaze on Maria. "Yes. A whip. You can ask him about it on the morrow."

Maria gave her father a questioning look.

"Aye," he said. "Kirkham has asked to call on you. I gave my consent. He will arrive at noon."

Chapter Sixteen

Maria's tumultuous emotions caused her to be ill the following morning. If she'd had but a moment between bouts with the basin, she'd have sent someone to find Nicholas and tell him she was too ill to receive him.

But she felt better later, and broke her fast as usual, with Alisia Preston. She did not take note of Alisia's curiously assessing glances, but ate her meal, taking care not to upset her sensitive stomach.

She took her usual morning ride at Westminster, and felt refreshed and optimistic as long as she did not have to think about seeing Nicholas later in the day.

How could she face him? She had practically melted in his arms in the garden at Fleet Castle last night, and was now mortified by her wanton response to him. Nicholas had to know what he'd done to her. He could not possibly misconstrue his power over her. He knew as well as she that she could not trust herself when he was near.

In fact, the scoundrel was probably counting on it.

Maria took comfort in the knowledge that her father planned to be at home when Nicholas called. He felt so strongly indebted to Kirkham for his intervention on the road the previous night that he planned to cut short his appointments at Westminster and return home early.

The duke's presence meant that Maria would not have to be alone with Nicholas. With her father there, she could manage the conversation, keeping it centered on her new experiences in London and the attack on the road.

She would make certain to avoid any discussion of Fleet Castle and all that had occurred there.

The attack on Sterlyng's carriage had been fortuitous for Nicholas. He had left Fleet Castle in a red haze of frustration, thanks to Maria Burton. He'd been anxious to return to his house in London when he and his escort had happened upon Sterlyng's ambushed carriage. The end result of the incident was that the duke trusted and respected him—at least a bit. Nicholas now had access to the duke's household, and he was sure he'd be able to maintain Sterlyng's good opinion of him.

Nick refused to dwell upon the possibility that Maria might have been seriously injured during the attack, though her image haunted him and woke him repeatedly throughout the night. To his dismay, he found himself yearning for her presence there in his bed, close enough that he could wrap his body around hers, hold her and convince himself that she was safe.

Which was absurd. He took women to bed for one reason, and it had nothing to do with their safety.

Still, he could not forget that she'd been in serious peril. Thoughts of Maria in danger plagued him. Those thieves had been harrying riders along the northern roads for weeks, and two men had already been killed during an attack. It was sheer luck that Nicholas and his men had been close on Sterlyng's trail when the scoundrels set upon them.

Nicholas assured himself that Maria's terrified scream would have pierced *any* man to the core, not just him. She had no special power over him, other than the fact that she was the one woman who could fall apart in his arms with barely a touch.

He would never forget the taste of her, or the sounds she made when he kissed the hollow of her neck or touched the tips of her breasts. The mere scent of her skin made him mad with desire.

But as her suitor, he would never be allowed to be alone with her. Never kiss her or taste her, never make love to her again. Since Nicholas had no intention of marrying her, she would wed someone like Bexhill, he supposed, though his jaw ached from tension at the mere thought of it.

In a quite fundamental way, Maria belonged to him. She had given her innocence to *him,* entrusted him with—

Nay, this was a path along which Nick did not wish to travel. His purpose in courting Maria was merely to gain entry to the Sterlyng household. Evidence of the duke's treason would be locked somewhere within, and 'twas Nick's sworn duty to find it.

When morning came, he rode to Sterlyng's house, dismounted and handed his horse over to a waiting groom. The front door was opened by the lady of the house, who greeted him politely, if distantly.

"His grace has not yet returned from Westminster, my lord," Alisia said, as she ushered Nicholas inside. "Lady Maria will join you for refreshments while we await the duke."

It seemed an eternity before Maria appeared. When

she finally entered the main hall, she was dressed in a gown that hugged her figure closely, except for its loose, graceful bag sleeves that fit snugly at the wrists. The gown's color was that of burgundy wine, and it was trimmed in a rich cloth that reminded Nicholas of fresh cream.

As did Maria's complexion. 'Twas too pale. He *knew* he should have ascertained her well-being himself last eve. Instead, he'd been so pleased to receive the duke's invitation to call upon Maria that he'd allowed Sterlyng to assure him that he would see to his daughter.

Mayhap Nicholas would have slept better if he'd seen for himself that she was all right. Mayhap those menacing dreams would not have harried and tormented him all night.

He stood and bowed, grasping Maria's hand, then took note as a fresh blush stained her cheeks. At least that was more healthy-looking than her previous pallor.

"Good day, my lord," she said as he touched his lips to her hand. She quickly tried to withdraw it from his grasp. Too quickly. Suspicious now, he looked at her hand, then pushed up her cuff, only to expose darkly bruised and abraded skin at her wrist.

"You were injured last night," he said, looking over every inch of her. "Your wrists..." he pushed back her veil to examine the skin there. "Your neck! My lady, your father assured me you were unharmed—"

"And I am, my lord," she protested, tugging her hand away and taking a seat near the fire. "'Tis nothing. I—"

"These injuries are not 'nothing,'" he said, crouching next to her knees. He took her hand, rubbed one thumb over the soft skin of her wrist and felt the pulse racing there. "I would never have left you if I'd known you'd been hurt."

Emotion flashed in her eyes. "Nicholas, these are naught but—"

A discreet clearing of a throat reminded them that Lady Alisia was still in the room, though they'd both forgotten her.

Nicholas wanted to throttle the woman. Could she not find something to do, someplace to go?

He locked his teeth together. Clearly, this audience was to be conducted in the most formal fashion, yet his body was coiled with tension. He wanted Maria. If there had been any possible way to get away with it, he'd have taken her hand and hauled her to a private place where he could kiss every inch of her. Soothe every bruise. Make her moan with the pleasure of his touch. "I trust you slept well after your mishap on the road last night," he said tightly.

Maria gave a little smile and replied all too formally, "Yes, my lord, thank you for asking."

"His grace should be home soon," Lady Alisia said. "Please, my lord, take a seat and finish your wine. We will dine as soon as the duke arrives."

Nick picked up his goblet and stood by the fire. There were circles under Maria's eyes, and he knew she lied. She had not slept well, in spite of her assurances otherwise. How could she sleep when she'd been bruised and battered so?

"These are the extent of your injuries, my lady?" he asked, strangely incapable of letting the topic go. Again he thought he should have been there to hold her all night as she slept, and soothe away the hurts that disturbed her. Had they lain together, Nicholas's sleep might have been cloaked in her soft scent, and the press of her body against his would have sweetened his slumber indescribably.

He believed his own presence would have done the same for Maria.

"Aye, my lord. 'Tis naught but a few scrapes where the brigand held my arms, and where he tore the chain from my neck..." Then she turned the subject from herself. "I understand you and your men helped our escort in rounding up the ruffians and delivering them to London."

He shrugged. A few wisps of her hair had escaped her veil. They teased her nape, and the sensitive skin below her ear. Would that he had leave to touch her there, and wind the errant locks around his finger. He would press his nose into her hair and inhale her soft scent, nuzzle her skin before turning his attention elsewhere.

"...and recovered the stolen valuables for us."

"'Twas naught," he said, though for a moment, 'twas difficult to find his voice.

"But my life, my lord...I did fear for it, and you arrived in a most timely fashion. I thank you now, as I did not have the opportunity to do so last eve."

She was gracious, and studiously distant—except for that one instant when she'd called him by his given name, and he'd seen that flash of fire in her eyes. She might have become the proper duke's daughter, but Nicholas knew what lay beneath her controlled exterior.

And God help him, though he knew 'twould be best not to dwell upon the intimacies they'd shared, nor the ones he'd *like* to share, he could not keep from doing so.

He reached inside his tunic and pulled out Maria's locket.

"My lord!" she cried when she saw her precious keepsake. She pressed it to her breast. "You retrieved my locket!"

"'Twas a simple thing."

"Nay, Nicholas," she said. "'Tis all I have of my mother, and I was sorry to lose it."

He'd known she treasured the locket, which was why he'd taken it to a goldsmith early that morn and had the broken links repaired. His collar grew tight as he watched her cradle the gold piece to her breast, and he could only wish his own hand was nestled there.

'Twas fortunate indeed when a footman opened the door and the duke entered. It forced Nicholas's concentration back to the issue at hand, which was merely to improve the duke's opinion of him, and begin to gain his trust.

It had naught to do with lockets and broken links.

"Kirkham," Sterlyng said, extending a hand to his guest. "My apologies for keeping you waiting."

"I only just arrived, your grace," he said.

"Lord Kirkham has just been lamenting Maria's injuries," Lady Alisia murmured.

"Ah," the duke said as he leaned over to kiss his daughter's temple. "She assures me they are minor. Shall we dine?"

Nicholas returned to his house at dusk in a completely frustrated state. He'd never had a moment alone in Sterlyng's home, so he'd had no opportunity to search through the duke's things. And he had a new reason for searching.

He did not believe Sterlyng was the traitor.

Nick had spent merely one afternoon with the duke and he could see that Sterlyng was a man of integrity and honor. 'Twas possible that his grace was a master at subterfuge, but Nicholas doubted it. He could not imagine the duke undermining England's interests in France. Nor would he betray his very good friends the Dukes of Gloucester and Bedford.

Still, the duke's seal had been found on an incriminating letter, and a letter from the mysterious "J" had been addressed to Sterlyng. There had to be some connection between Sterlyng and the traitor, if they, in fact, were not the same.

There was one other question that plagued Nicholas. Who knew that *he* would be interested in the duke's correspondence? Why would someone see to it that the letter from "J" was slipped under Nicholas's door?

He stepped into his study and sat down. A few ugly suspicions wound through his mind as he dropped his gloves on his desk and shuffled through the day's correspondence without really seeing anything.

For the first time that he could recall, his deceitfulness bothered him. He did not like lying to Maria about his reasons for spending time with her. After all the lies he'd had to tell over the years, all his double-dealing chicanery, everything about this matter left him with a sour taste.

He doubted Maria would ever speak to him again after she learned of his deception and his shameless use of her to get to her father. She would wonder if anything he'd said or done for her had been purely or honorably motivated.

Should he care?

"God's breath!" he muttered to himself, rubbing a hand across the back of his neck. He was well and truly in a muddle now, with little choice but to move forward.

"Tournay!" he called.

"Yes, my lord," the secretary said as he entered the chamber.

"Send someone down to the docks and find a ship with a cargo of fresh flowers," he said. "I want an armful of yellow roses sent to Lady Maria Burton."

"Roses, my lord?" Tournay asked. "'Twill be costly, sir, if any can be found."

"Cost does not concern me," Nicholas replied. He knew Tournay was ready to return to his own rooms, but felt no guilt keeping him later than usual. After all, he paid the man well to be at his beck and call. "Spend whatever is necessary. And while you're about it, find Sir Gyles. He and I have a tournament strategy to work out."

Maria rode through the park at Westminster the next morning with her groom following a discreet distance behind, as was her habit. She'd never known such freedom.

She enjoyed her rides since she'd had some lessons and now knew the proper technique for riding sidesaddle. She took quiet pride in her groom's observation that she had a natural ability on horseback.

The sky had cleared. The air was fresh here at Westminster, and the earth smelled wonderful after a light morning rain. The early blossoms were out, but nothing could compare to the bushels of yellow roses she'd received from Nicholas.

She was confused and torn by his gesture, coming so soon after the yards of silk that his secretary had personally delivered, and the indecent way he'd behaved with her in the garden at Fleet Castle.

Alisia had been scandalized by such a personal—nay, intimate—gift. No man with honorable intentions would

ever have sent such a thing to a lady, and Alisia made
certain that Maria understood that fact.

Maria had not needed to be told. She knew the kind
of man Nicholas Hawken was, and what he expected
from a woman. 'Twas certainly not marriage, though in
truth, she did not think he intended to be insulting with
his attentions. Wicked, perhaps, but never rude.

He would seduce her out of her clothes again if he
could, and make love to her until she had no will of her
own. Nicholas would want nothing more—*or less*—
than a passionate interlude of reckless, intense coupling.

Yet he'd sent her roses. The most beautiful, delicate
roses she'd ever seen. Maria had been astonished by the
color, assuming all roses were red or pink like the ones
in Alderton's gardens.

And she'd been touched beyond all reason that he'd
gone to such effort to find her such an exotic gift.

Still puzzling over his generous gesture, Maria can-
tered along the meadow path on the eastern edge of
Westminster. She did not think she would ever understand Nicholas. One moment he was heroic and noble,
and the next he was a taunting, beguiling, unprincipled
scoundrel.

And Maria's heart nearly stood still when she saw
him sitting astride his horse at the edge of the woods
before her. He sat so tall and straight, his shoulders
broad, his hair gleaming darkly in the morning sun-
shine.

To her credit, she did not alter her gait, but rode
confidently toward him, as if his presence on her path
meant naught to her. Again she looked to Cecilia's ex-
ample, and remembered Alisia's advice, too. She was
ready for him. He would never again corner her as he'd
done at Fleet Castle.

"Good morn, my lady fair," he said when she reached him. He turned his mount and fell into step next to her, riding at an easy trot.

She merely nodded a greeting as she continued to ride.

"'Tis a fine morn for riding," he said innocently. But when he caught her gaze, his eyes took on an intensely sensual expression. "Or strolling hand in hand alongside yonder brook…" He took hold of her horse's reins and pulled her to a halt. "I would steal your kisses in the grass, my lady fair," he said, taking her hand and peeling away her glove. He kissed her palm while his eyes held hers captive.

Maria's tongue stuck to the roof of her mouth. She knew full well what he was suggesting, but had no intention of making herself the fool again. Instead, she gave an impression of considering his invitation, glancing in the direction of the little brook that ran through the meadow. "Nay, I think not, Lord Kirkham," she finally said, pulling her hand away. She closed her fingers around the locket that hung from its repaired chain. "The path would likely be too muddy after the rain."

"You know me far too intimately for such formalities, Maria," he said. "Let us—"

"I meant to thank you, Nicholas," she said airily, though her heart was pounding, "for the roses. They are wonderful." She would maintain a polite distance, just as she had the last time they'd been together, but not give an inch on this. She knew what a rogue he was, and that he would take advantage if she did not keep him at arm's length.

She resumed a leisurely trot.

"They reminded me of you—your golden hair, your

beautiful eyes,'' Nicholas said as he nudged his own mount to keep up.

Maria laughed. ''You are a flattering knave, Nicholas,'' she chided. She turned and looked at him thoughtfully. ''But those roses touched my heart.''

At that, she dug her heels into the side of her mount and galloped away from him, regretting that she'd spoken her true feelings, afraid she would say more if she stayed. She could never allow Nicholas to know what she felt for him. 'Twas better to keep her distance, and keep her heart safe.

Nick watched Maria ride away, and did not follow, as he should have done. He knew he should pursue her relentlessly until he became as commonplace a visitor to her father's house as Henric Tournay, who was becoming so familiar with his delivery of gifts that he could now come and go at his leisure.

But Maria's words made Nicholas falter.

Nay, 'twas not just her words, but something he'd seen in those expressive eyes when she'd spoken of her heart, the way she'd touched the locket that rested at her breast. He did not care for the way it made him feel.

He did not enjoy lying to her—using her to get to her father. But, by damn, he had a mission to accomplish, an important task for England. If he lost sight of his purpose now, 'twould be at the peril of too many English knights, still fighting on French soil.

He had to admit that he had not been thinking of strategy when he'd suggested a stroll by the river. He'd only been able to think how it would feel to touch her and hold her close. It had been far too long since he'd kissed her, and Nicholas could swear she felt the same. He'd not seen disdain in her eyes when he'd touched her, rather a heat and a hunger that he knew only too well.

Maria's figure faded in the distance as Nick watched. Her groom followed faithfully behind, the man whose sole task was to see that his mistress came to no harm.

Nick only wished he could guarantee the same.

Chapter Seventeen

"I trust you slept well, my lady?" Lord Bexhill inquired as Maria strolled with him in the Sterlyng courtyard. Gardeners had been at work preparing the flower beds, and baskets of color adorned the archways that lined the walls.

"Quite well, thank you," she replied. Her hand was upon his as they walked, and Maria desperately tried to conjure some heat from their connection. To her chagrin, none existed. Bexhill was handsome and sophisticated, but he did not inflame her as Nicholas Hawken could do with merely a glance.

"You will attend the tourney on the morrow?"

She swallowed hard. She'd been dreading the day of the tourney, and had hoped to avoid it, but she and her father had been invited to share Gloucester's box, and could not refuse. "Yes," she said. "I shall be there."

Bexhill smiled. Though naught was unpleasant about the earl's face, his smile involved only his mouth and teeth. It did not touch his eyes, or effect the set of his head upon his neck, the way Nicholas's smile would do. When mirth took Kirkham, his entire body was alight with it. His head tilted at an engaging angle, and the corners of his eyes crinkled with merriment. 'Twas a thoroughly rascally smile, and Maria would do well to forget it.

They came full circle and sat at a wooden table that would soon be surrounded by flowers. A maid brought a tray of cider and sweetcakes, but as she set it on the table, one of the goblets tipped off and cracked.

"Stupid girl!" Bexhill said. He pulled Maria away as though she might be injured by the broken crockery. His grasp on her arm was a mite too rough.

"'Tis all right, Lizzie," Maria interjected, freeing her arm from Bexhill's grasp. She helped pick up the broken pieces. "No harm done."

"Oh, my lady, 'tis sorry I am—"

"'Tis sorry you ought—"

Maria placed her hand on Bexhill's sleeve. "Come, my lord," she said. "Let us join my father in his study."

Maria had made many a blunder over the years in serving her aunt and uncle, and understood the maid's nervousness. Bexhill's harshness with the girl rankled, and Maria wanted nothing more than to see the earl to the door. However, she could not expedite his departure without seeming rude, so she decided to shift responsibility for him to her father.

"Father," she said as she opened his study door, "I brought—"

Her thoughts deserted her when she saw Nicholas standing at the window, and her father seated at his desk. Judging by their expressions, they'd been engaged in some serious discussion, and Maria could not help but feel guilty at the interruption.

"Oh, I beg your pardon," she said, but Bexhill pushed past her and entered.

"Your grace," he said politely, but when the earl turned to Nicholas, he positively sneered. "Kirkham."

To his credit, Nicholas did not rise to the bait. He merely nodded at Bexhill and then caught her father's eye. Some unspoken communication flashed between them, and Nicholas moved away from the window. He came to Maria, took both hands in his and kissed the back of one. "You look lovely this morning, my lady fair," he said. "Your morning ride agrees with you."

She blushed at the reference to their meeting, but said nothing. "Father, I apologize for interrupting," she said. "I was unaware that you had a guest," she added, looking straight into Nicholas's eyes. She hoped to dispel any notion that his presence was what had brought her here.

"Ah yes, Kirkham and I have been hard at work," the duke said as he arose from the desk. "Bedford has asked for a new poll tax, and the Lords have been discussing how to present it."

"We shall leave you to it, then—"

"Nay, join us," Sterlyng said. "I've been so preoccupied with matters at Westminster these days, I've missed seeing you as much as I'd like."

Only then did Nicholas let Maria's hands go, and he held out a chair for her. Bexhill took the chair nearest her, and Nicholas returned to his perch near the window. There was none of the teasing rascal about him now, and Maria surmised that his discussion with her father had included more than just a discussion on a new poll tax.

Her heart thrummed when Nicholas's eyes found hers. She did not wish to be under his scrutiny as she was courted by another man, and Bexhill was clearly courting her. He would make an admirable husband, and Nicholas could not help but know it.

But it made her feel vulnerable, and open to his criticism. As if he had any say in her choice of spouse. Nicholas himself was utterly unsuitable, yet he took every opportunity to remind her of her unwise—yet oh, so breathtaking—liaison with him.

Nicholas swore under his breath. Bexhill acted rather too proprietarily with Maria for his liking. If the blond giant pawed Maria one more time with those beefy hands, Nick was going to shove the earl's nose into the back of his head. And never give it a second thought.

Surely Sterlyng would not have his daughter wed this man. Nick could not imagine anyone less suited to her, and if he ever got word of an impending marriage between the two, he vowed to intervene.

God's teeth! Nicholas himself was not a likely husband, and well he knew it. He had no right to come between Maria and the man of her choosing, even if 'twas an idiot like Bexhill.

Nick had made it clear to Maria that, though he'd be willing to resume their affair at any time, he was not in the market for a wife. There was no doubt that if he *had* been looking for one, she would suit him better than any woman he'd ever known. But the work he did for England was dangerous. He had taken great pains to avoid being discovered, but knew that he was in peril at all times.

He had no intention of changing his style of life at this point. He'd built a reputation as an infamous rogue, a ladies' man, one who took foolish risks and consorted with others of his kind—all done in order to eke secrets from the unsuspecting men of his class.

'Twas a dangerous occupation, as well he knew. A

Frenchman or an English traitor could expose him at any time, and then all would be lost.

Nicholas had no interest in leaving a widow...and perhaps children. 'Twas something to which he'd rarely given a thought, his mind singularly centered on his work for Bedford.

But the thought of children suddenly left him breathless. Maria as mother to Hawken children was all too appealing an idea.

His attitudes must be changing, he thought with chagrin, if he was thinking about getting Maria Burton with child. For even now, the idea of making children with her was extraordinarily tantalizing. So was the prospect of living a quiet life at Kirkham, of visiting Mattie Tailor in the village whenever he was of a mind to do so, of knowing that Sir Roger and Lady Malloy understood that Nicholas was not the wastrel they'd been led to believe.

He speared his fingers through his hair as he looked over at Maria, so lovely and poised. He knew he made her nervous. There was no doubt in his mind that his presence disturbed her.

God's blood, *she* disturbed *him* as well! His thoughts might be seriously muddled with regard to Lady Maria Burton, but one thing was perfectly clear. He could not bear the thought of her wed to another man.

At noon the following day, Maria was seated next to her father, sharing a private box in the gallery that overlooked the tournament field. Sitting with them were Humphrey, Duke of Gloucester, and his wife, Lady Eleanor.

Eleanor was a lively woman, different from any of the noblewomen Maria had yet met—and unpopular among many of them. Maria liked her, though. She was friendly and vivacious, touching her husband often, to his obvious pleasure. Her hair was only barely covered, and she wore vibrant colors that set off her complexion. The daring cut of Eleanor's gown made Maria envious of her audacity.

Various servants came and went from the observation box, bearing pillows to make their masters comfortable in their seats, and food and drink to refresh them.

Maria was nervous and on edge, knowing that Bexhill and Nicholas were to meet on the field. She comforted herself with the knowledge that this was to be a "tournament of peace," and that, in any event, Nicholas would not be mortally wounded. She'd heard plenty about Bexhill's mastery on the field of battle, but knew little of Nicholas's skills.

She knew of his courtly skills. And she knew of his skill in the bedchamber.

Neither of these would serve him now.

At least he was a competent brawler. He'd shown her that much when he'd rescued her and her father on the road from Fleet Castle. She could only hope that he would be equally skilled in formal battle, without his whip.

"The contest will run three courses, Lady Maria," Gloucester said. "The combatants will wield blunted weapons, since this is a tournament of peace."

"First is the lance contest," Sterlyng explained. "Then they'll fight with swords, and last of all with axes."

Maria felt a wave of nausea that was becoming all too familiar of late. If only events in her life would settle down, then perhaps her stomach would, too.

"But their weapons cannot do real injury, Father?"

"That is correct."

A knight in black leather armor rode into the arena on a gray roan. His head was fully covered by a black helm, but his colors were burgundy-red and white. The crowd in the stands cheered his arrival and watched as he rode to the gallery where Maria sat.

This was not surprising, for Gloucester—the king's uncle—was the highest ranking nobleman present at the tournament, and Maria happened to be sharing his box with her father. According to Sterlyng, 'twas customary for the combatants to pay homage to the king before beginning the contest. Since King Henry was not in attendance, the Duke of Gloucester would do.

The knight sat tall and straight in his saddle, with his sword at his side, his ax hanging from his saddle and his lance in front of him. He was broad shouldered and narrow hipped, and he rode with the easy confidence of a champion. Maria knew at once that this was Nicholas Hawken.

He stopped in front of Maria, then bowed to Gloucester and Sterlyng. Lastly, he raised his helm and afforded a view of his visage.

The crowd grew silent. Maria's heart gave a start when she looked into his eyes, now a stormy gray, and he spoke directly to her. "My lady," he said. "A small token of your confidence and esteem would honor me."

Smiling widely, Lady Eleanor leaned toward Maria and whispered, "Give him your veil, Maria."

The fine white silk of her veil had been made with the cloth that he'd sent her. It did not conceal Maria's hair, but the fabric had been so lovely...and it had been a gift from Nicholas. She could not deny she'd had the veil hastily made, along with a chemise that she now wore against her bare skin. 'Twas foolish, Maria knew, but still 'twas almost as if his hands caressed her while she wore it.

And almost as if he knew what lay under her gown as his eyes raked over her.

Refusing to be discomfited by the intensity of Nicholas's gaze, she pulled the veil from her chapeau and leaned over to hand it to him. With his gauntlets removed, he took the veil from Maria, keeping her hand in his for a long, heated moment. Then he slipped the cloth under his armor, to wear against his heart.

Maria felt a strange burning in the back of her throat as she watched this gesture, but before there was time to give it any further thought, Nicholas turned his horse and sped away.

"Upon my oath, I would swoon at so gallant a display," Lady Eleanor said. "How handsome a champion..." Then she added under her breath, "And what a superb lover he would be..."

Nonplussed by the lady's remark, Maria was saved from having to respond by Lord Bexhill, who rode up at that moment.

She wondered if Lady Eleanor had some particular insight into her past, but realized that she'd made the statement only because of Nicholas himself, of his handsome features and the dashing figure he cut. 'Twas true that Maria's heart beat a little faster, her palms were a bit moist, now that he was within sight. Why should it be different for any other lady? She tipped her chin up slightly and hardened her heart. She knew how popular he was among them.

Bexhill followed the same formalities as Nicholas. The only difference was that he turned to another gallery down the way and begged a token from some other lady. 'Twas given with much fanfare, and then the battle was on.

"Bexhill wears full armor," Gloucester noted, frowning.

"'Tis odd," Sterlyng agreed.

"Why is it odd?" Maria asked anxiously.

"Kirkham's armor is cuir-bouilli."

"Leather?" Maria asked incredulously. She looked with alarm at the combatants on the field. "But Bexhill wears plate armor. Does that not—"

"Nay, Daughter," Sterlyng said. "Kirkham's armor has been boiled and treated, and is quite sturdy. 'Tis customary to wear lighter protection in a peace tournament."

"But why does Bexhill wear plate?"

Sterlyng frowned and shook his head. It seemed that he was puzzled by the earl's attire, too.

"Look, they begin!" Lady Eleanor cried with excitement.

Maria braced herself as the two knights charged each other from opposite ends of the field. Each man bore a lance that extended well beyond his horse's head, aimed at his opponent. Unconsciously, Maria held her breath and grasped her father's forearm as she watched.

"What is the goal of this contest?" she asked, her voice betraying her worry.

"'Tis merely to unseat the opponent," Sterlyng replied. "In actual battle, 'twould be to kill."

The first clash had Bexhill nearly falling from his mount. Maria let out the breath she was holding as the two knights galloped away from their first charge and circled 'round to the far ends of the field.

Again they went at each other, but this time, neither

knight was compromised. The third charge was different.

Bexhill's lance dipped slightly, and the two horses collided. Nicholas's horse went down. Maria flew to her feet as Nicholas disappeared amid hoofs and screaming horses. "Father!"

Sterlyng came to his feet beside her, as did Gloucester. "What ho?" the king's uncle said, frowning.

"Something ails Kirkham's horse," Sterlyng replied. "'Tis odd for a horse to be so injured during a peaceful conflict." He called for a page and gave him instructions, and the young man quickly left the gallery.

Several men ran to the field to assist Kirkham, while Bexhill rode off to the perimeter. Maria did not care for Bexhill's arrogant posture, and wondered if the earl had done something to injure Nicholas's horse. Whatever had happened had not been clearly visible to her, nor to anyone else near her.

But Sterlyng and Gloucester exchanged a glance.

"What?" Maria asked, noticing the two.

"'Tis naught, my dear," Gloucester said cautiously. "Only fair strange that while Kirkham has come to the tourney wearing cuir-bouilli, Bexhill wears plate...with spikes. And after three rounds, 'tis only Kirkham's *horse* that's gone down."

Maria looked into her father's eyes, asking for clarification.

"Could be some form of deceit," he said, though he was puzzled. Maria knew that her father thought Bexhill beyond reproach, and would have trouble believing ill of him.

"But, Father—"

"Hush, Daughter," Sterlyng said, giving her the reassurance of his arm 'round her shoulders. Maria was too preoccupied with the events on the field to notice his speculative glance. "The lords' squires will deal with the situation."

She breathed more easily when Nicholas stood away from the fray, apparently unharmed, but her anxiety was renewed as the two knights unsheathed their swords.

Maria jumped as the swords clashed, but Sterlyng steadied her. "They are made of whalebone," he said, "and unlikely to cause lethal damage."

Maria had her doubts. With the way the two men struck at each other, she could easily believe that one would be hurt. Close to tears, she knew that even had Nicholas not worn her veil next to his heart, she would still have championed him. Her own heart was at peril with all she felt for him, but she could not distance herself from Nicholas.

She winced with every blow he took, and suppressed the urge to scream at them to stop this demented contest. *Men!* There was no purpose to this exercise, and Maria could only imagine the injuries they would suffer, even if there were no lethal blows.

"Your grace…" The page spoke quietly to Gloucester. Maria did not hear what was said, but Gloucester turned and spoke to a knight who stood nearby.

"What is it, Father?" she asked.

Sterlyng shrugged. "The page must have noted some irregularity and…look," he said, nodding toward the combatants on the field. "Kirkham has dealt the end blow."

Maria saw that Nicholas had, indeed, bested Bexhill, and the earl was lying supine beneath Nicholas's sword. "What now?"

Two knights entered the field on foot. One assisted

Bexhill to his feet and the other went to Nicholas's side. Without delay, they escorted the two combatants away.

"'Tis finished," Gloucester said angrily. "I will not allow such trickery to be employed in the royal tourneys."

"Trickery?"

"My page suspects that Kirkham's horse was gored by Bexhill's armor...mayhap his lance. He could not be certain, and Bexhill denies any wrongdoing. Insists that whatever happened was inadvertent."

The nausea hit Maria so suddenly, she had to sit down.

Chapter Eighteen

"Are you all right, Maria?" Eleanor asked. "Would you care for a sip of—"

Maria knew she must look ghastly if Lady Eleanor had noticed. She shook her head and pressed her fingers to her lips. "Nay," she whispered. "Give me but a moment."

"I declare the Marquis of Kirkham the winner of this tourney," Gloucester announced to the crowd. "The battle by ax is waived and Kirkham will receive the prize."

He showed the golden medallion that would be awarded to Kirkham, but Maria could hardly draw her attention to it. She was just relieved that Nicholas had not been maimed, or badly wounded.

"May we go home now, Father?" she asked.

Finally admitting to himself that he'd fought only for Maria, Nicholas swallowed bitter disappointment that she was not at her seat when Gloucester awarded him the prize. He'd wanted nothing more than to accept it, only to turn and present it to his lady fair.

Why he wanted to do such a thing... He shook his

head. There was naught but confusion when he thought of Lady Maria Burton.

Ah well, 'twas no matter that she had left the tourney before its end, he thought as he lowered himself into a tub of hot water. He was to be Sterlyng's guest tonight and would see Maria when they supped. There he would give her the prize Gloucester had presented to him, a golden medallion inset with rubies. Then he would see if she could remain indifferent to him.

He soaked his bruised body and smiled. At least one purpose had been served today. Bexhill had been exposed as the fraud he was. Though he'd denied any intentional wrongdoing, most everyone believed the earl had gored Nick's horse with a spike—an inexcusable offense during a tourney of peace, which was intended to be a mere show of skill, not a battle to the death.

And Maria would know what a lout Bexhill was.

Nicholas lifted the white silk veil that lay upon a table near the tub. The piece had been cut from the bolt he'd sent her and its significance was not lost on him. She'd had it made into a veil within a day or two of receiving it.

He held it close to his nose and mouth and inhaled, drawing in Maria's fragrance. 'Twas only a piece of silk, but it had been worn close to her skin. Not once had he considered returning it to her.

He concluded they'd had too little time together. That was why his mind was fixated on her and the intensity of the relations between them. One more night with her…nay, a trifling couple of hours…

His body hardened as he imagined her here, in this tub with him. Mayhap she would sit astride him with her marvelous hair flowing about her shoulders, her luscious breasts tantalizing him, her lips moist and tender.

Maria's interaction with him at Fleet Castle had nearly been his undoing. Never had he known anyone so exquisitely sensitive to his touch, so ingenuous in her response to him. She'd said it was a mistake that night, and had started to tell him he didn't want her.

She couldn't possibly be more wrong. He wanted her the way a starving man wanted food.

More.

He climbed out of the tub and scrubbed himself dry as he reined in his fantasy. This was not the time to engage in fanciful dreams about Maria Burton. He had an important job to do.

French troops had moved into position near Orléans. They now had a champion, the maiden Jehann. And as unlikely as she seemed, this "soldier-maiden" posed an actual threat to the English troops positioned there.

'Twas imperative that Nicholas discover the identity of the high-placed traitor, and stop the flow of sensitive information to France. If he failed to do his part, even more Englishmen would die in battle.

He considered confiding in Sterlyng, but decided instead to maintain the fiction that Sterlyng was the one suspected of the treason. That way, whoever was planting evidence was likely to continue doing so, and was also more likely to be caught. Then there would be no more messages to the dauphin's forces, telling them about numbers of troops, and food supplies, and morale. There would be no one to interpret the sentiments of the English people or Parliament with regard to the wars in France, or how Bedford's financial resources would change.

As Nicholas dressed, he considered ways to entrap the French informer. And he nearly succeeded in eliminating thoughts of his lovely Maria from his mind.

* * *

Maria slept part of the afternoon, tossing and turning with dreams of the tournament, and bloodshed that had never actually occurred. She dreamed all sorts of horrors, most of them having to do with Nicholas, swords and lances, and when she awoke, she was unsettled. She felt mentally, as well as physically, disoriented.

Besides all else, the cooking smells of fowl and fish that wafted through the house made her queasy. Looking for an escape, she and Alisia left the house and walked down to the riverside, where pleasure boats were available for hire, and young men wooed their ladies amidst the willows on the lawn overlooking the water.

"'Tis lovely here," Maria said to Alisia.

The lady nodded. "Your father said the tournament upset you."

Maria shrugged. "Seeing grown men going at each other with weapons was disturbing."

"I understand Lord Kirkham won."

"Aye. Lord Bexhill was no match against him."

"That is interesting," Alisia remarked. "One never hears of Lord Kirkham's battle prowess, but I know he served in France under King Henry's command years ago."

"He did?"

Alisia nodded. "His brother was killed while fighting by his side. 'Tis said Kirkham never recovered from the loss."

"I can well imagine," Maria said as they walked on.

"The king released him from service, but Kirkham did not return to England, as I recall," Alisia continued, remembering facts and rumor as she spoke. "'Twas thought that he blamed himself for his brother's death, and that he was unable to face his father after that.''

It pained Maria to think of his sorrow.

''He eventually returned to England after his father's death,'' Alisia said. ''And became marquis.''

They reached the river's edge and walked in silence for a time. ''Why do you suppose Ni—Lord Kirkham is so...''

''Disreputable?''

Maria nodded.

They strolled on for a moment before Alisia spoke. ''I do not believe he is quite so bad as he wants society to think,'' she said quietly.

Maria stopped. ''Nay?''

Alisia kept walking. She shook her head and waited for Maria to catch up. ''Nay. I sense too much principle, too much honor under the surface. Look at the deference with which he treats your father. Surely that is not feigned.''

''Nay, Alisia,'' Maria said with enthusiasm. ''And at Kirkham, he was so considerate of his old nursemaid. And of the old couple who manage his estates. My aunt and cousins at Alderton never showed any such consideration of their tenants.''

''I believe there is much more to Kirkham than meets the eye,'' Alicia said, carefully observing Maria's reaction to her words.

Maria watched her feet as she walked, and weighed Alisia's words. Life had been so simple before. She had never had to scrutinize motivations, though with Nicholas, she'd had no choice but to conclude that his sole purpose was to entice her into his bed again. She knew his reputation. Even if she hadn't been warned away from him here in London, she had learned at Kirkham that he was a most *un*virtuous host.

Nevertheless, Maria admitted that Alisia might be correct. 'Twas possible there was more going on between them than pure lust.

She dared not hope.

"Father says that large ships sail into London Harbor with goods from all over the world."

Alisia accepted the change of subject with a slight nod of her head. It seemed that there was more she would have said on the subject of Nicholas Hawken, but she let it pass. "Aye. They do," she replied brusquely. "And you'd best stay away from that part of the river. There's nary a rougher place on earth than the harbor waterfront."

Maria frowned. "Why?" she asked. "What makes it so dangerous?"

Alisia sniffed. "The worst sorts of men will be found there. Taverns and…low women. Harlots. They indulge in all sorts of vices. Too much drink, and fights… Every now and again you'll hear of some dark goings-on down there. Someone beaten, another one knifed…."

"Well, I'll never have reason to go to the harbor."

"See that you don't," Alisia said. "Maria…?"

"Hmm?" Maria replied absently as she gazed at the water. The day was uncommonly sunny and pleasant, and she relished the warmth of the afternoon sun on her skin. 'Twas a welcome diversion from her preoccupation with Nicholas Hawken, the unscrupulous lord who might not be as bad as he seemed.

"Look!" she said, pointing at the water. Two boats sped by, each with two young men at the oars. "They're racing!"

"Aye, that they are," Alisia remarked. She never

asked Maria the question that had been on the tip of her tongue only a few minutes before.

Preparations for the evening's company were in full swing by the time they returned to the house, and Maria went to her room to dress for the soiree.

Alone now, she found that visions of her earlier dreams plagued her once again. She saw Nicholas, bruised and bloody, and Lord Bexhill's face contorted in an evil grin. She did not know how the man could live with himself after what he'd done during the tourney. What kind of knight would ever think to injure another contestant's horse? How had he thought he'd get away with it? The man must not have one bone of integrity in him.

Daylight was fading, but Maria did not bother to light a lamp just yet. She removed the plain gown she'd worn for walking, and sat down on a cushioned bench, wearing only the thin silk chemise, which whispered softly against her skin. She pulled the fine bone pins from her hair and began to brush the mass.

Her discussion with Alisia as they'd walked by the river had made thoughts of Nicholas only more confusing. Maria closed her eyes and sighed, his face clearly visible in her mind. What a scoundrel he was, she thought. A comely, inconstant, remarkable knave, and she would do well to remember that.

Yet with very little effort, Maria could almost feel his hands upon her shoulders, his lips on hers. His scent would remind her of the spicy soap he used and—

A noise at the window shook her out of her reverie. She turned to look, and saw the man of her thoughts brazenly climbing through the open casement.

"Nicholas!"

"Hush," he said, quickly coming to her side and covering her mouth with one hand. "Don't scream."

She shook her head and pulled his hand away. "You should not be here! Why—"

He interrupted her words with a kiss, a long, searing kiss that made Maria's knees feel as if they were made of butter. "I would see you alone, my lady fair," he whispered. "And I knew it would not happen unless I…" His eyes bored into hers, then grazed the rest of her features. "Ah, my lady fair, you are so very lovely. My silken gift becomes you. 'Tis just as I imagined it." Then his mouth devoured hers again, and his hands slipped under the straps of her chemise, lowering the garment.

Maria could offer no resistance. As disreputable as he was, she could not keep from loving him, from taking pleasure in his touch. She trembled when his hands drifted down, teasing every sensitive part of her, until he cupped her breasts in his hands.

"Nicholas…" she breathed. "You are unharmed? Bexhill did not hurt—"

"Nay, lady fair," Nick said. "You may examine every inch of me if you must."

He bent and laved one nipple with his tongue, then sucked the entire bud into his mouth. She grabbed his dark hair and held his head in place while she reveled in the sensations that shot through her.

Heat pooled low, in her very center. Pressure built in her most private place. Suddenly, the same intense sensations she'd experienced in the garden at Fleet were upon her. Every muscle flexed, then her entire being dissolved into a state of pure pleasure. Euphoria took hold as each nerve awoke and hummed with joy.

With her thoughts in a haze, Maria belatedly realized

she would have fallen had Nicholas not caught her and
carried her to the bed.

Her chemise had slipped off entirely, and she lay naked upon the quilt, with Nicholas over her, his talented
hands and lips still wreaking havoc upon her body. She
should not allow this. She should send him away.
"Nicholas…" she moaned, unable to put any sensible
words together.

"Hush, love," he said as he kissed both breasts, then
the flesh at her waist. His hands skimmed down her
legs, and likewise, his lips followed a downward path.
Hot breath tickled her navel, then his mouth was teasing
and nipping her most sensitive flesh.

She pulled at his hair. "Nicholas, you must not!"

"Ah, but I *must*," he said, kissing her softly again.
"I have dreamed of nothing but this…making love to
you…since you ran from me at Kirkham."

"And I must run again," she murmured, even as she
moaned with pleasure. "You are wholly unsuitable for
me, Nicholas. I must find a proper husband and…oh!"
She shuddered with pleasure.

"Speak no more of proper husbands," he said. "Feel
what happens when I touch you."

She could do nothing *but* feel. He had turned her into
a creature of the moment, a wild woman, hungry for his
touch. Rational thought was an impossibility when he
seduced her this way, as he well knew.

The shadows in the room deepened. Maria could
scarcely see Nicholas's features as she writhed under
him, entirely at his mercy. 'Twas not right, she knew,
to allow him such liberties. Soon she would go belowstairs and entertain her father's guests, some of
whom were perfectly respectable prospective husbands.

Nicholas would be there, as well, she thought with

chagrin. How would she face him after this...this interlude?

A sharp knock sounded at the door. "My lady?"

"A moment, please!" Maria said in dismay.

"I've come to help you with your laces, and your hair," the maid said.

"I'm not ready," she called. "Please give me a few moments...."

"Aye, ma'am," the maid said. "If you'll just pull the bell cord, I'll return when you want me."

Maria swung her legs off the bed and jerked her discarded chemise in front of her.

Nick looked at her predatorily, but rose to his feet. "You hide nothing from me, my lady fair."

Maria was afraid that was all too true. "Nicholas!" she rasped in dismay. How had she allowed this seduction to take place? She should have pushed him back out the window before he'd even climbed all the way in.

"I will take my leave now," he said, kissing her quickly, "but I'll return."

"Nay, Nicholas!" Maria whispered. "You must not!"

He winked, then turned and climbed out the window.

Chapter Nineteen

Supper would have been deathly dull had it not been for Nicholas's presence. He made the room come alive with his personality, his jests, his knowledge of the workings of Westminster and all who toiled within.

Everyone seemed fascinated by him, especially, Maria noted, the ladies of the party.

That alone was enough to sour Maria's mood, as well as her memory of the moments Nick had spent seducing her in her own chamber. How dare he invade her privacy and treat her like a common harlot? She was not one of his loose women, to be so used and then discarded.

True, he had not spent himself, and Maria could only believe that was his just punishment for treating her so badly. She hoped he suffered mightily with his frustration.

"…a token of esteem for the fair lady Maria," he was saying. Maria had not paid attention to the words, but Nicholas was handing something to her. 'Twas a large golden medallion with the Lancaster seal tooled into the surface, and it was encrusted with red gems.

"Ah, my lady," he chided, "you have not been listening."

She blushed. Charmingly, to Nicholas's way of thinking. She'd been distracted and irritable all through the meal, though she attempted to be pleasant to all Sterlyng's other guests. Nicholas seemed to be the only one excluded from her charm.

He supposed he deserved that. He had not planned to invade her chamber uninvited. But he'd arrived early in Bridewell Lane, and as he'd bided his time, he'd seen Maria through the window of her chamber. He'd not been able to resist stealing a few moments with her, though he'd never thought he'd take those few kisses so far.

Her chemise had been made of the silk he'd sent her, and visions of her in it had plagued his dreams. Never again could he look at her without thinking of his silk caressing her naked form. It suited her so well, concealing yet enticing, all at once.

His body came to full alert when he thought of her in the throes of passion. She was the most beautiful creature when she responded to him, and he could not get enough of her. He would return later....

Nay, 'twas too soon for Maria. He'd breached her defenses once today, mayhap even earlier. For she'd left the tournament before its completion. Could it be that his lady fair felt more for him than disdain?

Even the duke seemed positively disposed toward him this evening, which would only work in his favor. As Sterlyng pinned the medallion to his daughter's gown, Nicholas smiled with satisfaction.

Then he slipped away from the gathering, ostensibly to use the privy.

* * *

Nicholas had been gone too long. Like a magnet, Maria was drawn by the powerful attraction between them. With his heavy medallion at her shoulder, she left the gathering in the great hall and went in search of him.

Considering the possibility that he would expect her to follow him, she went upstairs to her own chamber, only to find it empty. She glanced inside her father's room, too, but Nicholas was not there.

She frowned. Where could he have gone? He'd been absent much too long for a trip to the privy, so he must be somewhere in the house.

Maria skipped down the back staircase and wandered through the kitchen, then into the yard near the privy. No one there.

Back in the house, Maria searched the rooms at the back until she reached the end of the narrow corridor to her father's study. As she peeped in the door, Nicholas captured her wrist and pulled her to him.

Blistering her breathless with his kiss, he pressed her body into his, then whispered kisses across her jaw to her ear, then down her throat. "You'll not find a husband among these milksop sons of noblemen, my lady fair," he said.

"I most certainly *will*," she said, pushing him away. He did not need to know that she was reconsidering her decision to snag a husband so soon. "I will find someone who will respect me, and not ambush me in dark corners."

Nicholas grinned and shook his head.

Maria frowned in turn and glanced around the chamber. "What are you doing in here?"

He hesitated for an instant. "I took a wrong turn when I came in," he said. "I was just coming to find you."

She crossed her arms impatiently and tapped one foot. "You'll forgive me if I find that somewhat difficult to believe, Lord Kirkham," she said coldly.

"'Tis true!" he said with a laugh. "My, my, you are a suspicious woman." He attempted to nuzzle her neck, but she pulled away. She knew he was trying to distract her, and wanted to know why.

The chamber appeared undisturbed in the dim light, but Maria could smell the smoke of a candle recently extinguished. He'd had light in here, and she would know why.

"What were you looking for?"

"Looking—?"

"Do not attempt to placate me with kisses, Nicholas," she said as she pressed the tip of her forefinger into his chest. "I know better."

"You are mistaken, love," he replied, acting the wounded rascal. "It is as I told you—"

"Nay, 'tis not," she retorted. "I can think of only one reason for you to be alone in my father's study."

She paused long enough for Nicholas to read her meaning. When he finally spoke, 'twas clear he understood.

"Nay, Maria," he said, appalled to realize that she'd come to the correct conclusion. He had really bungled things!

What could he tell her? What excuse could he give? Without doubt, some version of the truth was necessary, but how much should he say? "Maria..."

"Nay, do not even think of lying to me, Nicholas."

"I have no intention of lying to you," he said, running his hands down her arms. He gathered her fingers into his hands. "'Tis just that...the more you know, the more...dangerous it is for all of us."

"Explain," she said, keeping her fists clenched, not budging from her position.

"To make it quick and to the point," he said, "I am in the service of the Duke of Bedford. There is evidence that important information is being transferred to the French…" He paused, but saw that Maria would not be satisfied until he'd finished. "…through your father."

She was silent for a moment, then let out a puff of air in dismissal. "That is preposterous," she said, turning away. "Ridiculous," she added under her breath.

He grabbed her arm. "It is deadly serious. Englishmen are being killed every day on battlefields because the French seem to know how many men we have, and where they are garrisoned. They know what provisions our soldiers have, when they were last paid, what our weaknesses are."

"You are serious," Maria said, shrugging away from him.

He gave a quick nod.

"And you think that my father is sending this information to the French king?"

"To the dauphin."

Maria stepped away, keeping her back to him. By the set of her shoulders, he could see that she was upset.

He cursed the bad luck that had kept him working at the sticky lock in Sterlyng's desk. Nicholas had gone through everything and found nothing, not one piece of incriminating evidence, not even in the locked drawer.

True enough, the letter from "the maid" was there, but that only gave proof to the notion that Sterlyng wasn't hiding anything. If he had another secure place within the house, Nicholas had no doubt that the maid's letter would have been hidden there, rather than in the desk.

Instead, all of the duke's valuables were stored in that single locked drawer, including his bronze seal.

Now Nicholas had proof that he must look elsewhere for the culprit. He had no doubt that the spy was a high-ranking sort—someone who had access to secret information. He would have to give this further thought.

He could not tell Maria of his suspicions or she might inadvertently thwart his investigation. If the culprit discovered that Nicholas knew of his treachery, he would likely become so careful Nick would never learn his identity. "Maria..."

She did not reply, but stood still, facing away from him. He walked around her, and discovered that she was blinking back tears and attempting to compose her facial expression.

"My father would never do anything so vile as what you've suggested," she said. "He is no traitor."

"Maria, I've come here to prove exactly that."

"You cannot possibly expect me to believe you."

"Well, yes—actually, I do." He gave her a sheepish smile that shot pain through her heart.

"I'll tell you what I believe, Nicholas Hawken," she said, sniffing. "You've come 'round, pretending friendship with my father, and—and an interest in me, while all the time, y-you—"

"Maria," he protested, "I did not know you were Burton's daughter while you were at Kirkham! When I...er, when we..." He sensed it would do more harm than good to mention the turn their relations had taken at Kirkham. "Maria, you must trust that that is not true. You are a lovely woman...and very special to me."

She looked up at him with glistening eyes, then glanced down, turned and walked out of the room.

Nick would have kicked something if he could have

done it silently. He could not remember a time when things had gone so badly with a woman. He usually managed his relations with the ladies with much more coolness than this.

He should have known from the first moment he'd seen her—when she'd cuffed him and knocked him off his feet on the road to Kirkham—that things would never be simple, or easy, with his lady fair.

Going on the assumption that Nicholas would not return to the party, Maria made his excuses for him, saying that he'd been called away. She half expected him at her chamber window later, after the house was quiet and all the guests had left, but he did not reappear.

She did not know whether to be thankful or upset.

Nay, she was thankful. Truly. She had no wish to see Nicholas Hawken again. He was a lying, sneaking blackguard who had no regard for honest and virtuous behavior.

Lying in her bed, and watching shadows dance on the walls, Maria thought through her disturbing conversation with the unscrupulous marquis. He'd as much as admitted to searching her father's study, but he'd also said it was for the purpose of proving him innocent. She did not know whether she could believe him.

Either way, it seemed that *someone* believed the Duke of Sterlyng was guilty of treason, else why would Nicholas risk searching through his things?

In the short time since he'd come for her at Rockbury, Maria had become fiercely attached to her father, and she was not about to allow anyone to discredit him now, just when they'd been reunited.

Maria wished she had a better grasp of politics, or knew more of the powerful men in Parliament. If she could get them to talk with her, perhaps then she would be able to piece together an understanding of what her father's involvement might be, or who was trying to ensnare him in this unethical plot.

Nicholas said he worked for the Duke of Bedford. Maria knew that Bedford, the Regent of France, was brother to the Duke of Gloucester. He was another of the king's uncles, the man responsible for conducting the French war. Alisia had said Bedford was the one who'd dismissed Nicholas from service years before. Was he also the one accusing her father of treason?

Maria frowned. She'd heard Sterlyng speak of Bedford, and knew they were close friends. What evidence could Bedford possibly have? And why would he believe the worst of her father?

There had to be some sign or actual documentation, else Nicholas would not have bothered searching her father's study and risk being caught. However, Maria would bet her life that her father was not involved in any way. He would never betray his friend Bedford— or his country.

Someone, the real culprit, had somehow managed to make Nicholas believe her father was guilty of treachery. And that was why Nicholas was engaged in pursuing her so diligently. He had done all that was possible to gain legitimate entry into her life.

Yet he was just as much a scoundrel as she had believed. What Alisia had seen beneath his surface was only more deception.

Maria's heart hurt.

She knew now, beyond a doubt, that he did not care for her. He had never cared for her. He merely wanted to make her so weak-skulled in his presence that she would not question any of his actions. And he'd been entirely too successful.

He had deliberately kissed her senseless, had consciously beguiled her to the point of abandon in order to make her so besotted, so completely overwhelmed that she'd let his prying go unnoticed.

He had nearly succeeded. Even now, when she did not want to think of the ways Nicholas could make her respond, Maria could feel his warm lips upon her skin. She could smell his scent upon her body.

She turned to make herself comfortable for sleep, but her gaze alighted on the window. 'Twas open.

Though she tried to tell herself she'd left it ajar because the night was warm, Maria knew she'd left it that way on the off chance that Nicholas would return. She told herself she only wanted to talk to him—to assure him that she would be making her own inquiries to absolve her father of any wrongdoing.

She sat up abruptly, then threw herself facedown on the bed. Rather than thinking about Nicholas, she needed to concentrate on this matter of treason, and try to figure a way to exonerate her father. She would not leave that knave, Nicholas Hawken, to his suspicions.

Maria considered going to her father about this, but decided against it. 'Twould only upset and embarrass him, and she did not want either. Nay, this was something she could deal with on her own—to show Nicholas how badly he'd erred. Then she would say goodbye to the marquis forever, and choose a husband from among the many suitors who had already spoken to her father, requesting her hand.

Punching her pillow into shape beneath her, Maria almost wished the duke would choose a husband for her. 'Twould make things that much easier.

Nicholas paced the length of his bedchamber, restless and edgy. He was tempted to return to Bridewell Lane and climb up to Maria's room, but he knew she'd be more likely to shove him out the window than welcome him with open arms.

He was worried. Maria had become far too important to him. The idea that she might take matters into her own hands was frightening. What if she managed to discover the identity of the traitor and confronted him? The danger to her would be enormous.

Nick slammed his knuckles on the table next to his bed.

His growing regard for Maria did not settle well. He'd never been so wrapped up in a woman that his purpose became sidetracked and muddled in his mind.

Mayhap 'twas time to gather his cronies for a night of carousing. A good binge would suffice in getting that little blond termagant out of his thoughts. There were plenty of other likely wenches who would just as soon take a marquis to bed than fight him.

But none would suit him half as well as Maria.

All diversions aside, he had to redouble his efforts to apprehend whoever was responsible for contriving the evidence against Sterlyng. If only Nick could discern some purpose to implicating the duke, he would have a greater chance of deducing who his true enemy was.

Unfortunately, no reasonable explanation came to mind, other than the possibility of throwing Nick off the trail. That in itself would occupy his time and efforts and keep him from discovering and thwarting the real traitor. There was a very good chance that this man was using the distraction to siphon even more damaging information to France.

Whatever the reason, somehow Nicholas would manage to keep Maria safe. She had no place in all this intrigue. He wished it were possible to go to her father with what little information he had, but until he had more than just a suspicion that the duke was innocent, he could not divulge what he knew.

The candles burned low as Nicholas thought again of Maria, and he cursed under his breath at the most recent turn of events. More than ever, he needed to stay close to her, but doubted she'd be disposed to let him, not after the way he'd bungled their encounter in her father's study.

Somehow, he'd have to convince her that he was not the enemy. On the contrary, he cared more about her than his own life.

Nearly a week passed with Nicholas unable to get close to Maria. When she went riding near Westminster, she was always accompanied by one of her many suitors. Walks along the riverside were never solitary affairs. One or more gentlemen accompanied her, along with Lady Alisia. Nick had gone to any number of fetes and soirees in hopes of seeing her, but she was not in attendance at any of them.

He finally had some luck when he learned of a boating party being hosted by Gloucester's wife.

Lady Eleanor was a lusty female with an adventurous nature. She had few inhibitions with regard to the men and women of her circle. 'Twas no difficulty at all to persuade her to help him press his suit with Maria.

A large group of festively dressed noblemen and women was assembled on the banks of the Thames not far from Westminster Hall. Here, couples would board small boats and row down to one of Lady Eleanor's favorite places, a park on the opposite shore. There the party would disembark and engage in a few rounds of *paille-maille,* and whatever other amusements Lady Eleanor had planned. Afterward, they would all sit on heavy cloths spread out on the ground, and eat a meal prepared and served by a score of servants.

Arriving there, Nicholas caught sight of Maria standing at the water's edge, talking with some other ladies. She was unaware of his presence.

His breath hitched at her loveliness.

She wore a gown of forest green trimmed in white, its neck cut low, exposing a vast amount of bare skin. An *excessive* amount of skin, to Nick's way of thinking. He bristled as he noticed each man in the party taking his turn gawking at her.

Maria still did not notice him, and Nicholas intended to keep it that way for now. He knew she would avoid him if possible, so he planned to commandeer a gig and get her into it with him, while Lady Eleanor distracted the others nearby.

Maria would then be his captive.

Nick smiled for the first time in days.

His timing needed to be impeccable, so he waited until Maria had been assisted into the gig, and her partner was about to board. As Eleanor got the attention of the young man who was to go with Maria, Nicholas bullied his way forward, took the other man's place and had pushed off from the quay before Maria had a chance to protest.

"Nicholas Hawken," she said, crossing her arms over her chest, "you had better have a very good reason for this, else you are a dead man."

Chapter Twenty

Nicholas gave her the grin that had the power to turn her knees to hot wax and her insides to melted butter.

However, she refused to be reduced to mush by him. This was the man who believed her father guilty of treason.

Even if his denials were true—which Maria had reason to doubt—he'd still used her to gain access to her father. And she was not about to forgive him that. His casual disregard for her heart was inexcusable.

"Well?" she demanded. He was too recklessly handsome. The muscles of his arms were too well defined through the sleeves of his tunic, his thighs absurdly powerful under his hose. Maria intentionally glanced away. 'Twas against her purpose to be reminded of the man's physical strength or prowess.

"'Tis a beautiful morn, love," he said. "I merely wanted to spend it with the most beautiful of women—Lady Maria Burton."

"Such truckling does not become you, Lord Kirkham."

"Nay? But what does?"

"Your absence, my lord."

''Ah, Maria, you wound me,'' he said, placing one hand against his chest.

''As if *that* were possible,'' she muttered.

He smiled and continued rowing the gig, his strokes smooth and steady, and so quick that he bypassed all the other boats headed down the river. He remained close to the west shore, while all the others headed across the Thames.

''You are not keeping up with the others,'' Maria said.

''On the contrary,'' he remarked, ''I am far ahead of them.''

''Nicholas, change course,'' Maria said, the motion of the boat making her queasy. ''Let us join the rest of the party.''

''I thought I would take you…'' He paused, and she looked down so he would not see her discomfiture. ''Maria?''

The wave of nausea overtook her so quickly she was not prepared for it. She felt chilled and clammy. She swallowed several times to keep from becoming ill, but knew she was losing the battle. She closed her eyes and covered her mouth with one hand. ''Nicholas, I think I'm going to be ill.''

She struggled to keep down her breakfast, while he did something with the boat. Suddenly they were no longer moving, and Nicholas was lifting her, carrying her away from the water.

He set her gently on the grass, in the sun. Then he sat down close to her and gathered her into his arms. Maria held one hand pressed to her stomach, and waited for the nausea to pass. He unfastened her chapeau and veil, and pulled her close. She heard him murmuring, and felt his lips upon her forehead and temple, but was so consumed by this wretched illness, she hardly noticed.

Finally, the awful sensations passed and she sat up, pulling slightly away from him.

"Better?"

She nodded, but said nothing. As much as she might want the comfort of his arms, she knew she must remain as distant as possible, to keep him from gaining advantage. He had too much sway over her.

"You turned quite green for a moment there," he said gently, as if comforting an ailing child. He frowned with concern. "Are you certain you are all right?"

"Yes, Nicholas," she replied. "'Twas just that awful boat ride. I'm unaccustomed to water travel."

A vertical line creased his forehead as he gazed at her, and it was all Maria could do to keep from smoothing it with her fingers.

"We'll wait here a bit and allow your stomach to settle before we go back."

"Go back?"

He shrugged. "To Lady Eleanor's assemblage on the other bank," he said. "Or home. I'll take you, either way."

"I do not want to get back into that boat," she said, eyeing the water warily.

The smile that quirked one corner of his mouth should have annoyed her, but she let it pass. She had no energy to argue with him now. "I don't blame you," he said. "Are you certain you're all right?"

"Completely."

"We could walk back to Westminster," he said, leaning toward her and brushing his lips over her hair. "'Tis not so very far."

Maria could not allow shivers of pleasure to influence

her opinion of him, though his lips had the power to make her weak. She knew what he wanted from her, and 'twas not her undying devotion.

She forced herself to tip her head away from him. "Have you learned anything about the...the traitor?" she asked, putting distance between them.

Nicholas sighed and loosened his hold on her. "Nay. And I would appreciate it if you would stay out of it," he said. "I have nightmares thinking of the danger in which you could find yourself in if—"

"Nicholas, 'tis my father whose reputation—his very life—is at stake here. I cannot sit idly by while you search for evidence against him."

"Maria, I am not looking for—"

She stood abruptly. "So you say, Nicholas, but I—" A wave of dizziness made her weave slightly, but Nicholas vaulted to his feet and steadied her.

"Maria, you are not all right," he said.

"I am," she said stubbornly. She tried to take a step away, but he held her fast. "And if you do not remove your hand from my person, Lord Kirkham, I shall scream."

"What? And not thrash me?"

In a huff, she turned and skulked away. She would not be baited by him, or seduced again. She had learned her lesson. Now she knew better than to allow him to use her as he'd done ever since following her to London.

In fact, she would return to Lady Eleanor's party. All that was necessary was to cross the Thames in the little boat. With Nicholas.

Maria was certain she could withstand that short length of time in the gig, but not so sure about spending any more time alone with Lord Kirkham. She was determined, however, to rejoin the gathering across the river. There were so many young people present, both ladies and gentlemen, and Maria had looked forward to this outing ever since she'd received the invitation.

Besides, 'twas a lovely afternoon and she refused to allow Nicholas Hawken's presence to sway her from her original purpose.

She changed course and began walking toward the bank of the river where Nicholas had pulled up the boat. He, of course, would follow, but Maria hoped he would not speak. She had nothing to say to him, and until he had new information regarding her father's innocence, then he had nothing to say to her, either.

"I thought you were going to walk to Westminster!" Nicholas shouted after her. No woman should have such an alluring gait, he thought as he caught up to her. His body responded to every move she made, just as if she were lying naked beneath him.

No one had ever had this effect on him before, and it behooved him not to think of such things now. Maria could be in danger if she rattled the wrong person with her questions, and he felt 'twas imperative to get her promise that she would stay out of it.

"I changed my mind," she said, without turning to look at him. "I wish to return to Lady Eleanor's gathering."

"Maria, we must talk," he said, falling into step next to her. "That was my reason for coming today." At least he had thought that was the reason.

"I have naught to say to you, Lord Kirkham."

"Nicholas."

She shrugged, and he decided not to argue the point.

"Have you done anything...spoken to anyone about—"

"Nay," she replied, "not yet. I have no intention of causing my father so much as one moment of grief over these…these rude accusations."

"Maria, I have not accused his grace of anything," Nick said.

"Mayhap not yet, but if naught else, you are a persistent one, Lord Kirkham," she said. "I have no doubt you'll find what you're looking for, and then 'twill be up to my father to prove his own innocence."

"Maria, I have no intention— Will you stop a moment and discuss this with me?"

"I have naught more to say to you, my lord."

"Oh, but I think you do." He stepped in front of her and put his hands on her shoulders. He would get her to listen if he had to tie her to a tree to do so.

Instead, he kissed her.

He felt a moment's resistance, but then her lips softened and her hands quit pushing against him. "Maria," he whispered, taking his mouth away for but an instant. His tongue teased her lips until she parted them and allowed him entry. He groaned with arousal and slipped one hand down to her hips, pulling her close.

Her hands encircled his neck, and her body pressed against his as she kissed him back. He sensed no reluctance, in spite of the words they'd exchanged so far.

God's breath, he had missed this. Touching her, tasting her. His fingers rediscovered the fine muscles and bones of her throat; his mouth relearned her flavor.

His skin burned everywhere her hands touched. He ached for her, yet he would not make love to her here, on the public path. Instead of crossing the river to join the party, he would take Maria back to his own house in London, where he would make love to her all afternoon. He would make her so weak with passion that she would forget about her questions, and concentrate all her attention upon him.

What a glorious day 'twould be.

Suddenly, she groaned and pushed away from him. "Nay, Nicholas!" she cried. "You will not do this to me!"

"Do what?" he asked. "Do what to you?"

"Seduce me until I have nary a thought in my head," she said, whirling away from him and storming down the path to the river on shaky legs.

Nick felt rather shaky himself. But he smiled at the thought of making Maria mindless. 'Twas good to hear her admit that he had such power over her.

He caught up to her once more.

"Please do not touch me again, Lord Kirkham."

He smiled.

"I am serious, Nicholas," she said. "Until this matter is resolved, I think 'tis better if we do not see one another."

"I disagree."

"It does not matter whether or not you agree," she stated coolly. "I will not be at home when you call."

"But you need not be at home, my lady fair, for me to spend time with you," he said, enjoying her discomfiture. He would have her in his bed when the time was right, and not a moment later. Clearly, she was powerless to resist him.

"I will avoid you in public as if you were a leper."

He snorted. "I will have you in bed again, Maria. Whether yours or mine is of no consequence. But rest assured, it will happen again. Soon."

"Nay, Nicholas," she said, "it will not. 'Tis my father's wish that I choose a husband and—"

"*Choose* a husband!" He knew this, but did not care

to have it thrown in his face after they'd just shared the most mind-numbing kiss within his memory.

"Yes. My father says I've had too few choices in my life and he wishes to remedy that." Maria reached the reedy bank and eyed the gig. She did not look forward to floating across the river in it, but could see no other option. She hoped it would be a mercifully quick trip. "He says that, even though 'tis unconventional, he believes 'tis only right that I decide for myself—"

"Do not climb in without help, Maria."

The exasperation in Nicholas's voice was unmistakable. Good. He seemed annoyed enough to refrain from talking. He took her hand as she stepped over the side of the gig. Then he slid the little boat out onto the water, stepping into it when it was just deep enough to push off.

Chapter Twenty-One

Maria tried not to watch him as he sat in front of her in the gig, but she found that her nausea diminished when she kept her eyes on him, rather than on the water or the moving riverbank.

She went only slightly green during the crossing, and refused Nicholas's attentions. He in turn ignored Maria's request that he leave the party. He pulled the boat in, then helped her out of it and escorted her to the group. She studiously ignored him when several of Lady Eleanor's female guests fawned over Nicholas and pleaded with him to stay. He seemed more than willing to satisfy their wishes.

Naturally he would, Maria thought, *being a master at seduction.*

She could only shake her head at these ladies, *and herself,* for falling prey to such transparent cajolery. Nicholas flirted shamelessly, winning approval from all the young women he encountered. His smile was too engaging. His words too charming.

And he was too obviously appreciative of the attributes the ladies displayed for his edification.

Maria could not watch. Deliberately forcing her attention elsewhere, she mingled with Lady Eleanor's guests, meeting as many of them as possible, and keeping her distance from Nicholas. *She* intended to marry. And a likely bridegroom could very well be present here at Lady Eleanor's party. In the meantime, Maria was going to enjoy every minute of the festivities.

Pointedly, she ignored the tittering laughter that surrounded Nicholas. She did not care to dwell on the likelihood that several of those ladies had already graced Nicholas's bed. Nor did she care for the pang of jealousy that came with the thought.

It had naught to do with her. Nicholas was a callous womanizer. She would not fall prey to him again. She was here to socialize with as many of her newfound peers as possible—not to pine over what could never be with Lord Kirkham. Her father wanted her to marry, and he'd given her the uncommon luxury of making her own choice.

She would do so. Soon.

After a few rounds of *paille-maille,* the guests milled about while acrobats tumbled across the lawn. Jugglers tossed colorful balls, while festively dressed minstrels played harp and drums, trumpet and fiddle. It all seemed very much like Dunstan Fair, with the notable lack of stalls displaying goods for sale.

After the meal was served, for which Maria could muster little appetite after her bout of seasickness, Lady Eleanor declared that everyone should prepare to participate in a demonstration of skills. Each member of the party was to choose something at which he or she was an expert, then give a performance of that skill.

This sent a round of excited chatter through the ladies, but a frisson of dread through Maria. She had no particular skill, besides bearing trays of refreshments that were half again her weight. Maria doubted anyone would be impressed by that.

"Archery targets have been set up yonder," Lady Eleanor announced, "and there is a ring for fencing. Musical instruments are here for your pleasure, and for those who would regale us with song, our minstrels will be pleased to accompany anyone."

Nicholas sat down on the wool-covered ground behind Maria. He leaned close and said, for her ears alone, "'Tis unfortunate that your most provocative skill is best saved for the bedchamber."

Maria gasped but said naught. Her heart pounded with this reminder of their intimate encounters, and her eyes darted to either side to see if any of her companions might have heard. Luckily, none had.

"Archers!" Lady Eleanor called. Her timing could not have been better. "The targets are ready!"

Everyone stood up from their places, straightening their clothes, and began walking toward a copse where huge bales of hay had been set up. Brightly colored cloth squares were attached, providing challenging targets. Squires stood together, holding bows and quivers of arrows, awaiting their masters.

"Have you ever shot an arrow, my lady fair?" Nicholas asked, walking next to her.

"Nay, Lord Kirkham," she replied, refusing to let him ruffle her.

"Shall I show you how?" he offered, placing her hand within the crook of his arm. "I would make it a most *personal* lesson."

Maria pulled her arm from his grasp and increased her pace, moving well ahead of him. She would not fall prey to his advances, no matter how he made her heart flutter. He was not the man for her—not with his seductive ways, and his distasteful clandestine activities. She would stay clear of him at any cost.

The archers took their places and shot at the targets, amid the cheers and applause of their squires and the other guests.

"Lord Kirkham," Lady Eleanor cried, "do you not shoot?"

Nicholas smiled and gave a shake of his head. "Nay, the bow is not my weapon, my lady."

"Swords, then?" she asked slyly.

"If you wish," Nicholas said good-naturedly.

Maria watched as he doffed his tunic and stood in his shirtsleeves, rolling up the sleeves to bare his muscular forearms, which, along with his hands, were liberally sprinkled with dark hair. She was aware of the strength and power in those hands, as well as their capacity for tenderness.

She closed her eyes in dismay when he picked up his sword.

"'Tis like the tournament of peace, Lady Maria," Eleanor said, taking note of Maria's anxiety. "The swords are blunted. The opponents will merely fence."

Lady Eleanor's reassurances gave little relief to Maria, who recalled all too well the events of that tournament. An unprincipled opponent could do a great deal of damage before being discovered.

Not that Nicholas's well-being was of any concern to her. She merely disliked the idea of seeing either contestant injured.

"Lord Mydelton," Eleanor said, turning to speak to a handsome young nobleman. She handed a stringed instrument to him. "Your forte is the fiddle, is it not?"

"Aye, my lady," the young man replied, taking the fiddle from her. He began to play a lively carole as the swordsmen began their contest. The other musicians followed Mydelton's lead, providing a lively background during the fencing match.

To Maria's great relief, the contest was held in good fun, amid jesting and laughter. Neither Nicholas nor his opponent took the contest too seriously, but called it a draw after only a few rounds.

"Well done, my lords," Lady Eleanor said as she awarded both men a ribbon and mock medallion. "'Tis my understanding that your weapon of choice is most unconventional, Lord Kirkham."

"And what would that be, my lady?" Nicholas took a dry cloth and wiped the light sheen of sweat from his face. His hair curled slightly over his forehead, and Maria found herself unable to take her eyes from him, even though the man's very presence vexed her.

Eleanor gestured toward one of the squires, who disappeared behind his companions. "The whip, my lord," she said, "as you well know."

Nicholas turned out both hands in mock frustration. "Ah, but since there is no whip here, I—"

"On the contrary," Lady Eleanor said. "I took the liberty of sending one of my young men for your whip. 'Tis here."

Maria did not think any of Lady Eleanor's guests took note of Nicholas's irritation with her announcement, but she saw his lips quirk in a certain way, and his brow descend. She knew he had had enough of being Eleanor's spectacle.

Yet Maria was intrigued. Before the incident when Nicholas had rescued her and her father on the way home from Fleet Castle, she had never heard of the whip being used as a weapon.

The crowd made noises of approval as Nicholas took

the whip from the page and followed Lady Eleanor to the riverbank, where targets had been set up. "Do not scowl so, Kirkham," Lady Eleanor chided. "This will be amusing for all of us."

Maria stood aside as Nicholas unwound the whip and eyed the targets. Colorful bottles had been set on low tables, forming small towers.

"The object is for you to remove the top bottle without disturbing the rest."

It appeared to Maria as if Nicholas was thoroughly bored with the prospect of demonstrating his skill, but every spectator seemed to hold his breath. With utter finesse, he held the base of the whip in one hand, then slid the length of leather through his other hand before he struck.

His sudden movement was quick and agile. With a *snap,* the topmost bottle was gone! Maria could hardly believe her eyes.

In rapid succession, he snapped the whip again and again, and each target bottle was tossed from its tower, never disturbing the rest. No wonder the thieves on the road from Fleet had been outmaneuvered, Maria thought. They had likely been taken completely by surprise by Nicholas's tactics.

Applause rang out. Nicholas handed the whip to the attendant and removed himself from the center of attention.

This was easy to do, since Lady Eleanor had moved on to her next diversion. In the meantime, Nicholas headed toward the place where he'd dropped his tunic. Maria followed, fascinated—in spite of herself—with his expertise.

"Was this how you stopped the highwaymen on the road from Fleet Castle?" she asked him. Her father had said she should ask him about his whip, but she had forgotten all about that.

He nodded and pulled on his tunic.

"'Tis a strange weapon, is it not?" she asked, walking beside him as he laced his clothes.

"Somewhat."

"Where did you learn such a thing?"

"In Italy," he said, "years ago."

"After your service in France?" she asked.

He looked at her sharply, then took her hand and placed it in the crook of his arm as if it belonged there, but had somehow slipped out. "What do you know of my service in France?" he asked.

"Nothing really," she replied. Alisia had mentioned it, as well as his brother's death, but Maria did not want to speak of these things. She did not want to know anything more of him, or to care about his losses, his sorrows. "Lady Alisia once mentioned that you served under King Henry in France. When she saw how worried I—er..." She fumbled, unwilling to betray her feelings.

Now he looked curiously at her blushing face. "And why would you be worried, my lady fair?"

"'Twas the tournament, if you must know," she said, pulling her hand away. "I took no enjoyment in those contests against Lord Bexhill."

He laughed. "And here I thought you were a bloodthirsty wench!"

"Whatever would give you such an idea, Nicholas?" she said with exasperation. "I have never—"

He took her arm again and suppressed a smile. "Nay, you are merely the feistiest woman I've ever known."

Maria bristled, fully aware that his words were anything but complimentary.

When they rejoined Lady Eleanor's party, a carriage was waiting. One of the servants approached Nicholas. "My lord," he said, "the carriage you ordered has arrived."

"Thank you," he said as the music and festivities continued around them.

"Lady Maria," Eleanor said, "you must give due appreciation to your champion."

Maria frowned. "My cham—?"

"Lord Kirkham, of course!" she said, laughing. "You had such difficulty on the water, he sent to London for a carriage."

Maria turned and threw a puzzled glance in his direction.

"Indeed, you may return to Westminster by boat if you prefer," he said in jest. "But if you are inclined to suffer my presence awhile longer, I will take you to Southwark, then across London Bridge, and back to Bridewell Lane."

Chapter Twenty-Two

Lord Bexhill was exonerated from any wrongdoing at the tournament, claiming that the goring of Kirkham's horse had been accidental. He made a public apology to Nicholas, nonetheless. Even so, Maria eliminated him from her collection of suitors. She could not help but feel his actions at the tournament had been underhanded, no matter what the official conclusion was.

Still, several likely suitors continued to court her. Most were young, comely and well connected. And they did not seem to be deterred by her advanced age.

Nicholas had not reappeared at her door after escorting her home the day of the river trip, nor had Maria expected him to do so. No doubt he was too busy skulking in dark corners, looking for enemies where there were none.

Maria did not change her mind about keeping Nicholas's suspicions to herself. For her father to learn that the Duke of Bedford did not trust him would be too damaging a blow. Maria would spare him that. She knew Nicholas's suspicions and accusations were unfounded, and regardless of his request that she stay out of it, she intended to discover the truth, by whatever means necessary.

It rankled, knowing that he thought badly of her father.

Yet why she should care was a mystery to her. His actions and words should have effectively eliminated any feelings she had for him, but alas, they had not. He'd been so solicitous the other day when the boat ride had made her so ill, as well as being fascinating and attractive. He had nearly managed to seduce her again.

Then he'd deliberately toyed with every available woman at Lady Eleanor's outing, flirting outrageously and playing the cocky rogue.

Maria wondered if her body would always betray her when he was near. He had some strange power over her, and she did not know how to combat it.

Worse yet, she did not know if she truly wanted to combat it. None of her suitors roused her passions the way Nicholas did. Not one could make her tremble with merely a touch of his hand. None of them ever stole kisses that took her breath away.

By the third morning after the river trip, when Maria was ill again, and for no good reason, she began to have suspicions as to the cause of her nausea.

She carried Nicholas Hawken's child. It had been weeks since she'd lain with him at Kirkham, and it would be weeks still before the pregnancy showed. But to Maria's dismay, she realized she had become pregnant with the lord's bastard, just as might happen to any common serving girl.

The blood rushed from her head at the discovery, and she sat down on her bed, putting her head down on her knees. She fought the urge to weep, for weeping would serve no purpose. Rather, she had to decide upon a course of action, one that would assure that she brought no dishonor to her father's name.

Maria took a few deep breaths to calm herself. Though her pregnancy was a problem, 'twas not a complete catastrophe. At least it did not have to be. When she stopped trembling, she examined what courses were open to her.

A nunnery would not have her, certainly not while she was with child. She could not run away, not after she and her father had just found each other, nor could she remain a spinster and bear her child out of wedlock.

She considered her final option. There were plenty of suitors from whom to choose. Only a few were actually distasteful—most were pleasant enough young men who did not think of her as a provincial bumpkin. Any one of them would do.

She would choose one, and marry.

"My lord." Sir Gyles entered Nicholas's chamber at Westminster, ushering in a cloak-clad man. "Here is the fellow we nabbed carrying the message."

Nick stood near the window. The weather was bleak, with rain coming down in torrents. He stepped over to his desk, leaned against its edge and crossed his arms over his chest.

"Where were you headed with this letter?" Nicholas asked the man who stood dripping rainwater on his chamber floor.

"To a ship in the 'arbor," the fellow replied belligerently. He was a scruffy, small-boned fellow, with dingy brown hair and teeth to match. He was none too clean, either. He kept his eyes downcast and fingered his hat as he stood before Nicholas. 'Twas clear he intended to give no more information than absolutely necessary.

"And the name of the ship?"

"'Ey, now," the man said. "I weren't doin' nothin' wrong. Just carryin' a message—"

"What was the name of the ship?" Nicholas insisted quietly. In spite of his civil tone, the messenger could not possibly mistake the seriousness of the question. He was being questioned by a lord of the realm, and could not help but know what the consequences of lying would be.

"The *Santa Clara*," he finally said.

Nicholas looked over at Sir Gyles with a question in his eyes. "I've already sent a man to check on it," the knight replied.

"Who gave you the letter?" Nicholas asked, holding the folded white vellum in his hand.

"A man...outside the 'all," the messenger said haltingly. "Give me tuppence to see it reached the *Santa Clara*."

"What did this man look like?" Nicholas asked. "How was he dressed?"

"'Twere rainin', m'lord," the man said. "An' he wore hisself a heavy cloak, with 'is 'ood up. I couldn't rightly see him."

Nick exchanged a glance with Gyles.

"Was he tall or short? Stout? Lean?"

The man shook his head. "'E was about regular, I'd say. Not too big, not too small."

Nick sighed, running his hand through his hair in frustration. "What about his speech?" he prodded. "Did you note anything unusual about the way the man spoke?"

The messenger shrugged and shook his head. "Nay,

m'lord. 'Tweren't nuthin' unusual about it. Sounded like you.''

"But he handed you this letter right outside the hall…in plain sight."

"Aye, m'lord," the man replied. "That 'e did."

The vision of a man's face flashed through Nick's mind. He'd seen this other fellow several times outside the hall of late, but his presence had not seemed suspicious.

Until now.

Could he have been sent to keep watch at Westminster and stir up what mischief he could? It seemed likely.

Nicholas did not doubt that he had been meant to discover this man with the letter. Whoever was responsible for setting up this little drama in the rain had succeeded in distracting him for a time. He felt certain that had been the purpose of this exercise.

But from *whom* or from *what* had he been distracted?

"Were you to meet someone at the *Santa Clara?*"

"Nae, m'lord," he said grudgingly. "Just go to the ship and stand on the quay and someone would be down to take the letter from me."

Nicholas seriously doubted they'd discover a ship called the *Santa Clara* in the harbor, but he did not keep Sir Gyles from sending someone to investigate.

Nicholas flipped sixpence to the fellow, who caught it handily. "If you see the man who set you upon this errand again, or if you even think you recognize him…come to me."

The man's dull eyes lit up at the sight of so much coin. "Aye, m'lord, that I will!"

Gyles led the man out while Nicholas examined the intercepted letter once more.

Though the wax was thicker than expected, the seal seemed to be Sterlyng's, but Nicholas could not be certain. The letter *J* was drawn on the opposite side of the seal. The text of the message was short: "As predicted, Commons against any new tax. England will be hard-pressed to raise the funds Bedford needs to pay the armies." There was no signature.

Who had sent this missive? And how had he gotten Sterlyng's seal? Was it counterfeit or real? Nicholas looked at the wax more closely. If this seal was a replica of the one Sterlyng used, then the forger had done excellent work.

The message was unimportant and not exactly secret. Anyone with connections to Parliament had to know that the men who made up England's governing body were against an increase in taxes to raise money for Bedford. This fact alone lent weight to Nick's argument that it was all a ruse, intended only to keep him distracted from the real villain, and to keep his suspicions on the Duke of Sterlyng.

Nick had a man watching Sterlyng's house, and knew that the duke had not left his residence since late yesterday morning, when he'd returned home from Westminster. Yet servants had come and gone several times. Any one of them could have carried the letter.

But Nicholas did not really believe that was the case. He paced the length of his office and waited for Sir Gyles to return. He was now certain there was no point in continuing to watch Sterlyng's house, unless he stopped every servant who came and went.

Unfortunately, there was also no reason to keep watch at Westminster, since there was always so much foot traffic over the paths here. Nick knew he would never learn anything of substance from watching who entered and exited.

He had men watching the ships at the docks, too, though he now believed that was nearly useless. Ships entered the harbor, and seamen frequented the taverns and brothels along the waterfront and down Cock Lane. 'Twould be no hardship to receive or deliver a letter that had changed hands several times before reaching its destination.

If he pulled Sir Gyles's men from their points of observation, 'twould become obvious that Nicholas was aware of his enemy's ruse, however. The traitor would also realize that Nicholas knew his own ploy for gleaning information—acting the profligate nobleman—had also been discovered.

He sat down abruptly. If 'twas known that he was not really the dissolute rogue everyone thought him, he would be useless as Bedford's spy. He frowned at the thought, and should have been disturbed by it, but he was not.

His reaction surprised him.

'Twas actually a relief to think he might finally give up his pretense. It did not usually wear on him—except when he was at Kirkham and had to subject Sir Roger and his wife to his antics. Or when Mattie Tailor heard the rumors of his dissipation....

And Maria Burton. She believed the worst of him. Both that he was a villain who had used her to entrap her father, *and* that he was a dissolute womanizer. He smiled. Mayhap Maria would now consider— He stopped short. What did he want Maria Burton to consider?

Himself as a serious suitor?

God's teeth, *yes.*

The notion of seriously courting Maria had been dancing at the back of his mind for a long time. Mayhap it had been ever since their encounter at Fleet Castle. She was beautiful and sensuous and responsive. She melted every time he touched her. She charmed him with the boldness of her spirit, as well as the kindness of her heart.

He had not been able to keep himself away from her, even though she'd demanded it.

Rain pelted the window, but provided no distraction as he thought of how Maria felt in his arms. There was no other woman who could delight him and exasperate him the way Maria Burton could do.

And she was about to choose a husband.

This was something Nicholas would not allow. There was no question in Nick's mind: Maria Burton was *his*. He intended to do whatever was necessary to make it impossible for her to choose anyone but him.

Chapter Twenty-Three

The rain lasted all day, making Maria more pensive and restless than ever.

Knowledge of her pregnancy with Nicholas's child filled her with joy one moment, then threw her into the depths of despair the next. She debated whether to confide in Alisia, but finally decided against it. Alisia was so loyal to Maria's father, she would feel compelled to tell him, and Maria was not ready for that.

Better to choose a husband and wed hastily, rather than cause her father undue turmoil. After an appropriate length of time, she would inform her father that she was with child and...

She sighed as she paced the floor. 'Twas Nicholas's child. Was it not his right to know when his son or daughter was born? Could she, in good conscience, keep the knowledge from him?

Maria stopped in her tracks. Certainly she could, she decided, wringing her hands and resuming her pacing. Nicholas had never shown any interest in gaining a wife or family. His conquests were legendary among the noble classes in London, and Maria knew he would likely see this new turn of events as a burden.

Contrary to what Alisia thought, the only aspect of Nicholas Hawken that did not meet the eye was that he was deceitful and underhanded. He engaged in clandestine activities gauged to harass and molest the most innocent of noblemen, such as her father.

Which led to Maria's other problem. How would she prove the duke innocent? Nicholas had forbidden her to act in this matter, but Maria had not changed her mind about learning whatever she could.

Her subtle questions had so far yielded nothing, and at this point, she was unsure how to proceed. She thought perhaps Lord Bexhill would have information—or at least connections—but she'd refused any contact with him after the debacle on the tournament field. She wondered if there was any way to change that.

Bexhill was a high-placed nobleman. He would have information, and would be aware of all that occurred at Westminster, would he not? She could ask him if anyone ever followed her father, or had access to his chambers at Westminster. Determined to have the earl invited to their home again, Maria went looking for her father. She ventured into his study, only to find Henric Tournay there.

"Oh!" Maria said, startled.

Tournay appeared just as startled by Maria, but quickly composed himself and stood, greeting her. "Good day, my lady. I—I await your father."

"I expected to see him here."

"Someone went for him, I b-believe." His eyes darted around her, past the door.

"Is there something with which I might help you?" she asked as stepped fully into the room.

Tournay shook his head. "I—I have a message f-from Lord Kirkham, and it, er, requires a response."

"Ah…" she said. "We have not seen Lord Kirkham in several days."

"I trust your sire has seen him in the House of Lords, my lady," Tournay remarked.

"I am certain you are correct," Maria said, taking a seat. Tournay seemed flushed, perhaps with fever. And he was perspiring, though 'twas not overly warm in her father's study. Maria wondered what ailed the man, for he had always seemed so well composed. "Are you unwell, Master Tournay?" she inquired.

"Nay, I…well, yes, I admit I am a bit under the weather," he said nervously.

At that moment, the duke entered his study, and Maria did not pursue the conversation. She watched as Tournay handed her father a letter. He read it, then penned a reply, sealed it and handed it back to Nicholas's secretary with hardly a word passing between the two.

Then Tournay took his leave and was gone.

"Father," Maria said, returning to her original purpose, "I wonder if you might invite Bexhill—along with a few others—to dine with us tomorrow?"

The Duke of Sterlyng sat back in his chair and studied her. For the first time, Maria felt uncomfortable under his scrutiny. She was deceiving him—if only by omission—and it did not settle well.

"You must know it pains me to say you nay," Sterlyng said, "but Bexhill lost my trust with his antics at the tourney."

Maria swallowed. "But, Father, he—"

"He acted in a most *unchivalrous* manner," he said, "and even though he was exonerated from guilt, I will never trust the man again. Not in my home, certainly not with my daughter."

"Oh."

"Let it rest, Maria," the duke said. "We are well rid of Lord Bexhill."

There was naught Maria could say. There were no arguments to give. She had heard that the earl had been exonerated only because Gloucester needed his continued support in the House of Lords. The duke could not afford to alienate the man, even though he was guilty of the grossest transgression.

Her father was right in banning Bexhill from his home. The earl was a toad.

Still, Maria needed to find a source of information. She did not want to tell her father of Nicholas's suspicions and accusations. She knew the pain it would cause him to know that Bedford did not trust him—especially after all the hard work and long hours he spent working for Bedford's causes.

She would not push her father to invite Bexhill. In truth, Maria did not know if even she could stand to have the errant lord near. Nay, she would glean what information she could from other powerful lords who would be welcome in their home.

Sterlyng leaned forward and folded his hands together. "Maria...have you developed any particular...*attachment* for Bexhill?"

"Nay, Father!" she said, startled by his question. 'Twas the last thing she had expected him to ask. "'Tis only that—that Lord Bexhill was always so...er, quick-witted and jolly. His presence seemed to enliven a party."

Sterlyng nodded. "Quite true, but I'd rather forgo the man's company for now. Perhaps in time he will vindicate himself with a few good deeds." Deep lines bracketed the duke's mouth. "But I will be honest with you and say that I could not abide him as a son-in-law."

"As you wish, Father."

"Tell me, Daughter," Sterlyng continued, "is there no young man who has yet caught your interest?"

"C-caught my interest?"

"As a bridegroom," Sterlyng said. "You know I would see you well married, child, but not before you have found the man who best suits you, and certainly not before you are ready to wed."

"Father...I..."

"I will not rush you, Maria," Sterlyng said. "I would have you make your own choice when it is time for you to wed."

"Yes, Father."

Sterlyng ran a hand across his mouth and jaw. "When your mother and I married, 'twas without the consent of her family. I loved her more than words can describe, and she cared deeply for me. Our match had naught to do with estates or dynasties. We chose each other, Maria."

She touched her mother's locket and knew that her parents had had a treasure in each other, something that did not often occur.

"It is that kind of choice that I wish to afford you."

"I understand, Father," Maria said quietly. The custom was that young women of her station would have a husband chosen for them, and their own feelings in the matter would have naught to do with the decision.

Her father wanted her to love the man she wed, to have the kind of affection and caring that he'd shared with her mother.

"Is there no..." He sat back and frowned. "Have

you met no young man here in London who has struck your fancy?''

Maria felt the blood rush to her cheeks. She would *not* think of Nicholas Hawken. The marquis was absolutely not a candidate for marriage, even if she did carry his child. Nay, the man had baldly accused her father of treason, and was even now working toward uncovering some evidence against him.

She'd been mistaken in thinking she loved him. She *would not* love him.

There were plenty of other young men from whom to choose—men who did not believe the worst of her father. Men who would be faithful and true.

''N-nay, Father,'' she stammered, giving a slight shake of her head.

''Well, perhaps in time you'll meet the one for you.'' Sterlyng stood suddenly. ''I agree that we should entertain tomorrow evening,'' he said. ''I'll ask Alisia to plan for a party of...what? Say, fifteen? Twenty?''

''Whatever you think, Father,'' Maria said. She tried to sound bright and interested, but had difficulty garnering much enthusiasm. Her attention was torn—between finding a husband and discovering who her father's enemy was.

And there was some urgency to both questions.

Maria had thought Bexhill would be her best source of information, but now that her father had banned him from their house, she would have to look elsewhere.

She could only hope that somehow she would be able to gain information from one of the gentlemen who attended their soiree the following night. She would do anything to prove Nicholas Hawken wrong.

''Is there no one in particular you'd like me to invite?'' Sterlyng gently chided. ''No one has piqued your interest, child?''

''Nay, Father,'' she said hastily, kneeling next to his chair and placing her hands in his. '''Tis not that I am uninterested. Merely that the changes in my life have come about so swiftly. I've only just found you... I do not care to marry and go away from you so soon.''

Sterlyng gave her a quick hug and smiled. ''It does my old heart good to hear you say it, Maria. But do not wait too long.'' He stood, then, tucking her arm in his, he turned to walk her out of the study. ''The years pass by, and suddenly you are old and alone. I would not wish that future for you.''

''Nay, Father,'' Maria said, her heart contracting at the thought of his painful losses so many years ago. ''I will marry.''

''There you are!'' Alisia said as she encountered Maria and her father coming out of his study.

''Ah...just the lady we wanted to see,'' Sterlyng said.

Maria had difficulty sleeping that night. She could not forget the wistful tone in her father's voice as he'd spoken of her mother.

She ached for the losses he had suffered in his life, first losing his wife, then his infant child. She knew he'd loved Sarah Morley passionately, and that her death had shattered him. True enough, he'd put himself back together over the years, but there was an innate sadness that she sensed in him still.

Maria knew that he'd grieved over the loss of his child, but he especially missed his love, Sarah. How awful to live without the one person who had the power to make the sun shine, or the moon rise, in his heart.

'Twas fortunate she did not feel so strongly about

Nicholas. There was nothing so special about him, not that half smile he gave when he found her amusing, not the care with which he touched her.

He was a knave of the very worst kind—a flirt who made love to any woman foolish enough to let him. Caring, commitment, responsibility—these had no part of Nicholas Hawken's life.

The night was warm, and Maria climbed out of bed. She padded barefoot to the window and sat on the cushioned seat, resting her arms on the sill, gazing out at the night sky.

She was embarrassed to think how naive and foolish she'd been all those weeks ago when she'd met Nicholas. Imagine thinking he would want to take her to wife, when he knew naught of her besides her given name. She suppressed a sad laugh when she thought of that. She'd been a serving girl named Ria when she'd met him. Certainly not a well-bred, potential wife.

She swallowed the lump in her throat and wiped ridiculous tears from her eyes. She had naught to weep about. She had a father who loved her and had given her the security of his name and his home. She had Alisia, too, who cared for her like a sister. And suitors? She had rooms full of them, and soon one would become her husband.

She had no need of Nicholas Hawken.

Preparations for the party Maria had suggested went on all the following day. Since the weather had turned fair, Lady Alisia decided to move the festivities out-of-doors. Tables were set up in the Sterlyng courtyard and lanterns hung along the rails to illuminate the space. Minstrels were hired to provide music for the guests, and there would be dancing, games and countless other amusements.

'Twas all overwhelming to Maria, who had thought only of having a few visitors whom she could subtly question regarding Nicholas's accusations. Now she was faced with the prospect of having to entertain fifty guests. Her attentions would be so divided, 'twould be a miracle if she learned anything useful.

But she might gain a prospective husband.

That was something she could not put off much longer. Soon the pregnancy would begin to show, and Maria knew she needed to be wed before that happened.

"'Twould behoove you to rest awhile, Maria," Alisia said, bustling her charge up the stairs and into her chamber. "If I'm not mistaken, the evening will prove to be a long one, and we cannot have you looking peaked."

Maria allowed herself to be cosseted. After her difficulty sleeping the night before, it felt good to have Alisia remove the pins from her hair and comb it until it crackled. Alisia's gentle kindness did much to soothe her frayed nerves.

"Much has happened to you these last few weeks, my lief," Alisia said affectionately. "'Tis only natural for you to feel unsettled...restless, mayhap."

"Nay, Alisia," Maria said. "I feel more settled than I've ever felt in my life. Here, with you and Father, I have finally found my home, my place in the world."

"Aye, 'tis good to hear you say it, Maria," Alisia murmured as she gently combed through the golden masses of Maria's hair, "and 'tis truly wonderful for your father to have you here, but I want you to know..."

Maria looked up and caught Alisia's gaze in the mirror. "Yes?"

"...if aught troubles you, you have only to come to me, and between us, we can work it out."

Maria swallowed. *Alisia knew!* The truth of it was in her eyes. She was too polite to come out and say it, but now that Maria thought of it, Alisia had to know of Maria's frequent bouts of illness...and her lack of menses. How foolish she had been, thinking her condition had been hidden from all. 'Twas likely that everyone in the household had their suspicions.

She could only hope her father did not yet know.

"Thank you, Alisia," Maria whispered shakily. She wondered if Alisia realized Nicholas Hawken was the father of her child, but was unprepared to speak of it now. "I will be fine once I rest awhile."

Maria had not yet seen him.

Nicholas leaned one shoulder against an open archway and observed as she went from one guest to another on her father's arm. He wondered how she would react when her eyes finally lit on him.

He'd likely be fortunate to get out of Bridewell Lane with his ears still attached.

She sparkled. Nay, she glowed with a light that emanated from within.

Nick's mouth went dry as he watched her smile, then laugh, then tip her head just so. Her hands were delicate, expressive. And he could only think of how they'd touched him, so intimately, so lovingly.

He'd seen her last eve, leaning out the window of her bedchamber, watching the moon as it rose. She had not seen him, for he'd stood in the shadows below, pondering whether or not to breach her chamber—and her ire—again.

He had just decided against it when he'd seen that

she was weeping, and he'd nearly lost his resolve to leave her alone. He knew he was the one who had caused her pain—'twas his suspicions of her father's integrity that saddened her.

He'd known she would not want to see him.

Nicholas had promised himself he'd stay away from her until his task was accomplished and he had vindicated her father. But when Sterlyng had invited him to this spring fete at his home, he'd been unable to refuse. He needed to see her. If there'd been any way possible, he would have touched her again. He would have kissed her into oblivion, caressed her and made her come apart in his arms once more.

He would show her without a doubt to whom she belonged.

"Kirkham!" The friendly voice was accompanied by an unwelcome slap on the back. "Looking a bit down in the mouth. Drink up, man!"

"Thanks," Nick said dryly as the young man, Viscount Wardale, shoved a mug of ale into his hand and gave him an elbow in the ribs. He'd never liked Wardale, though the viscount frequently hung about the fringes of Nicholas's circle. He'd never really become part of the group that provided Nicholas with his deceptive front, and Nick now knew why. The man was as irritating as a thistle.

"Word is the duke's allowing his daughter to choose her own husband," Wardale said. "Ha! What I wouldn't give to lay hands on that one! Even without the estate and the dowry." When he made a rude sound by snapping his cheek with his teeth, Nicholas considered dragging the man to the river and dumping him in.

"I would not recommend it, Wardale," he said through clenched teeth. "Touch her and you and I will meet at St. James's with swords at dawn.'' Without a thought to Wardale's reaction, he slammed down his mug and stalked off to yet another arched door frame, where he propped himself and watched as Maria fascinated all the young suitors who wanted her wealth…and her body.

What was wrong with Sterlyng? Nick wondered as he speared his fingers through his hair. *That he would allow Maria to become fair game among all these— these buffoons?*

Nicholas could not abide the idea of Wardale—or any of these others—with his hands on her. Nick surveyed Sterlyng's courtyard, sizing up every one of the unmarried men present. Not one was worthy of her.

Viscount Rudney seemed to be dominating Maria's attentions this evening. He was an honorable man, a good-natured sort, Nick thought, without any vices that Nicholas had ever been able to discover in the course of his work. Maria could do worse than to choose him.

Though Rudney's color was a bit sallow for Nicholas's liking, and his tastes a mite bland, he would make a decent husband, Nick supposed. He didn't imagine Maria would be put off by the man's delicate hands, or the light down of his beard. The viscount would likely install her at his country estate in Wessex and—

Nick slammed the palm of one hand against a post and turned away from the crowd. He could not continue here, watching her move from one suitor to the next. Deciding there was no sense in prolonging this agony, he turned to leave.

As he made his way toward one of the courtyard gates, he turned back for one last look and saw Lady Alisia slipping gracefully through the crowd toward him.

"My lord," she said, "how lovely to see you. Have you eaten?"

Nicholas looked past Alisia to the platters of meat and puddings, fruits and cheese, that were set out on the trestle tables. He had no appetite for food this night. His only hunger was for the golden-haired lady who would shun him if she knew of his presence.

"Nay, Lady Alisia," he finally replied, "I came only to pay my respects to the duke and his daughter."

"But you have not done so, my lord."

Nicholas's expression darkened, but he said nothing. He stood quietly with Lady Alisia for another moment, listening to the minstrels and the light chatter going on all 'round them, while his frustration grew.

"You care for her, my lord," Alisia said, looking inquisitively at him, "do you not?"

Nicholas's throat closed. It did not matter what he felt for Maria Burton. She was beyond his reach. She would never have him, not when she believed he had merely used her to get to her father. Not when she thought he was a bastard ruthless enough to unjustly accuse her father of treason.

Nick knew he could not pursue her until that matter was closed and the villain exposed. Until then, he would have to continue in his role as the wicked Marquis of Kirkham. In the meantime, Maria would likely choose another man.

"Of course I care for her, my lady," he said, forcing a lightness to his tone. "She is lovely…a credit to her father."

"And would you consider—"

He laughed and backed away in the true style of a bachelor unwilling to be caught. "Do not think to ensnare me in a feminine trap, Lady Alisia. More determined mothers have tried...and failed.''

He did not notice Alisia's speculative expression as he turned away and unlatched the gate.

''My lord.''

Nicholas nearly groaned aloud. He had not moved fast enough.

''She cares for you.''

He crossed his arms over his chest. ''You are mistaken, my lady,'' he said tightly. ''She wants naught to do with me.''

''She may well believe that now, Lord Kirkham,'' she countered, ''but there is more depth to her than you might imagine.''

''I have some notion of Lady Maria's depth,'' he replied tightly. He knew her better than Alisia suspected, and that knowledge did naught but torment him.

''Lord Nicholas,'' Alisia said, ''I do not know what caused the breach between you...but I believe I might help to heal it.''

Nicholas let out his breath. ''How?''

''You must tell her how you feel.''

''Lady Alisia,'' he said, ''Maria will not allow me within five feet of her. How do you propose—''

''You must wait until all of his grace's guests have left,'' Alisia said. ''I will see that the side entrance of the house remains unbolted. His grace has chambers at the far end of the hall from Maria's bedchamber, and he sleeps soundly—especially after a few mugs of wine. Come to her tonight....''

Nick knew he would have to be a dolt to refuse this chance, yet his suspicious nature could not accept the invitation without question. ''Why do you provide me this opportunity, Lady Alisia? This very *improper* opportunity?''

''You must understand...I have come to love Maria as I would my own sister,'' Alisia said. ''And it hurts me to see her so very unhappy. She cares for you, yet...she refuses to acknowledge this.''

''And if I should go up to her chamber—''

''Your intentions toward her are honorable, are they not?''

He nodded.

''Then you would see that she comes to no harm.''

He quickly decided. ''I give you my word.''

Chapter Twenty-Four

Maria's chamber was illuminated by the light of the full moon. Dressed only in the long chemise she'd had made from Nicholas's silk, she sat again by her window and sighed. Her hair was loose upon her shoulders, and she toyed with one stray lock.

She would choose a husband from among the young men who'd been present tonight. Lord Singleton was a likely prospect. He had visited her several times in past weeks, and he'd been very solicitous at Lady Eleanor's river party. He was clever and always entertaining, even if his eyes were so beady they reminded her of a hawk hunting its prey.

She bit her lip. Perhaps Lord Frompton would suit better. He was good-looking and friendly enough. Nay, she thought, he spat his food between a gap in his front teeth when he ate, and she did not believe she could tolerate that fault for a month, much less a lifetime.

She considered all the young men she'd met of late, and each one had some shortcoming that made Maria think she'd be better off bearing her bastard somewhere far from London. At Rockbury? Mayhap she could return there. Surely her father would visit often, and Ma-

ria would not find herself bound to a man she could not
abide.

Another deep sigh penetrated the silence.

Nicholas had come tonight. She had seen him across
the courtyard, yet he had not sought her out. He'd
stayed on the perimeter of the gathering, sipping from
a mug, speaking to all who approached him.

One tear slipped from her eye as she thought of him
standing in the shadows, unwilling to come too close to
her. Of course he would not approach, she reminded
herself. She had warned him to stay away, and he would
not want to create an unpleasant disturbance.

But why had he come?

Surely he had other amusements to occupy his time—
such as searching out incriminating evidence against her
father, she thought bitterly. Or finding some lusty young
female to warm his bed.

With the back of her hand, Maria brushed the tear
away and decided she must choose one of the suitors.
Lord Rudney was a likely candidate—at any rate, he
was the least offensive of the lot. He was fair and not
too tall, his brown eyes were kind and his appearance
did not in the least remind her of...

Nay, this would never do. She reorganized her
thoughts and pictured Viscount Rudney again. He was
good-natured and jovial, a lively young—

"Nicholas!" she whispered, flying to her feet.

He'd made scarcely a sound, but when she heard the
squeak of the floor, she turned to see the handsome
marquis standing just inside her doorway. He closed it
quietly. Had her thoughts so preoccupied her that she
had not noticed him?

"I could not stay away."

Her hand went to her throat as she glanced at the

door, then back to Nicholas, worried that somehow his presence would rouse the household. He'd been so quiet, though....

Maria could not find her voice.

Yet she could almost feel the babe within her stirring, recognizing his sire. She resisted placing a hand over her womb, unwilling to call attention to her condition, even though she knew there was no outward sign of it.

Nicholas took a few steps closer. Maria stood her ground, although she was trembling. She did not want him to touch her now, mere moments after deciding upon Rudney for her husband. Lord Rudney was a man of honor, a man who would never dream of making the kind of outrageous accusations Nicholas had made against her father.

Nor would he have used her to sidle his way into her father's good graces.

And now that she'd decided upon her mate, she had every intention of being true to him. She would not allow Nicholas to so much as touch her. For she knew that if he did, her power of will would fade. She never had the strength to deny him.

"Y-you should not be here," she stammered.

"Seems to be the only place where I might see you alone."

"But my father...should he a-awaken..."

"He sleeps soundly."

"I—I told you I did not wish to see you again," she said, taking one step back. The backs of her knees touched the window seat.

"You know by now that I am not a man who listens."

He kept coming toward her, giving her little room to slip away. She reminded herself that he had used her badly. He had no right to invade her private chamber, nor had he any other rights in this house. "Please go, Nicholas," she said. "We have naught to say to one another."

"Ah, but there is much that I would say to you, my lady fair."

"Please do not mock me," she said, lowering her eyes to the floor. She'd always known he'd called her that in jest—that she was anything *but* a lady fair.

He tipped her chin up with one finger. "'Tis not mockery, Maria," he said. "You are my fair one."

Maria swallowed and blinked back tears. Standing so close to him, she knew she loved him. She wished she could believe his words, but knew she could not trust anything he said. He'd lied to her, used her. He believed her father capable of treachery against England, against his oldest friend.

"L-leave here."

"Nay, Maria. I cannot." He took her hand and sat her down next to him on the window seat. "I am not the villain you have built up in your mind."

"Nay?" she said warily. She knew better than to let him this close. All her good sense flew from her when he touched her. And a part of her wished he would do it.

Make her mindless.

He shook his head in reply. "We spoke briefly of my service in France."

"Yes..." she whispered. He should go. Now, before he could say any more. Before her heart could become any more tightly bound to him.

Yet his hand was clenched around hers, and she did not possess the power of will to pull away.

"I convinced my elder brother, Edmund, to go to

France with King Henry. 'Twas years ago... I was young. Foolish. Anxious to earn a glorious name for myself, just as my father had done before me.

"Edmund was killed by my side in a surprise attack."

"Oh, Nicholas," she cried, touched—and torn—by the lines of pain etched on his face. She looked into his eyes, even as she wished she had the strength to turn away, to make him leave.

"We were each to cover the other's back. When the attack came, I failed him."

The words were stark, and there was naught Maria could say to counter them. "I am so sorry, Nicholas," she said quietly, placing her palm against his cheek.

"I was to blame for his death," Nicholas said steadily. "Had I not convinced him to go along with me, he would be marquis now. He would be happily wed to Alyce Palton, the maid he loved since he was a lad, and I would have a brood of nieces and nephews in residence at Kirkham."

He brushed a hand over his face.

"My father was devastated by Edmund's death. I could not face him, coward that I was, so I went to Italy for a time...."

"Oh, Nicholas..."

"I tell you this not for your pity," he said quietly, "but for your understanding."

"Pity is not what I feel," she said, though she would not say exactly what it was that she *did* feel. She was far too vulnerable already.

"While I squandered my time nursing my grief in Italy, I eventually realized there was something I could do that might help prevent more English lads from meeting their deaths on the battlefields of France.

"I went to work for Bedford. 'Tis my job to…*discover* the secrets of powerful men. The information I ferret out often determines the conduct of the war. It usually has little to do with specific battles. But 'tis my hope that my efforts will help Bedford bring about an end to the conflict. It has gone on far too long."

Maria nodded. He'd told her some of this before, though now she had a better grasp of it. She knew what drove him to act the wastrel, to associate with the worst men of his class.

"The work I do is dangerous. I would not have involved you for any reason," he said, "but someone has gone to a great deal of trouble to make it seem that your father is guilty of treason."

"He would not—!"

"I know this, Maria," he said, touching a finger to her lips. "I do not accuse your father of anything."

Mayhap not. "Yet you used me, Nicholas," she said. "Used me to gain access to my father."

"I will not deny that I did, but—"

She stood abruptly, unmindful of her state of undress. "You have been dishonest and underhanded in your dealings with me."

"Aye, Maria." His voice was quiet, resigned. "I admit it."

"You must go, Nicholas," she said, shoring up her courage to do what she must. "There is no good purpose to your presence here."

"Maria, someone is working very hard to convince me that your father is a traitor," he said, coming to his feet to face her. "I cannot—"

"Go, Nicholas," she said. She hated the way her voice trembled now, but there was no way around it.

She could deal with no more lies. "I have chosen a bridegroom, and I will wed as soon as my father arranges it."

Nicholas said naught for a moment, but Maria noticed a muscle clench tightly in his jaw.

"Rudney," he finally said, his voice was flat and humorless.

She nodded. "He is a g-good man," she said. "Honest and true."

Nicholas looked as though he would speak, but then changed his mind.

"You must go," Maria whispered.

He stood abruptly and breathed deeply. He ran a hand over his face again, then reached out to gently brush his thumb over her lower lip, cradling her jaw in his fingers. Then he kissed her lightly, sadly.

"Farewell, my lady fair," he said, his voice deep and quiet.

Before Maria could even think, he had turned and walked out. She stood unmoving, her hand over the place he'd last touched. His kiss had touched her deeply, but had not made her mindless.

Nay, hot tears finally fell as she tried to shut off the flood of thoughts and questions that overwhelmed her now. She tried to quiet her brain with images of Lord Rudney, but found herself unable to call his face to mind.

'Twas Nicholas's visage—and words—that dominated her thoughts. He had not disputed her claim that he'd used her and been dishonest with her. He'd gone to great lengths to tell her the reasons for his clandestine activities.

She supposed he had good reason for all of his deceptions. Yet it still hurt to know he'd been so dishonest with her. How could she ever trust a man like him?

Yet another inner voice asked how could she wed Lord Rudney when she loved her scoundrel, Nicholas Hawken, and bore his child?

She dropped to her bed and wept for all she had lost and all she could never have.

'Twas late, but Maria knew she would never sleep, not with her emotions in such a state of upheaval. She took a light shawl and pulled it 'round her shoulders, then stepped out of her room. She passed her father's chamber as she walked toward the stairs, and heard his loud snores within. She smiled gratefully for the noise. 'Twas no wonder he'd slept through Nicholas's visit.

With feet bare, she slipped soundlessly down the stairs. She knew her father kept a bottle of strong wine in his study, and one cup would surely help her to relax. Mayhap she would even fall asleep, without dreams of Nicholas to plague her.

The servants had retired hours ago, and all was quiet in the house. But when Maria reached the study, she found the door slightly ajar, and a light emanating from within. *Nicholas,* she thought as her heart clenched with pain. *He was searching her father's things again!*

Yet it was not Nicholas she saw through the crack in the door. 'Twas Henric Tournay. And he was bent over the drawer that her father kept locked.

With hardly a conscious thought, Maria turned and fled. She climbed the stairs silently once again and ran to her chamber. Throwing a deep blue kirtle over her chemise, she quickly pulled the laces and tied them, then slipped on a pair of shoes.

She would follow Nicholas's minion wherever he led,

and confront the Marquis of Kirkham—once and for all—with her damning discovery.

Nicholas felt frustrated enough to bang a few heads together.

He had always considered himself a civilized fellow—else he'd have thrown Maria over his shoulder and carried her off like some Viking barbarian of olden times. Since she was obviously unwilling to listen to reason, he could think of nothing he'd rather do than take her to a stronghold somewhere in the North Sea and spend days making love to her.

As that was out of the question, he decided 'twas a good night to get drunk. Rip-roaring drunk.

He'd found a carriage for hire, then collected his wastrel associates and begun a valiant attempt at numbing his brain. Dissatisfied with the first two wineshops they sampled, Nicholas's party moved on to the waterfront and found a thoroughly disreputable establishment, run by a brawny wine keeper with a shiny bald pate and only a few teeth in his jaw.

When they entered the dingy wineshop, Nicholas decided he wouldn't mind a good brawl tonight. And this rundown place was ripe for it.

"Here'sh to Kirkham!" Lord Lofton said in a slurred voice. "Besht drinkin' companion in all of jolly London!"

"Hear, hear!" muttered the others, already well on their way toward a state of sloppy drunkenness.

A buxom bar wench set a second mug down in front of Nick. He hadn't managed to get drunk yet, but intended to give it a good effort here. The place suited him and his black mood.

The wineshop smelled strongly of fish, fermented cider and unwashed bodies, mingled with other unsavory aromas. But broken windows, blackened walls and tables with carvings etched onto their surfaces added to the setting.

A lone piper—an Irishman, by the look of him—played a haunting tune in one corner. A group of sailors tossed dice against one wall, and two unbelievably disgusting whores plied their trade where they would.

The rest of the men sat hunched over platters of food and tankards of ale, while a few sailors stood at a makeshift bar. Nick took note of the way each man eyed the others, as if to size them up in case anything untoward should occur.

And Nick had every intention of causing a distinctly untoward incident.

He threw coins on the table and ordered drinks for all.

A melee broke out when every man in the place scrambled for the coin as well as the promised ale. The whores squealed in protest at the distraction, then began to clamber over each other, and the men, to get to the money.

'Twas not long before the first punch was thrown.

Nicholas jumped into the fray with relish. His comrades were not so drunk as to be useless, and every one, to a man, enjoyed a good brawl. Nick, too, fought with a vengeance, playing out the night's frustrations on his opponents, bloodying their noses and bruising their eyes.

As he fought one opponent, two jumped him from behind. He quickly bent at the waist, throwing the two off his back, and causing his first opponent to miss his punch. The man yowled in frustration. Nick made a quick move, putting his back against a wall, then dealt with the three at once.

"Need help, Kirkham?" Lofton shouted over the tumult.

Nicholas's first man went down. "Hah!" he barked, ducking a fist, "these puny louts have naught that I cannot handle."

Incensed by the insult, his two attackers went after him with even greater relish, but to no avail. With one booted foot, Nick shoved one of them across the room. The man flew over a table and crashed into another brawling pair.

Nick had no time to appreciate his handiwork, for another attacker took a swing at him. He ducked. The fellow's luckless companion took the blow, which threw him against the wall, knocking him senseless.

'Twas only then that Nicholas used his own fists. He took immense satisfaction in each blow, both given and received. He grinned with wicked delight when another opponent turned up to give assistance to his comrade, and Nick dealt with him as well.

For a good quarter hour the battle raged on. It was not until all the participants had their fill of cuts and bruises that things finally settled down again. The two harlots had disappeared. The sailor with the dice pocketed them and left with his companions. The Irishman's lip was too swollen to resume playing his pipe, so he sat quietly in his corner, nursing his bloodied knuckles.

Nicholas and his group tipped a table back onto its legs. They found a few unbroken chairs and sat back down, congratulating themselves on finding such good sport. Nicholas coiled his whip on the table before him.

"'Tis a fine blackened eye you've got, Kirkham," Lofton said.

Nicholas winced and dabbed at his eye with his sleeve. It was only slightly bloody, but the swelling was increasing by the minute. At least it gave him something to think of other than Maria and his futile visit to her chamber.

"I'd say the lot of ye owe me a good bit o' coin fer all this mess." The tavern's burly wine keeper leaned over their table and placed two beefy fists on the surface next to Nicholas.

Naturally, Nick intended to pay for any damage, but the man's belligerent attitude irritated him. He'd just as soon go a round or two with him.

"Here's my part," Lofton said, throwing a few coins onto the table. The rest of Nicholas's companions anted up, as did Nick, after weighing the prudence of resuming the brawl.

He'd gotten only a temporary respite from his dour thoughts, but he now knew that another fight was not going to satisfy what ailed him.

Rudney. She was going to wed Rudney.

He took a huge swallow of the ale in his mug. Why had he left her chamber without telling her that he cared for her? That he loved her?

What a fool he'd been. It should have been so simple. He should have told her that his work for Bedford could not continue because a French informer knew of it. And that meant Nick was free to act as he chose, no longer having to play the wastrel for the benefit of any man who would underestimate him.

It meant he was free to marry.

He jabbed his fingers through his hair and grimaced in discomfort when he scraped a tender spot. What in Hades was he doing here? Why had he not hastened back to Bridewell Lane and gotten down on his knees to beg Maria to have him?

What a fool he was. She *must* care for him, else there would not have been tears in her eyes when he'd entered her chamber. He would tell her he was finished with all deception and intrigue.

He would return to her now and demand that she give credit to his suit. He would not allow her to wed Rudney—nay, he would forbid her even to speak to the man again!

Determined to take his leave, Nicholas was about to bid farewell to his companions when a man with a vaguely familiar face entered the wineshop. Nick paused for a moment, trying to recall where he'd seen him before, and then realized he was the same one who'd been hanging about Westminster these last weeks.

There was a good possibility he was involved in the deception involving the letters!

As the fellow raised his cup to drink, he saw Nicholas eyeing him. He bolted.

Nicholas did not think twice. He grabbed his whip and ran after the man.

Chapter Twenty-Five

Maria's anger propelled her.

Just thinking of Nicholas's nerve, showing up in her room, telling her about his brother and his work for the duke of Bedford—while his secretary burglarized her father's study—was enough to make her fume.

For once, Maria felt fortunate that she had not had the typical upbringing of a gentle maid. She had always been free to run and scrap with the servants' children, and in later years, she had run from Geoffrey and his friends more times than she could count.

'Twas late, and dark in the streets. Stealthily, Maria pursued Tournay as he walked down the cobbled lane. She kept him in sight as he turned down the Strand and headed east, toward the main part of London.

She assumed he was headed toward Nicholas's house. Where else would he be going with his ill-gotten booty from her father's study? Not Westminster, for that was in the opposite direction. It had to be Nicholas's.

Tournay continued on, a bit more casually now, confident that he'd not been caught. Maria followed him as he progressed along the Strand, past Temple Church and St. Paul's. She made certain he never caught sight of her, maintaining a safe distance behind him and keeping to the shadows near buildings. He had no idea he was being followed.

The odor of the river became quite strong, and Maria began to wonder if her guess as to Tournay's destination had been correct. Surely Nicholas did not live in so rank a neighborhood as this. The buildings were small and mean, some with fowl roosting in the front yards. Another yard had pigs snoring together. The pavement was rough and she had to walk carefully to avoid the offal in the road.

Tournay turned down a narrow lane, heading toward the river itself. Maria nearly gagged with the foul odors. Buildings seemed to grow straight up from the broken cobbles, and she paused a moment, pressing her back up against a wall.

This was the forbidden waterfront, the district Alisia had warned her about.

There were voices in the distance, and the hollow, creaking sounds of ships rocking in their moorings in the harbor. Maria pressed her hand to her mouth and fought the wave of nausea. She would master it. She was not about to let Tournay get away from her now, not when she was so close to discovering what was going on, who was behind the suspicions cast upon her father.

Tournay continued to move toward the water, and Maria pushed away from the wall and got back on his trail. There were men out and about even at this late hour, and she made a determined effort to remain in the shadows and out of sight. She was glad her kirtle was so dark in color, else she'd be seen too easily.

As it was, no one accosted her.

Two men stepped out of a shop, talking loudly together. Tournay stopped and pushed his way through the door. Maria crouched beside a nearby barrel to wait for him to reappear, hoping he would not leave by a back door.

She knew she really should follow him in, but could not imagine how she would get away with it. 'Twould be impossible to keep her presence secret once she stepped inside, and she did not want Tournay to know she'd followed him.

But how to discover what transpired within? The side of the building that faced Maria held two dingy windows. She decided to creep over to one and see if she could rub away a bit of the grime, mayhap see what Tournay was up to…or at least who he met inside.

She slipped away from the barrel and, keeping her crouch, moved to the wineshop. With the corner of one sleeve, she began to rub at a window, but it did not help much. She could hardly see anything, other than men in dark tunics hunched over cups of ale.

Tournay was not in sight, until half a moment later, when he stepped outside again. Maria held perfectly still as he moved away from the wineshop, then she began to follow him cautiously once more.

They walked on along the waterfront, and Maria was certain they'd reach the Tower itself if they continued much farther. They passed Dowgate, and were nearly to Ebbgate when Tournay stopped at another wineshop.

Maria concealed herself again as he went within. This time she was able to peek inside.

The place was a wreck, even for the low standards of this downtrodden locale. Tables were turned on their sides, and broken chairs littered the floor. Most of the men inside stood to drink their mugs, but a few sat at righted tables.

Maria watched as Tournay went in and searched the place with his eyes, then swiftly turned and left.

Still she followed, though she was weary of the chase.

No longer did she believe Nicholas was the man who would be at the end of Tournay's quest. For all his faults, Nicholas had never directly lied to her, and she could not imagine him coming to her chamber in order to perpetuate falsehoods. He admitted to being dishonest with her. Yet he'd come to her chamber to…

Why had he come? Certainly not to seduce her, for he'd have managed that without difficulty.

Maria covered her belly with one hand. Nicholas's child rested beneath her heart, and it suddenly seemed too unfair, too dishonest, to keep it secret from him. He'd been as honest as he could be when he'd visited tonight, and Maria had to credit him for that. He'd even told her that he did not suspect her father of treason, but rather, someone else. If only she could believe—

Tournay!

Maria's eyes grew wide. The secretary was a traitor! He was the one who had arranged for Nicholas to suspect her father! The French must have learned of Nick's clandestine role, then somehow managed to place Tournay in Nicholas's service. The secretary had then used his proximity to confound matters, and keep Nicholas off his own scent.

Giddy with the truth of her realization, Maria watched as Tournay once again surveyed the interior of the wineshop before leaving. As far as Maria could tell, no one inside the tavern took note of his entrance, or his exit.

She gave him a head start, then took up position behind him, determined to follow him and discover as much as she could for Nicholas.

There was no doubt that Nicholas had seen the fellow before. The man had been hanging around Westminster for the past couple of weeks, but his presence had not registered in Nick's mind as being particularly strange.

Yet now, everything and everyone was suspect. Someone was sending him signals that implicated the Duke of Sterlyng. The same person was intentionally muddling the situation in order to distract Nicholas from the real traitor.

Nick was not about to give Maria up to Rudney, but he knew that in order to win her, he would have to find the true culprit and prove to her that he had not maliciously "created" evidence against her father. Nick had to show her that he was an honorable man.

Or at least that he could *become* an honorable man.

He had no doubt that the man who'd left the tavern was involved, else why would he have run the moment he'd met Nicholas's eyes?

He stepped away from the wineshop and looked both east and west, his vision only slightly hampered by the swelling of one eye. But he could not see the fellow. The man had disappeared into the darkness.

It did not matter. There was only one way to go if one wanted to get lost—deeper into the docks, where ropes and nets, barrels and boxes of cargo would provide adequate cover for a man who wished to hide.

Nicholas began walking toward the wharf, keeping his eyes sharply tuned for any stealthy movement.

The ships were rocking quietly in their berths, the sailors either asleep or absent. Nicholas spied a man and woman in a small alcove, performing an act that, in this case, was best left to the imagination. An orange-striped cat wandered by, but as Nicholas stood still, surveying all about him, he noticed no other movement, heard no other sounds but the quiet slapping of water against the wood of the piers.

There was a sudden crash and a burst of activity on the quay. Nicholas turned and saw his prey jump out from behind a crate, then sprint eastward down the wooden dock.

Nick pursued him, his bruised and aching muscles protesting every move.

The main wharf was a wide boardwalk, with long wooden piers jutting out like fingers between the ships. Some of these had buildings on the end, hovering above the water.

The purpose of these structures was unclear, though Maria supposed 'twas possible that cargo might be stored there until it could be taken to its inland destination, or loaded on board for export. Mayhap the buildings were used by port officials for some purpose.

It did not matter now, as Maria watched Tournay heading toward one particular ship. She kept well behind him and took note of where he seemed to be headed. She tried to decipher the ship's markings, but there was little light—only a faint glimmer that emanated from a few lamps on board.

She was unafraid. Mayhap foolishly so, but to this point, Tournay had shown no inkling that he suspected that anyone was following him. And if he turned and gave chase, she was certain she could outrun him. She was no fool. She'd taken note of several hiding places along the way, and could easily slip into one of them if he happened to notice her.

Her plan, however, was to avoid all that. She wanted to see where Tournay went, then hasten back and find Nicholas as quickly as possible, and tell him that she'd discovered Tournay was the French informer. Nicholas would know what to do about it.

Aware now of Tournay's game, Maria regretted that she had not seen more clearly that Nicholas had been manipulated into believing the worst of her father. Tournay had been in the perfect position to fabricate whatever tale was necessary to keep Nicholas interested in the Duke of Sterlyng, and off his own track.

Reluctantly, Maria credited the secretary for his cleverness.

She wished she could speak to Nicholas now, to apologize for her harsh words. She would tell him she understood his dilemma and no longer condemned him for suspecting her father.

She would not blame him if he refused her apology. She had not trusted him, had not given enough credit to his words when he'd explained his reasons for working for Bedford. Maria should have known his motives could not be dishonorable, and that he would do the right thing.

Foolishly, she had not trusted him. She had believed the worst of him, only because of the reputation he'd cultivated among the noble classes.

Tournay stopped abruptly and flattened himself against a building. Maria dropped down beside a pile of refuse and waited. 'Twas then that she heard footsteps pounding hollowly on the wooden walk. Someone—perhaps more than one person—was running toward them.

Maria looked to her right, in the direction from which the footsteps came. A man suddenly appeared, and kept on running, turning toward the ship. Tournay stooped down for a moment. Maria could not quite see what he was doing, but doubted that his action boded well.

Another man came into view, chasing after the first. He was tall, dark haired and sturdily built, his white linen shirt uncovered by a doublet, making his form visible in the murky light. Yet Maria could not discern his features.

He turned toward the ship where Tournay seemed to have been headed before this interruption, and ran down the boardwalk, coming close to catching the first man. The pursuer turned slightly, and Maria recognized him.

'Twas Nicholas!

In no more than the blink of an eye, action erupted on the dock. Tournay swiftly crept up behind Nicholas and raised his arm. Maria started forward in order to intervene, but without hesitation the secretary struck Nick a blow on the back of the head, and Nicholas went down.

Maria bit on her fist to keep from screaming. She knew she would be of no assistance to Nicholas if Tournay discovered her presence. She hoped he and his cohorts would board the ship and sail away; then she would be free and safe to attend to Nicholas.

That was not to happen.

There were shouts, and several men came down the gangplank. Nicholas lay motionless on the wharf, and Tournay stood near him, talking in low tones with the men from the ship. Finally, they seemed to reach a decision, and two men took hold of Nick's arms. They dragged him into the building at the end of the quay.

For the first time since beginning her pursuit of Tournay, Maria knew true fear. What were the men planning to do with Nicholas?

She gathered her wits and all of her courage, and moved out of her hiding place. She was not going to allow these men to harm Nicholas in the isolation of that building. She had no idea how she would stop them, but was certain there must be something she could do.

The approach to the building would be difficult because there were still men on board the ship, watching for their comrades to reappear. If Maria ran openly to the building, they would be alerted to her presence, and she wanted to avoid that.

She looked around and plotted a safe route to the place where Nicholas was being held, praying all the while that the men had not seriously harmed him.

A light fog started to roll in off the water, and that, along with the darkness, played in Maria's favor. Wishing she had thought to bring her dark shawl in order to cover her bright hair, she stepped quietly to a stand of barrels and crouched behind them for a moment.

Her next step would be to grab the whip Nicholas had dropped, then make it to the cover of a large crate that stood partway between her and the storage building. Glad that there were no lanterns on the quay to expose her, she crept forward, picked up the whip, then scurried over to the crate to wait. She slowed her breathing and calmed herself. Only a few more feet until she reached the building.

Without warning, the men who'd taken Nicholas came crashing out, shouting at the men on the ship. They all seemed to speak at once, and Maria could not make out what was being said.

Then she smelled smoke.

They'd torched the building!

Chapter Twenty-Six

Nick was choking.

And his throat was on fire.

He knew he had to stand up and move, but his muscles would not work. His bones felt soft. His brain ached and he could see out of only one eye. He could not remember where he was, or what had happened.

Smoke enveloped him, and he realized he was going to burn to death if he did not rouse himself. He slid his hands under his chest and pushed himself up, closing his eyes against the explosion of pain in his head and the dizziness that assailed him. He had to move!

"Nicholas!"

He must be hearing things. It could not be Maria's voice, no matter how desperately he wanted to see her before he died. He tried to get to his knees, but fell back to the ground, coughing.

"Nicholas!"

He forced himself up again. He could hear the hiss and crackle of the blaze nearby, and knew he had to move quickly. He had to find his way out of the inferno before it consumed him.

Unsteadily, he came to his feet and looked around.

Fire was all around him, no longer a few small flames, but a conflagration. He could see no doors or windows beyond the smoke and flames, so did not know which way to go.

But he knew that if he made a mistake, it would be fatal.

"Nicholas!"

There it was again. Only this time, Nick did not think the voice came from his imagination. It truly was Maria, and she was inside. She had to be inside, else he would not be able to hear her.

Damnation! Where was she?

The fire roared around him. He looked for something to use to break through one of the flimsy-looking walls, but there was nothing.

Something tall and dark loomed ahead of him, and he realized it was a winch. The pulley ropes went both below and above him, through holes in the floor and ceiling. If he could just drop down to the floor below, the fire might not be as bad, and 'twas possible that he could find a way out.

But first he had to find Maria.

"Nicholas!" Praise God, her voice came from below.

He made his way to the winch and looked down. Maria stood there, nearly enveloped in smoke. He judged the distance and realized it was too far to jump without suffering serious injury. On the other hand, he had few choices.

"I have your whip!" she cried. "You can use it to lower yourself down!"

She wasted no time, but held one end and snapped the length of the whip toward the opening where Nicholas crouched. It did not reach him, but came close.

"Try again!" he called. Flames crept nearer, and he could hardly see for the hot smoke that burned his eyes.

He lay flat on the floor near the hole and stretched out his arms. Cracking the whip once more, Maria tried again to send one end to him. It took several tries before he was able to catch hold of it.

The flames were nearly upon him. Smoke circled his head, making it difficult to breathe.

Blindly, he tied the whip to the base of the winch, then quickly grabbed the opposite end. Wedging himself through the small opening in the floor, he lowered himself down, using the strip of leather. When he neared the end, and was dangling high above the floor, the whip came loose from its mooring, and Nicholas fell the final eight feet.

Maria cried out and ran to him. "Nicholas!" she exclaimed. "I thought I'd never find you!"

He wasted no time. Standing quickly, he picked up the whip and took her hand. "Where's the door?"

"There!" she shouted over the roar, pointing to a wall of flames. "We can't go that way!"

She was right. There were flames all around now, and they'd be seriously burned if they moved. "What's below?"

The pulley ropes went through another hole in the floor.

"The river," she replied. She pulled up her skirt and covered her mouth with one edge in a futile attempt to keep out the smoke.

"Is there a platform down there?"

"I don't know," Maria replied. "Nicholas, you're bleeding!"

"That's the least of my worries," he replied, ignoring

the trickle of blood that ran down the side of his face. "Come on, let's get out of here."

He tied the whip again and fed the length through the opening in the floor. "Wrap this around your wrist, then hang on. I'll lower you down. There's bound to be a platform for loading and unloading cargo."

She did as she was told. "Nicholas," she said, just before she slipped through the hole. "Master Tournay is behind all this."

"Tournay?"

"Aye," she replied. "He's the one who bashed you and had you dragged inside—"

"*Damn!* We'll talk later, love," he said. "For now, just move!"

A fiery beam crashed down next to Nicholas's head. He ducked and began to lower Maria toward the water. Suddenly he heard a ripping sound and a squeal, and then Maria's weight was no longer at the end of the whip. With his heart in his throat, he took the leather cord, wrapped it around a post that he could only hope would hold firm, then slid down its length to the end.

Maria lay on a platform near the water. She was on her back, her arms and legs akimbo, her eyes closed.

With his heart in his throat, Nicholas crouched next to her. He ran one hand over her forehead. "Maria!" he rasped, attempting to rouse her.

She did not move. Not a moan or a sigh could be heard, but the roar of the fire would have masked any small sound she might make.

Nick glanced quickly around. Flames were spreading to the outer walls and support posts down here. Smoke would smother them completely if they did not move soon.

Coughing, he slipped an arm around her shoulders

and grabbed one of her arms, then pulled her over his shoulder and stood. Staggering for a moment from the dizziness and headache caused by the blow he'd taken, he carried her to the end of the platform.

Nicholas could hear voices now, over the raging inferno—men shouting in panicked tones. He heard hammering, too, and realized that the men were chopping at the wooden platform on which the building rested, hoping to send it into the Thames before any more damage could occur.

Soon the structure would come crashing down upon them, if Nick did not act immediately.

He saw several dark shapes in the water. He prayed they were boats, because swimming out into the current would be impossible, carrying an unconscious Maria. A few more steps and he was at the edge of the platform. Here he was able to see more clearly that there were two boats. Only one was within reach.

'Twas enough.

Nicholas stepped gingerly into it, keeping Maria balanced on his shoulder. The boat wobbled dangerously, but settled down as soon as Nick laid Maria on the bottom and sat down. He found the oars, then started rowing away from the quay.

The vision of the burning building was terrifying. If the men did not chop it loose from the dock, the entire wharf could catch on fire...and then all of London could easily follow, going up in flame. Nicholas was sickened by the knowledge that Tournay would burn London intentionally to support the French. Yet property destruction was the least of it.

Too many people—women and children included—would be killed.

Once he got the boat out in the current, Nicholas

could not spare a moment to attend to Maria. He rowed for their lives, anxious to get away before anyone saw that they'd escaped from danger. If Tournay or any of the men on the ship knew he'd survived the fire, they would come after him. Nicholas could not afford that, especially with Maria lying hurt and unconscious. He had to get her to safety.

Nick continued steering the little boat until they got well beyond the harbor, nearer Temple Church. 'Twas not much farther before they'd reach the area near Bridewell Lane, and there he could pull the boat up into the shallows.

Then he would try to awaken Maria before he took her home.

"My lord!" Lady Alisia cried, pulling a wrapper around her. 'Twas nearly dawn now, and Maria lay nestled, and still unconscious, in Nicholas's arms at the door of her house in Bridewell Lane.

Nick knew his expression was grim. He was bruised and filthy, and his clothes were torn. Maria was in the same condition, which clearly alarmed Lady Alisia.

The lady pulled open the door, and Nicholas walked in past a footman who held a lamp. With the faint glow to light the way, Nick climbed the steps to Maria's room, entered it and carefully laid her on the bed.

"What's amiss?" Sterlyng asked as he came into the room. His tone was anxious. His white hair was disheveled, his feet were bare and he wore a long shirt that had been hastily donned. "Maria?"

"Your grace…" Nicholas's voice was harsh from burns. A spasm of coughing overtook him and he was unable to say more.

''Kirkham!'' Sterlyng frowned as glanced from Nicholas to Maria. ''What's happened?''

'''Tis a long story, your grace,'' Nick finally replied. ''Lady Alisia, did I hear you send the footman for a physician?''

''Yes, my lord,'' she replied, frowning with concern. ''He is to fetch Sir John.''

Unmindful of his filthy, tattered clothes, Nicholas sat down on the edge of Maria's bed. With blackened but gentle fingers, he brushed her hair away from her face. She was so pale, so vulnerable. Soot covered her clothes, and her gown was torn. Her hands and face were as filthy as Nicholas's own.

He would give his right arm to have her well again—conscious and spitting fire, telling him to go to the very devil.

Silently, Alisia gathered clean cloths and a basin of water, and set them next to the bed.

''Kirkham?'' 'Twas not a question, but a demand from Maria's father.

Nicholas looked up at Sterlyng, who stood holding a lamp. The firelight flickered, causing shadows to play over his features. Nick had never before noted such deep lines in the duke's face. He did not doubt that seeing his daughter brought in like this had aged the man. If it could have been any other way...

Nicholas's throat was closed and he still felt choked, but knew 'twas not merely due to the smoke he'd inhaled. Emotion paralyzed him—fear and panic, love and tenderness for the one woman whose life meant everything to him.

''Your grace...'' Nicholas began again as he took Maria's hand in his own. Her skin was so soft, so delicate now. He recalled that, when he'd first met her at

Kirkham, her hands had been reddened and chafed, and he'd wondered about it....

Should he spend a moment now trying to explain everything to Sterlyng, or leave immediately for the docks to see if he could apprehend Tournay?

Nay. He would not leave Maria. For any reason.

"Might I send a message?" he asked. "'Tis urgent."

Sterlyng paused a moment, then gave a slight nod of his head.

"I will explain as much as I am able," Nicholas said. "Maria...when she awakens...will have to tell the rest."

Sterlyng pulled up a chair next to his daughter's bed and listened while Nicholas told of his work for Bedford, of the recent events that had caused suspicion to fall on Sterlyng. As Nicholas spoke, pen and vellum were brought to the room. He interrupted his narrative to write a quick missive to Sir Gyles and hand it to the footman.

"Your grace, my lord..." Alisia said, "if the two of you will quit the room for a few moments, I will see to Maria...get these filthy clothes off her and bathe her before the physician arrives."

Nicholas hardly heard her words. Maria looked so small and fragile. Alisia had washed most of the soot from her face, but her brow remained unnaturally dark, and there were smudges under her chin.

Still, Nicholas did not think he could have loved her more. She'd risked her life to get him out of the burning storage building, cleverly making use of his whip. He wished he'd tied it around her waist before lowering her down to the water, rather than having her hang on to it.

But there'd been no time. He'd had to get her out before they were both burned alive.

ia Morley—her aunt—insisting that Maria's property belongs to her son? The woman is delusional.''

''*No one* will take anything from her again,'' Nicholas said vehemently. He paced the floor, restless, angry. He wanted naught more than to tear back up the stairs and shake Maria awake.

She could not remain unconscious much longer!

Sterlyng leaned back in his chair and observed as Nicholas moved impatiently across the room. ''How was she injured?'' he finally asked.

Nicholas shrugged in frustration. ''I cannot imagine how she happened to show up in that warehouse tonight, your grace,'' he said, stopping his pacing for a moment. ''Or how she learned of my secretary's part in the conspiracy. I only know that she saved my life. If anything happens to her—''

At Nicholas's words, Sterlyng stood and commenced pacing in turn. ''Naught more will happen to my daughter,'' he said, his voice breaking as he spoke. ''Not when I've only just found her.''

''Aye, your grace,'' Nicholas breathed. ''I pray that is so.'' Nay, nothing more would happen to Maria. He vowed to keep her safe and cherished as she should be.

He was relieved that Sterlyng seemed to feel no animosity toward him. If it had been his own daughter brought home in such a condition, Nicholas was certain he'd be shouting down the walls. Or throttling the man who carried her.

Sterlyng stopped in front of Nicholas, running a hand over his whiskered jaw. ''Your eye...it does not look good, Kirkham.''

''No, your grace,'' Nicholas replied absently. ''I don't imagine it does.''

''And your hands are burned.''

For the first time, Nick glanced at the blisters that had already begun to form. He had not noticed, nor did it matter. He could think only of Maria, of her courage...of her continued unconsciousness.

The arrival of the physician roused the two men from their dour thoughts, and they hastened to the front door to greet him.

"Has someone taken ill, your grace?" he asked.

"Not exactly, but my daughter has been injured. She is in need of your skills, Sir John," Sterlyng replied as he took the man's elbow and started walking up the stairs with him.

"She took a fall and was knocked unconscious," Nick said, climbing right behind them.

"She has not yet come 'round, and it's been some time since the fall...."

"How long?" the physician asked.

"More than an hour," Nicholas replied. "Possibly two by now."

The physician pursed his lips and shook his head. "Show me to her."

When they reached Maria's room, Sterlyng held the door open for the physician and followed him inside. Nicholas went, too.

Alisia had gotten all the soot from Maria's face and hands. The bedclothes covered her nearly to her neck, though Nick could see that she'd been dressed in some sort of gown, laced up to her chin.

The physician set down his satchel, took one of the lamps and held it close to her face. He opened each eyelid in turn, then touched the pulse in her neck.

Nicholas shuddered at the sight. He could almost taste that pulse. He'd recently had his tongue on that sensitive spot. He gritted his teeth and vowed he would do so again.

He would not lose her now.

Suddenly, the physician turned. "Gentlemen, if you would be so kind as to give me a moment with Lady Maria…"

Nicholas stared blankly at the man, but Sterlyng was slightly better composed. He put his hand on Nick's shoulder and turned him, then ushered him out of the room. Nick heard the healer ask Alisia to stay.

The waiting was interminable. Nick and Sterlyng remained in the passage on the second floor outside Maria's room while the physician made his examination. The two men did not speak, but every now and then one sighed in frustration or ran a troubled hand through his hair.

Finally, the door opened.

"Stay with her, my lady," Sir John said.

"What?" Sterlyng asked. "Will she…recover?"

"Let us retire to your study, your grace," the healer said. Then he turned to eye Nicholas. "There, we shall talk."

Chapter Twenty-Seven

"'Tis a nasty bump on the back of her head," Sir John said. He lifted the cup of wine to his lips and sipped. "And though she has a number of bumps and bruises and burns...I believe she will recover from them."

Nicholas heard the physician's unspoken "but" and refused to credit the possibility that Maria had sustained any lasting damage. She would be all right. She would soon awaken and he would wed her and take her to Kirkham, and—

"'Tis her child I fear for."

The silence in the room was palpable.

Nicholas felt as if the air had been forcibly siphoned from his lungs. The heart that used to beat so strong and steady in his chest faltered.

"Her child?" Sterlyng finally said. His voice was strained, and Nicholas was still speechless.

Sir John nodded. "There is some bleeding...only a few spots, mind you, but I've seen this sort of thing progress," he said. He set down his mug and stood. "She must be watched carefully. If there is an increase in blood loss, send for me immediately. Or if a good midwife is known to you…?"

Since neither Sterlyng nor Kirkham seemed capable of further speech or movement, the physician saw himself out. Sterlyng was the first to recover from the shock. He turned to Nicholas and spoke. "You'd know about this, I suppose."

Nick shook his head. "Nay," he whispered in awe. "She never said anything. But it is mine. The babe is mine."

A flurry of recent memories suddenly swamped him. Maria turning green in the boat at Lady Eleanor's party. Holding her stomach and running from the baker's stall at Dunstan Fair. Other times when she'd looked peaked for no good reason.

He knew now there'd been very good reason.

She carried his child!

"I care for her, your grace," Nicholas said. "With all my heart." He turned on one heel and hastened from the duke's study, heading for the stairs. He took the steps by twos, and when he reached Maria's room, he opened the door and stepped in without knocking.

If his entrance startled Lady Alisia, she did not show it. She pulled open the drapery and let in the dawn. "Lord Kirkham?"

"You knew…."

Alisia tipped her head slightly. "I suspected."

"She will be my wife," Nicholas said firmly. He sat on the bed beside Maria and took her hand. "As soon as she is able to stand, the priest will be summoned and we will wed."

A throat cleared behind him. "Have I aught to say about it?"

Nicholas did not leave his place at the edge of the

bed. He turned slightly, to look into the duke's startlingly amber eyes. The older man's expression was grave, but Nicholas was determined that there was naught the duke could say or do to dissuade him from his course. "Nay, your grace," he said. "She may be your daughter, but I believe the lady has been mine since the moment she set foot on Kirkham land."

"My daughter has had ample opportunity to choose you as her spouse, Kirkham," Sterlyng said. "Yet she did not."

"You know her reasons for being angry with me," Nicholas said. "'Tis only that—"

"My daughter will have her choice of husband," he said, walking 'round to the opposite side of the bed. "'Twas my promise to her, and I mean to keep it."

"You may rest assured that she will choose me," Nick said. And he hoped his words were true.

Alisia nursed her all through the day, moistening her lips with a wet cloth, wiping her brow when she became warm.

Nicholas never left her side. He'd written to Sir Gyles, explaining the most recent turn of events, and set him the task of apprehending Henric Tournay. Beyond that, he had not given Tournay another thought. His attention was fixed on Maria.

He would not leave her again. He paced, he sat, he even dozed once or twice. A servant was sent to bring him fresh clothes, and he even took a few moments to bathe.

His mind was overcrowded with thoughts of the future, with Maria as his wife. There were improvements to be made to Castle Kirkham. A nursery to furnish, servants to hire. Mattie Tailor's daughter was the most competent midwife in the district, and Nicholas decided to move her and her mother into the castle while they awaited the birth. The child would be born in winter, and Nicholas would brook no delay in—

"No!"

Nicholas started at the sound of Maria's frantic whisper, even though she remained unconscious. He took her hand again and leaned close. "Hush, love," he said. "You're safe now, open your eyes."

She did not open her eyes, but murmured unintelligibly. It seemed then that she moaned every time she was touched or was moved, and Nicholas took this as a good sign. Alisia said there was no further indication of miscarriage, so he felt assured that the babe rested peacefully again within its mother's womb.

If only she would awaken.

Late in the afternoon, a footman knocked and was admitted to the chamber. "Lord Kirkham," he said. "A gentleman awaits you downstairs."

Though he did not want to leave her, Nick pressed a kiss to Maria's forehead and stood. Following the footman, he arrived in the duke's study to find Sterlyng sitting at his desk, and Sir Gyles standing before him.

"My lord," Gyles said, giving a slight bow of respect.

"Sir Gyles has much to report," Sterlyng said.

Nicholas looked to Gyles for an explanation, hoping for a quick one so that he could return to Maria's chamber.

"We seized the ship you described," Gyles said. "And arrested all aboard."

"Good. And Tournay?"

"Since we were certain they thought you'd been killed in the warehouse fire," Gyles replied, "we assumed Tournay would be feeling safe and secure, his treachery undiscovered.''

"But…?''

"He was not on board the ship.''

"By God!'' Nicholas swore. "Where is he?''

"Unknown, my lord,'' Gyles said. "We have the rest of the crew at London Tower and they're being questioned even as we speak. But at the moment, Tournay is at large.''

"He cannot hope to insinuate himself at Westminster,'' Sterlyng observed. "Not when everyone knows of his treason.''

"But where is he?'

"Several ships left the harbor during the fire,'' Gyles said. "We do not yet know if all have returned. Mayhap he was on one of the others.''

"Check on it.''

"Aye, my lord.''

"See if he left anything at his lodgings,'' Nicholas said. "Anything of value that he'd return for.''

"Yes, my lord,'' Gyles repeated. "By the way…you never gave Tournay any reason to suspect you were working for Lord Bedford.''

Nicholas shook his head. "Nay. I did not.''

"Then he must have known this before securing a position in your employ. Your ruse must have become known to the French some time ago.''

Nicholas had already considered this and knew that it was true. The French had to have known of his ploy before sending Tournay to him. His days of working covertly for Bedford were over.

Nick had no regrets. He'd spent many years in the duke's service, and though his work was nowhere near finished, he'd grown tired of acting the debauched nobleman. 'Twas time to move on. Maria and their child needed him.

"That's correct," Nicholas said, finally replying to Gyles's remark. "My usefulness to Lord Bedford, at least in this capacity, is finished."

"I must take my leave, your grace, my lord," Sir Gyles said. "There is still much to do."

Sterlyng followed Gyles and saw him out, while Nicholas returned to Maria's chamber. She was still unconscious, but more restless now.

"Has she spoken?" he asked Alisia.

"Nay. Just a few moans, like before."

Nicholas knelt next to the bed then and put his face level with Maria's. He kissed her lips and lightly touched her hair.

"Nicholas..." she breathed.

Pain shot through Maria's head like a red-hot poker touched to the nerves behind her eyes. She heard voices, but they sounded like echoes—distant and unclear. She moved her legs and tried to move her arms, but her shoulders hurt, and her legs felt as weak as sickroom broth.

She could not imagine what was wrong with her. Why could she not open her eyes or move her body?

One voice was particularly comforting. She was certain 'twas Nicholas, but she wanted him in the bed with her. She wanted naught more than for him to hold her in his arms, to keep her warm and safe.

But it seemed that all he would do was hold her hand and touch his lips to hers. She tried to speak, to tell him to come closer, to lie with her, but the words did not come.

She did not know if he would even want to. She'd

been so awful to him when he'd come to her room. She'd told him to go away, that she'd chosen Rudney for her husband.

What a fool she'd been.

She understood now how Nicholas had been misled, how Tournay had assured him that her father was suspected of treason. It had been unfair for her to accuse him of using her. She should have been above believing all those rumors about him.

She should have trusted him.

Maria attempted to open her eyes, but the light hurt.

"She awakens, your grace!" someone cried. Maria recognized Alisia's quiet voice.

"Open your eyes, sweetheart," Nicholas said.

"Can you hear me, Maria?" It was her father's voice.

She felt confused. They all spoke at once, so Maria shut out every sound but that of Nicholas's voice, his breath near her ear. She nearly wept with relief that he was actually here, that he hadn't abandoned her because of their parting words.

Suddenly, the events on the wharf returned in a flash of memory. She and Nicholas had nearly been trapped, yet they'd somehow gotten out of the fire. What had happened?

She could not quite remember.

The light hurt, but she squinted against it as Nicholas's face came into view. "Your eye!" she whispered. She wanted to touch him, but her hand would not obey her command.

She felt movement at the other side of the bed and shifted slightly to see that her father had sat down next to her. "You're back with us again," he said simply, though she could hear emotion thick in his voice.

"Would you like a sip of water, Maria?" Alisia asked.

Alisia fussed over her awhile. The duke touched her head and her hands, and spoke a few soothing words. Then suddenly, she was alone with Nicholas.

Her father had said something like, "Have a care, Kirkham," and then the door had closed behind him and he was gone.

Maria did not bother to wonder at that, but curled into the warmth of Nicholas's body when he lay next to her. She felt cold and hot at the same time, and her throat felt as if 'twas still on fire.

Her eyes adjusted to the light, and the throbbing in her head subsided a little. She felt ever so much better when Nicholas wrapped his arms around her and pulled her close.

"You saved my life, love," he said quietly.

Maria did not speak. There were so many half-truths, untruths and unspoken truths between them, she did not know where to begin.

He cupped her cheek and kissed her forehead.

"How did you know I'd be on the docks?" he asked.

"I didn't," she replied, basking in the warm security of his arms. "I followed Tournay there."

"Tournay? But how—?"

"Tournay was here…in the house."

"What?" Nicholas demanded.

"After you left me…" She felt the heat rise to her face when she thought of their encounter, and was glad she'd pressed her cheek to his chest so he could not see her embarrassment. "I was too restless to sleep. I went downstairs and saw Tournay rummaging through my father's desk," she said. "When he left, I followed him. Despite what you told me, I—I thought he was in your employ, doing your bidding. I was going to follow him to you, and confront you...."

Nicholas did not speak, but Maria felt his breath catch. She'd hurt him with her distrust, and she wanted naught more than to make amends.

"You told me someone was trying to convince you that my father was a traitor, but I did not believe you," she said. She sniffed once and swallowed the lump in her throat. She was ashamed to have thought the worst of him. "But a-as I followed Tournay, I realized that you'd been truthful with me last night. I—I am so sorry, Nicholas, for not trusting you. I should ha—"

"Hush," he said. "'Tis over now, love. 'Twas difficult to know what to think. I *cultivated* that reputation. I *intended* that everyone believe the worst of me. Little did I know it would work so well."

"I've been so foolish."

"Nay, prudently cautious."

"Oh, Nicholas..." She sighed. A lock of his hair had fallen over his forehead and she reached up to push it back. "'Tis one of the things I love best about you—your understanding nature."

"I am not as understanding as you may think."

"Nay?"

"What you risked in following Tournay...the thought of it terrifies me even now. I was so afraid I'd lose you," he said, holding her close. "When I saw you standing beneath me in the warehouse, my heart dropped to my toes."

"It could not have been worse than when I saw Tournay hit you from behind."

"Ah, Maria..." He pulled back in order to see her face. Then he tipped her chin up with one finger and brushed his lips over hers. "We made a fine pair, don't you think?"

"Aye, Nicholas," she said, fighting tears.

"How is your head?" he asked. "Still hurt terribly?"

"Mmm. A bit," she replied. "But there is one thing you could do to help it."

"What would that be, my lady fair?"

"Kiss me again."

He brushed his lips lightly over hers once again, but Maria wanted more. She took hold of the front of his tunic and pulled him close, touching her tongue to the corner of his mouth.

He groaned and pulled away.

"Maria, I promised your father I would behave."

"And you're behaving exactly as I wish."

"I don't think this is quite what he expected," Nicholas said. "Besides, we have not settled things between us."

Maria lay back. 'Twas true. Naught was settled. She still had not told him of the babe.

"My work for Bedford is finished," he said. "'Tis no longer necessary for me to associate with the scoundrels and knaves who have been my companions these last few years."

"Why did you associate with them?"

"To learn their secrets," he replied. "And the secrets of anyone else who would underestimate me."

"Very clever, Nicholas," Maria said. "Is that why you kept me from them at Kirkham? Because they were scoundrels?"

"Aye. They—"

"And what of the women you had there?"

"I had no... Ah, you mean the one who stood outside

my window with Lofton and Trendall the morning you left me?''

Maria smiled deceptively. ''Aye, *Lord Nicky,*'' she said. ''The one whose wares you apparently sampled just before you lured me into your bed.''

Nicholas ran his hands up Maria's arms. ''I've sampled no one since I met you. My heart, my body and my mind have been tied in knots since the day you knocked me on my arse outside Kirkham. Put me out of my misery and become my wife, Maria.''

She believed him, for she, too, had been confounded since meeting him that day. Maria bit her lip. She still hadn't told him of their child, and he was likely to be very angry when he discovered she'd kept it from him, and that she'd planned to wed another man.

There was naught to do but tell him now. ''Nicholas...'' she began. ''There is something you must know.''

He raised his head and propped his chin in his hand. He looked down at her. There was a mischievous light in his eyes that worried her. ''I wondered if you'd ever get 'round to telling me.''

''T-telling you?'' she asked guiltily. ''You know?''

''Of the pregnancy?'' he asked, drawing her close once again. ''Aye. I know.''

''How?''

''There was some fear of miscarriage—''

''Oh, no!'' she cried in alarm. She covered her belly protectively with her hand. ''Not our—''

''Nay, sweetheart. Not now,'' he said, kissing her forehead. ''But when I first brought you home this morning, there was some light bleeding. Alisia assured your father and me that all is well now.''

Relief flooded through Maria, even as embarrassment and chagrin took its place. "So, my father knows?"

Nicholas smiled. "He does. 'Tis the only reason he's left us alone…in your bedchamber."

"Nicholas—"

"You're not still planning to marry Rudney."

"Nay, Nicholas," she whispered into his chest. "Only you."

"'Tis a very good thing, my love," he said. "Rudney's not a bad sort. I would hate to have to kill him."

"Nicholas," she warned.

"I am only teasing," he said, then he turned serious again. "I care for you as I have no other, Maria. Please do me the honor of becoming my wife."

"Oh, Nicholas," she breathed. "'Twill be my greatest pleasure."

"There will be no more secrets between us," he said, hugging her close.

"Aye," she answered sleepily. "Absolute honesty."

He kissed her tenderly and held her close until she fell into a natural sleep. Both she and the babe needed to rest.

Nicholas slept, too, but awoke in the darkened room sometime during the night, his muscles cramped and sore. He got up from the bed and stretched, gazing out the window at the stars above.

Some slight movement caught his eye and he stepped back, looking down at the cobbled walkway. He might be mistaken, but he believed he'd seen a cloaked man standing in the shadows.

Nick could think of no legitimate reason for anyone to be watching Sterlyng's house, so he slipped out of Maria's chamber and went down the stairs. He made his way through the dark house to one of the back doors. Letting himself out, he silently skirted the wall of the house, keeping to the cover of the shrubs.

When he reached the corner, he crouched low and looked toward the opposite end of the lane, where he'd seen the man.

He was still there.

Nick slipped back the way he'd come and cut away from the wall, toward the neighboring house. If he could get 'round it, then cross over and come up behind the man, the element of surprise would work in Nicholas's favor.

Moving quickly, he put his plan into action, praying that the watcher would not leave—*or act*—until Nicholas managed to get to him. His presence was ominous, though Nick could not imagine his intent.

He crossed over to the neighboring dwelling, moved up the side of the building to the front. Silently, he advanced across the way without calling attention to his actions. The man still remained in place, although Nicholas had the distinct impression that he was getting ready to move.

A short distance from the watcher was a path that went down to the river. There were bushes and shrubs that had recently come into bloom, and Nicholas made use of them to cover his progress as he crept along.

When he'd gone far enough, he doubled back, just as the man started walking stealthily toward Maria's house.

The fellow dropped his cloak, and Nicholas saw that he was slightly built and his hair was light. Nick had no doubt it was Tournay.

But he could not figure out why his erstwhile secretary would be here. Did he hope to harm Maria? Mayhap Sterlyng? Or had he come to finish whatever he'd been doing in the duke's study?

He would have answers, Nicholas thought as he came upon Tournay from behind. He threw one powerful arm around the secretary's throat and yanked him down.

Tournay pulled out a long, thin dagger and rolled away from Nicholas. He quickly came to his feet and brandished the knife at his opponent.

Nicholas gave a quick laugh at the pathetic weapon.

"You will not laugh when you find this blade in your gullet, my lord," Tournay threatened.

"You'll have to spear me in the back, Tournay," Nicholas scoffed, "just as you had to attack me last night. You're not man enough to fight face-to-face."

Tournay grasped the dagger and lunged, but Nicholas had no difficulty dodging the blow. He grabbed Tournay's arm and twisted, though the secretary went suddenly limp and threw Nicholas off balance. He lashed out with his foot and tripped Nick, sending him to the ground.

So, Nicholas thought, *the man was not the untrained weakling he appeared.* 'Twas no matter. Nick had underestimated him once, but 'twould not happen again. He would best the man and disarm him in short order.

"What were you doing in Sterlyng's study last night?" Nicholas asked.

"Making impressions of his seal," Tournay replied. Then he lunged again. "Prepare yourself for death, Kirkham."

Nicholas threw a kick, catching the secretary in the belly, sending him head over heels. The fall knocked the wind out of the man, and Nick quickly came to his feet.

"How does Sterlyng's seal serve you, Tournay?" he

asked as the secretary got to his knees and brandished the knife once again. Nick spread his arms and moved slowly, attempting to catch the man off guard.

"I can put *anything* into a missive," Tournay said, catching his breath. "Once the sealing wax is melted, I set Sterlyng's seal into it. No one ever guesses the one is affixed to the other."

"I wondered why the supposed letters from Sterlyng had such thick seals."

"And now you know," Tournay said through clenched teeth, "just in time to die."

"I think not, little man."

This enraged Tournay, and he charged again with his knife, nearly catching Nicholas in the side. But Nick was faster, evading the blow at the last instant.

They parried for a few moments, with Tournay thrusting the dagger and Nicholas avoiding it. "Clearly, your little ruse worked for a while, Tournay," Nicholas said. "But from whom were you diverting my attention? That's the most interesting question."

Tournay sliced again, cutting only air, but his movement gave Nicholas the advantage. He grabbed Tournay's arm and pulled it down hard over his raised knee, knocking the knife from it. He slammed the secretary against the wall of the house and closed one hand around his throat.

The pressure of Nicholas's hand was too great, and Tournay's voice was choked. "No one!" he rasped.

"I think you're lying, worm," Nicholas said. "I think there is someone you're protecting. And if you have any inclination of drawing another breath, you'll say his name."

Tournay gave a negative shake of his head.

Nicholas increased the pressure. "Apparently you do not believe I am serious."

Tournay gagged and fought Nicholas with all his strength, but he could not budge the larger, more powerful nobleman. He finally nodded as much as he was able, and Nicholas let up on the pressure, just enough to allow the secretary to speak.

"Bex—"

"Repeat yourself!"

"Bex—" He gagged again, and Nicholas eased up a bit more.

"Bexhill!"

Chapter Twenty-Eight

London. Autumn, 1429

A footman cleared his throat and apologized for intruding on the lord and his lady. "There are guests, my lord."

Nicholas sat near the fire. Maria's feet rested in his lap and he leaned across her body to feed her morsels from the supper tray. Though her pregnancy had not advanced so far for her to need such coddling, she did not say him nay.

Nicholas was glad, for he enjoyed every moment of touching her.

"Is it Sterlyng?" Nick asked. He would be welcome to share their meal before the fire.

"No, my lord," the footman replied. "But...*relations,* I believe."

"Who could it be?"

Maria had no sooner asked her question than a handsome older woman pushed into the room, past the footman. She was well groomed and richly dressed, and Nicholas had no recollection of ever having met her.

"Ria!" she cried.

When Maria recoiled, Nicholas set her feet aside and stood abruptly. "Madam, you intrude."

"How can I possibly intrude, my lord?" the woman asked. "I am Olivia Morley! Ria's aunt."

Stunned that the woman had the gall to show up at their house in London, Nicholas was nearly speechless. And she'd brought her two offspring, who hovered near the door, obviously awaiting the outcome of their mother's invasion here.

"My wife has no aunt," he said tightly. He would never forgive the woman for her low treatment of Maria. Nor would he accept her into his home.

"Ah, but she does," Olivia continued, coming to sit next to Maria. "And 'tis so long since we last saw you, darling Ria."

Maria did not speak, and Nicholas saw that the color had drained from her face. He knew that months ago Olivia had denied Maria's existence to the justice who'd tried to find her. He also knew that Olivia Morley had tried to take Rockbury from her, claiming that it was the rightful possession of her son, Geoffrey.

Sterlyng was correct about Lady Olivia. She had delusions.

"Adrick," he said to the footman as he gently pulled Maria's aunt from her chair, "please escort Lady Olivia and her children out."

"But my lord—" Olivia objected.

"My wife has no need of relatives beyond her father...and me."

"But we're here in London to see her!" Olivia protested as the footman and Nicholas each took one arm to usher her out. She resisted slightly, as if unable to comprehend that she was being shown the door. "'Tis her duty to introduce us to all of London soci—"

"Her duty to you is fulfilled many times over, Lady Olivia," Nicholas said as they finally reached the door. He sent her out, then gave a little push to the young man's back. His sister followed. "Have the grace never to darken our door again, Morleys," he said. "Your presence is unwelcome here."

Nicholas shut the door on them with great relish and returned to Maria. He sat down with her again, and resumed his position as if they'd never been disturbed.

"Put your feet back in my lap, love," Nicholas said.

The shock of Olivia's visit had subsided to some extent, Maria's color had returned, though she seemed far from settled.

"Ria?" he asked, frowning. The way the aunt had said it made Nicholas believe 'twas not exactly a pet name.

"I don't believe she ever knew my real name," Maria said. "I was just her sister-in-law's bastard."

Nick's temper seethed. Even if she had truly been a bastard child, there was no reason for the mean manner with which she'd been treated at Alderton. He cringed at the thought of his own child suffering such mistreatment.

No chance of that. The child Maria carried would be well and truly loved. *And legitimate,* thanks to their marriage, which had taken place with little ado as soon as Maria had recovered from her fall.

She had never asked, and Nicholas had never told her of Tournay's demise. In her condition, 'twould not have been prudent to regale her with tales of the traitor's execution, nor did she need to know that Bexhill had also met an untimely end. Bedford and Gloucester had

"Your grace?" Lady Alisia prompted.

"Very well, Alisia," Sterlyng said, though he was clearly reluctant to leave. He put a hand on Nicholas's shoulder. "Kirkham, come with me."

The two men retired to Sterlyng's study, where Nicholas resumed his explanation of recent events as they pertained to Maria's condition. He told Sterlyng that Maria had become aware of his suspicions and had taken it upon herself to prove him wrong.

"And you allowed this?" Sterlyng demanded, grabbing a handful of Nicholas's tunic.

"Nay, your grace," Nicholas quickly replied. He made no move against Sterlyng, whose distraught state was plainly understandable. Besides, Nick felt guilty for involving Maria, however inadvertently. He did not blame her father for holding him responsible for her injuries. "I told her that 'twould be too dangerous for her to pursue it. Yet I know she was anxious to show your innocence."

Sterlyng sighed and let Nick go. "She has her mother's temperament," he said. "My Sarah was headstrong. She often acted before thinking."

"Aye, Maria is a fiery one."

"And I know she had to scrape for her living at Alderton," the duke added. "She was treated as less than the lowest servant there. Once her old nurse died, Maria had to fight for everything she received."

Nicholas had suspected as much, after hearing the rumors surrounding Maria's arrival in London. Knowing how she'd been treated by her mother's relations made him fume inside.

Sterlyng let himself drop into the chair near his desk. "Do you know, I've actually received letters from Oliv-

seen to it that Lord Bexhill would never again imperil Englishmen's lives.

Nick took a morsel of pastry from the tray on the table and fed it to her by hand. Maria caught one of his fingers between her lips and swirled her tongue around it, eliciting a groan from Nicholas.

"Do you want to finish this meal, wench? Or just proceed directly to the bedchamber?"

Maria dropped her lashes seductively. "Oh, I intend to finish...*Lord Nicky.*"

The room suddenly seemed too hot. He pulled his tunic over his head. "That's better," he said, rolling up the sleeves of his linen undershirt. "'Tis warm by the fire."

He shifted, then leaned over and touched a kiss to her lips. "What, exactly, do you intend to finish, my lady fair?" His voice was low, seductive, and he did not back away.

"My meal, of course," she said, though a secretive smile crossed her lips. She pulled his head down for another kiss, and was rewarded with a scorching meeting of mouths that made her breathless.

"Mayhap later, my lady fair," he said. "Much later."

*   *   *   *   *

Take a jaunt to Merry Old England
with these timeless stories from
Harlequin Historicals

On sale March 2002

THE LOVE MATCH
by Deborah Simmons
Deborah Hale
Nicola Cornick
Don't miss this captivating bridal collection
filled with three breathtaking Regency tales!

MARRYING MISCHIEF
by Lyn Stone
Will a quarantine spark romance between a
determined earl and his convenient bride?

On sale April 2002

MISS VEREY'S PROPOSAL
by Nicola Cornick
A matchmaking duke causes a smitten London
debutante to realize she's betrothed to the
wrong brother!

DRAGON'S KNIGHT
by Catherine Archer
When a powerful knight rushes to the aid of a
beautiful noblewoman, will he finally conquer
his darkest demons?

 Harlequin Historicals®

This Mother's Day Give Your Mom A Royal Treat

Win a fabulous one-week vacation in Puerto Rico for you and your mother at the luxurious Inter-Continental San Juan Resort & Casino. The prize includes round trip airfare for two, breakfast daily and a mother and daughter day of beauty at the beachfront hotel's spa.

INTER·CONTINENTAL
San Juan
RESORT & CASINO

Here's all you have to do:

Tell us in 100 words or less how your mother helped with the romance in your life. It may be a story about your engagement, wedding or those boyfriends when you were a teenager or any other romantic advice from your mother. The entry will be judged based on its originality, emotionally compelling nature and sincerity. See official rules on following page.

Send your entry to:
Mother's Day Contest

In Canada
P.O. Box 637
Fort Erie, Ontario
L2A 5X3

In U.S.A.
P.O. Box 9076
3010 Walden Ave.
Buffalo, NY
14269-9076

Or enter online at www.eHarlequin.com

Two ways to enter:

• **Via The Internet:** Log on to the Harlequin romance website (www.eHarlequin.com) anytime beginning 12:01 a.m. E.S.T., January 1, 2002 through 11:59 p.m. E.S.T., April 1, 2002 and follow the directions displayed on-line to enter your name, address (including zip code), e-mail address and in 100 words or fewer, describe how your mother helped with the romance in your life.

• **Via Mail:** Handprint (or type) on an 8 1/2" x 11" plain piece of paper, your name, address (including zip code) and e-mail address (if you have one), and in 100 words or fewer, describe how your mother helped with the romance in your life. Mail your entry via first-class mail to: Harlequin Mother's Day Contest 2216, (in the U.S.) P.O. Box 9076, Buffalo, NY 14269-9076; (in Canada) P.O. Box 637, Fort Erie, Ontario, Canada L2A 5X3.

For eligibility, entries must be submitted either through a completed Internet transmission or postmarked no later than 11:59 p.m. E.S.T., April 1, 2002 (mail-in entries must be received by April 9, 2002). Limit one entry per person, household address and e-mail address. On-line and/or mailed entries received from persons residing in geographic areas in which entry is not permissible will be disqualified.

Entries will be judged by a panel of judges, consisting of members of the Harlequin editorial, marketing and public relations staff using the following criteria:
  • Originality - 50%
  • Emotional Appeal - 25%
  • Sincerity - 25%

In the event of a tie, duplicate prizes will be awarded. Decisions of the judges are final.

Prize: A 6-night/7-day stay for two at the Inter-Continental San Juan Resort & Casino, including round-trip coach air transportation from gateway airport nearest winner's home (approximate retail value: $4,000). Prize includes breakfast daily and a mother and daughter day of beauty at the beachfront hotel's spa. Prize consists of only those items listed as part of the prize. Prize is valued in U.S. currency.

All entries become the property of Torstar Corp. and will not be returned. No responsibility is assumed for lost, late, illegible, incomplete, inaccurate, non-delivered or misdirected mail or misdirected e-mail, for technical, hardware or software failures of any kind, lost or unavailable network connections, or failed, incomplete, garbled or delayed computer transmission or any human error which may occur in the receipt or processing of the entries in this Contest.

Contest open only to residents of the U.S. (except Colorado) and Canada, who are 18 years of age or older and is void wherever prohibited by law; all applicable laws and regulations apply. Any litigation within the Province of Quebec respecting the conduct or organization of a publicity contest may be submitted to the Régie des alcools, des courses et des jeux for a ruling. Any litigation respecting the awarding of a prize may be submitted to the Régie des alcools, des courses et des jeux only for the purpose of helping the parties reach a settlement. Employees and immediate family members of Torstar Corp. and D.L. Blair, Inc., their affiliates, subsidiaries and all other agencies, entities and persons connected with the use, marketing or conduct of this Contest are not eligible to enter. Taxes on prize are the sole responsibility of winner. Acceptance of any prize offered constitutes permission to use winner's name, photograph or other likeness for the purposes of advertising, trade and promotion on behalf of Torstar Corp., its affiliates and subsidiaries without further compensation to the winner, unless prohibited by law.

Winner will be determined no later than April 15, 2002 and be notified by mail. Winner will be required to sign and return an Affidavit of Eligibility form within 15 days after winner notification. Non-compliance within that time period may result in disqualification and an alternate winner may be selected. Winner of trip must execute a Release of Liability prior to ticketing and must possess required travel documents (e.g. Passport, photo ID) where applicable. Travel must be completed within 12 months of selection and is subject to traveling companion completing and returning a Release of Liability prior to travel; and hotel and flight accommodations availability. Certain restrictions and blackout dates may apply. No substitution of prize permitted by winner. Torstar Corp. and D.L. Blair, Inc., their parents, affiliates, and subsidiaries are not responsible for errors in printing or electronic presentation of Contest, or entries. In the event of printing or other errors which may result in unintended prize values or duplication of prizes, all affected entries shall be null and void. If for any reason the Internet portion of the Contest is not capable of running as planned, including infection by computer virus, bugs, tampering, unauthorized intervention, fraud, technical failures, or any other causes beyond the control of Torstar Corp. which corrupt or affect the administration, secrecy, fairness, integrity or proper conduct of the Contest, Torstar Corp. reserves the right, at its sole discretion, to disqualify any individual who tampers with the entry process and to cancel, terminate, modify or suspend the Contest or the Internet portion thereof. In the event the Internet portion must be terminated a notice will be posted on the website and all entries received prior to termination will be judged in accordance with these rules. In the event of a dispute regarding an on-line entry, the entry will be deemed submitted by the authorized holder of the e-mail account submitted at the time of entry. Authorized account holder is defined as the natural person who is assigned to an e-mail address by an Internet access provider, on-line service provider or other organization that is responsible for arranging e-mail address for the domain associated with the submitted e-mail address. Torstar Corp. and/or D.L. Blair Inc. assumes no responsibility for any computer injury or damage related to or resulting from accessing and/or downloading any sweepstakes material. Rules are subject to any requirements/limitations imposed by the FCC. **Purchase or acceptance of a product offer does not improve your chances of winning.**

For winner's name (available after May 1, 2002), send a self-addressed, stamped envelope to: Harlequin Mother's Day Contest Winners 2216, P.O. Box 4200 Blair, NE 68009-4200 or you may access the www.eHarlequin.com Web site through June 3, 2002.

Contest sponsored by Torstar Corp., P.O. Box 9042, Buffalo, NY 14269-9042.

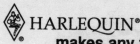